Polarium; a huge fictional star visible to all planets and featured in all four stories in our Star Chasers anthology. Polarium's purpose differs depending on where the story is set
but has a huge influence over the lives and loves of the characters involved. Treat yourself, stowaway with us and
transport yourself to the stars with some of eXtasy Books'
top authors.

Star Chasers
Copyright © 2018 Viola Grace, Taryn Jameson, Gabriella Bradley, Belinda McBride, Astrid Cooper
ISBN: 978-1-4874-2146-5
Cover art by Angela Waters

Published by eXtasy Books Inc or
Devine Destinies, an imprint of eXtasy Books Inc

Look for us online at:
www.eXtasybooks.com or www.devinedestinies.com

Star Chasers

By

Viola Grace, Taryn Jameson, Gabriella Bradley, Belinda McBride, Astrid Cooper

FROZEN EMBER
BY
VIOLA GRACE

CHAPTER ONE

Ember Velar looked around and waited as calmly as she could. Mimicking the wall behind her was a strange request, but she did it.

The Ontex recruiter stared at her and blinked slowly. "You were not exaggerating. You really do mimic your surroundings."

She smiled. "It works with people, too, but that can get disturbing."

"I see. Well, the first shipment of Volunteers has already left, but if you want to be on the next shuttle, you have a place, Ms. Velar."

Ember wasn't sure she had heard him. "The next shuttle? When does that one leave?"

"Six days. You have two days to make up your mind."

Ember shook her head. "I have made up my mind. I am going. I just need to write a letter, and I have to figure out how to have it delivered in two decades."

Recruiter Norz inclined its head. "We can make sure of that."

She blinked. "You can?"

"Of course. It is a little enough thing for the Alliance to do considering what you are about to surrender in the name of your world's honour and potential."

Ember nodded. "Right. I will have the letter for you on the day I leave. I am not leaving until I know it is in your hands."

"I accept that. I will be at the shuttle and confirm your

request."

"Thank you. This is a hard letter to write, and I want it to get to her if she goes looking."

"May I ask who it is for?"

Ember looked at Norz calmly. "My daughter. She was taken from me two years ago, and I am not allowed contact."

"How is that possible?"

"Her father's family had money to make her go away. I didn't have any means to fight them. So, I am doing what I can and making a new home for us in the stars. If she gets this and we get our champions, she can join me if she likes. There will be a place for her, wherever I go."

Norz nodded. "I will be there to take on the letter. It will get to your child the moment she turns eighteen."

"Thank you. Now I just have to go home and write it."

Norz tapped her lightly on the arm in comfort, and Ember's body identified something in the contact. Norz had a human soul. Ember could feel it. The rest of the body, that was up for debate. It didn't matter. That recruiter was her ticket to being able to live her life in the stars and to have a message sent to her daughter when there was no one around to threaten.

If her daughter wanted contact, the Alliance would get a message to Ember. She was sure of it. She had to be. There was no other option.

The day she left the Earth, she handed Norz the fat envelope with every hope and dream she had for her daughter. It was a hard day, but the hardest had been the day she went to the nursery and found out that her baby wasn't there.

Her asshole ex-boyfriend had gotten his congresswoman mother in on the situation and the conscious decision to hide the pregnancy after it had already happened. A lovely couple had adopted the child the moment that Ember had been declared unfit by the congresswoman's golfing buddy. The family court judge. Her baby had been removed out of state within hours.

She kept the focus for the letter to be that she did not give up, she merely decided to wait and see if her child had any of her characteristics. If she came looking, Ember would be waiting.

Two years of legal battles had exhausted her finances, her social contacts, and her friends, so this was the only move she had left. The breakdown that she had had before she came to this decision had been short, powerful, and left her with the knowledge that her daughter was safe, healthy, and she would grow up. When she was eighteen, she would get the letter, and she would know that Ember didn't give up on her. Ember just chose to wait instead of fighting a losing battle. No child needed that much anger and acrimony in her life.

As she left the Earth behind, she put her emotions, anger, frustration, and pain into a small part of her soul. They might be useful in the future, but right now, they were making her cry.

Ember turned from side to side and checked out her reflection in the mirror. She looked like she was starring in a sci-fi flick.

"Right. I am actually living one."

She twisted to check out her butt in the skin-tight fabric. "Well, it isn't a mom bod. That is for sure."

Her hips were curvier after having her daughter, and her breasts were bigger. Ember had scraped her dark hair into a ponytail, and it was high on the back of her head. It swung when she moved.

She looked into her eyes and tried to see anything extraordinary in her gaze. There was nothing. The hazel was the same colour on the warship that it had been on Earth.

Aliens. She had already seen more than the Ontex and his bodyguards. She had seen dozens of species, all in the same uniform of the warship.

There were aliens who looked like they had feline genes, scales, all the colours of the rainbow, and maybe a few that she had never imagined. She was here to blend in as her job and assignment. She had quite the task on her hands.

Ember suddenly laughed. "I am an alien."

Any planet she landed on, she would be an alien. It was a heady thought. She was going from walking around and being lost in the crowd, to standing out because she wasn't just like everyone else. She was going to be alien wherever she went. She had to get used to the idea.

The chime rang, and she snapped out of her preoccupation. It was time to meet for lunch. She pressed her hands over her belly in the reinforced suit. She had no idea how she was going to fit any food in with the suit on.

She stepped out of her room and followed the directions she had been given to the dining room. A few other humans from her class met up with her in the hallway, and they all went to engage in some of the most basic education in what was safe for them to eat.

Ember laughed and chatted with some of the other women and men, but she kept her eyes on the basics of what she was allowed to consume, and which species had toxic components in their daily meals. It was her first class, and she was eager to learn more as they cruised through the stars.

CHAPTER TWO

Instructor Mfalla smiled brightly. Her mouth was on her forehead, so it took getting used to. "This is your reflex stasis capsule. You don't test well for full sensory deprivation, so your implants are now rigged to feel a toned-down version of what the capsule is engaged in, and you will be able to remain aware of what is going on around you. It is experimental, so you are going to be the first long-run trial of the technology. It is set to send data bursts, so we can keep track of its performance."

Ember looked into the capsule that was going to house her for the next six months while she travelled. She was only scheduled to wake up once every three months while the pod did its maintenance. It was going to do everything for her while it slowed her biological processes down to barely discernable.

"I have never heard of pre-emptive therapy before."

"It is called training, Ember." Mfalla sighed. "You have been in training."

Ember crouched to examine the controls. "I know. I also know I can rewire this thing in my sleep. Well, maybe not then."

Mfalla stamped a hoof and shook her head. "Enough. You won't be on the outside for more than a few minutes tomorrow. Get in and see how it feels."

Ember was suspicious, but her instructor would never do anything to hurt her. She had had plenty of opportunity.

"So, the port suit works just like the simulator?"

"Yes. It is loaded with saline so nothing will happen. Well, you might get bloaty." Mfalla smiled.

Ember chuckled and climbed into the low capsule. It was three feet wide and seven feet long inside, with a gel bed that could be activated once she was plugged in.

She got the worst connection over with. The suit was highly invasive in the crotch region, but it would have to be, or she would have a toxin issue.

She hissed as it activated and then went on to set the plugs in either thigh and her fingers trembled as she inserted the whisper-thin needle into the port at the back of her skull. When that was done, she used the jacks in her suit's sleeves and lay back, pressing the switch that swelled the gel around her. She was locked in place.

Mfalla had been smiling, but now her lips pulled flat. "Excellent. Another one that immobilized themselves. Enjoy the pickup."

Ember wanted to scream, but a cool flood ran through her. She got cold, she got sleepy, and then everything went dark.

Mfalla murmured into her coded com. "Preparing to jettison trash."

"Standing by. Time of expiry?"

"Seventy-two hours."

"Confirmed."

Mfalla looked at the pod behind the force screen. The moment that she pushed the button, another payment would be sent to her family. It was too bad. She liked Ember.

She hit the button, and the pod fell into the void.

Ember's dreams frosted over. She was holding her baby and

running down a hall coated with ice and snow, and it was getting colder with every step.

She finally found a doorway and tried to get through it, but the metal of the frame warped around her and held tight.

"Are you sure that this case isn't empty?" One of the collection agents looked into the pod.

"She is in there. Mfalla would never dare to betray us. Look again."

He looked again, and there against the blue gel was a faintly blue creature, lying motionless in deep slumber. "Are we sure she is Terran?"

"Definite."

He whistled softly. "She is talented. This is going to be the haul of a lifetime."

"You are joking."

"I am not. She is some kind of chameleon."

His companion clapped him on the shoulder. "What we have here, is a scavenger's treasure. Take care of the pod systems. We want a good price for her when we get to the trader outpost."

The collection agent swiftly connected the pod to the ship's systems and let it share their life support. There was a long journey ahead of them. She had to stay fresh.

Ember felt the connection to something much larger than herself, and she used the sensors along the capsule to gain access to the information systems of the ship that she was on.

Her first month in space and she was already a cliché.

First, she was able to pick up on energy signatures, traces

of oxygen and carbon filters, and then she stumbled into the database. Alien species, logs of pickups, finances, everything was exposed to her. She started reading, keeping her presence as small as she could, and worked out that she was on board a vessel piloted by folk who made their living by stealing and selling others.

Fuck.

They had flagged her capsule and were looking forward to selling her at a trading center. *Double fuck.*

She hung out in the information station and learned everything she could about the people who had her, the ship she was on, and how long they had been travelling. When she had learned everything she could from their systems, she started over with special attention to crew files.

She felt the ship docking, hands on the capsule, and everything went silent.

Three months later, she woke during the pod's scheduled maintenance and she used her link to test where she was and what condition the pod was in.

She was pinned between layers of other stasis pods on a bulk slaver ship. That was all the information that she could access. Great. Her first day free of the grasp of the pod and she was stuck.

The air was still circulating in her pod, the cryo-fluid was moving slowly in her veins, and she was immobile. She had made it off her planet and into space, and she was stuck in a can.

She would be dead before her daughter ever got the letter.

Ember relaxed into the gel and controlled her breathing. She sent the sensory connection out through the pod and broke through the firewall of the ship. She wanted to know where she was and what she was doing.

She pulled the data that she needed and uploaded it into the small storage buffer that they had created in her brain.

She could go through that data at her leisure and learn a bit more about what they planned to do with her.

She counted the times that the pod woke her so it could do its maintenance. Fifteen times she had woken, trapped in a stack of pods. They were storing her until they had a proper buyer, and in the meantime, they had left all Alliance space and were moving off into uncharted territories where she and those with her would fetch the best price.

The details on her file were shocking. She had been sold three times and handed on from what appeared to be a wholesaler and into the boutique retail market.

The next time she woke, she was alone in the hold. The other pods were gone. There was no pressure on the sides of her pod, but it was humming along happily. The levels of supplies must have been restocked because it was showing that she could last in the pod for another twenty years.

She really did not want to be in the pod for another twenty years.

The direction of the ship was toward a huge star. The designation was Polarium, and the area was surrounded by dangerous stellar phenomenon. The payday for delivering her was more money than she could imagine, but she had no idea why someone untrained like her was generating such a large price tag.

The pod was giving her feedback. Ember kept her eyes closed as the wrappings of ice spun around her. She was in space again. She was floating and in space again.

As the pod rotated, she saw the wreckage of the ship that had housed her, huge chunks of the hull had been removed, and there was nothing left to support life.

Ember watched the stars spin past as her pod rotated and

felt the encompassing light of the huge star nearest to her. She hadn't gotten the latest directional update, so she had no idea where she was.

The pod woke her twice more as she was in an intense orbit around the star. Radiation exposure was a possible setup, but she couldn't do anything.

She watched a star come toward her and smiled at the fancy spectacle. It looked for all the world like a star was moving around debris and coming toward her pod.

Ember couldn't move and didn't know how much of this was a hallucination, but the star coming toward her had a person in it. The pod twisted away, and she lost sight of the oncoming blaze. At least she wouldn't have to watch her death coming toward her.

Warmth wrapped around the pod and suddenly her view of the wreckage was very clear. The ship that she must have been on had been torn open. Something had ripped metal into shreds, and there were a few bodies floating around.

Whatever had happened must have been recent.

She was moved from the site of the destruction to a base floating in the center of nothing.

She had seen images of Alliance space stations and this was nothing like it. A sphere with a spire running through it from top to bottom was a strange white-silver that reflected the light around it. The station was getting rapidly larger, and she had to wonder if she was going to be smashed into it.

The thing holding her slowed down just when she was getting nervous. Part of her mind laughed hysterically that it took the threat of being smashed to make her nervous. She had no idea how many times she had been woken by the maintenance cycle, but this might be her last.

A door opened in the station and her transport system

flew right into it. What had looked so small from a distance turned into a hundred-foot-high doorway that was two hundred feet wide. The hangar inside was mind-boggling, well, the floor was. She could only see what was right in front of her and now that she was being pulled through the space she could admire the smooth polish of the metal that was the same as the exterior.

The tug of gravity made her glad for the gel restraining her. Even inside the station, the fireball was still flying, and it was a dizzying ten minutes of working toward the center of the station before he set the pod down and rolled her over.

Ember could hear him humming to himself as he plugged the unit in, and she just about screamed when everything faded to black once again. *Fuckity, fuck!*

CHAPTER THREE

Cross looked into the pod and had to focus to see the creature inside.

She is not a creature, she is a Terran. I have been waiting for her for some time.

Cross snorted. "If you were waiting for her, why did you tear that ship apart?"

They were threatening to destroy her pod. I had to act.

"You acted them into chunks. There is nothing left."

Polarium chuckled in his mind. *She is left. I have waited decades for her to arrive.*

Cross peered into the pod. "Are you sure it is female? It looks blue and flat to me."

She is in a support gel. Set the pod to release her in two days. That should be more than enough time for the station to fill with atmosphere.

Cross crouched and keyed in the waking time. Why this particular woman was so important to Polarium was not his business. If the star wanted her, the star would have her. Cross was just how the tremendous intellect and power got around.

Ember opened her eyes, and everything was different. There was no feeling on the outside of the pod. A chime rang out. "Welcome to your destination."

Ember carefully wiggled her left arm over, and when she grazed the controls, the gel released her limbs. The skull jack released, and she hit the pod lid, blasting it free.

The air that rushed in wasn't that of a ship or Earth. She could taste minerals in the wrong quantities with every breath.

Ember released the jacks in her arms and legs. The connection to her groin was removed with a lot of shrieking and cursing, but eventually it was stowed with the others for sterilization.

Wherever she was, it was silent. There were no sounds, no whirring of machines, no chirps of computers. Nothing.

Standing up was not going to be an option after all that time, so she grabbed the outer edge of the pod with her feeble arms, and she started to pull.

Inch by inch, she heaved her body out of the pod. The fall and the thud was almost welcome after the strain of getting free of her prison.

Ember breathed heavily as her limbs were shaking. "Where the hell am I?"

"You are on the Polarium orbital station. Security clearance required is level forty."

The voice came from the walls themselves.

"What is my clearance?"

"Level fifty."

Lying on her back, she looked up at the pattered ceiling twenty feet above. "Who are you?"

"I am the monitor. I have been supplied with provisions and a replication station. Are you injured?"

Ember chuckled, wheezing slightly. "Can't you tell?"

"No. Your baselines were not included in my programming."

"Check the pod. It has all my scans."

"Ah. Of course. Checking."

A moment later the monitor spoke. "I have it. Yes, you have suffered nerve damage and neural interference. I will take you to medical."

"Oh, goody. I thought it was just me."

A whirring broke the silence, and a hulking bot rounded the corner. It rolled up to her and stopped short, folding nearly in half and extending flat tines similar to that of a forklift. The tines slid under her knees and shoulders, and the bot straightened.

The change in altitude made her dizzy, but she would be damned if she passed out again. She needed to know what was going on.

"Based on your scans I am amazed you were able to get out of the pod." The monitor was surprised. It showed in its voice.

"I was motivated. I had slept long enough."

"I would say so. Barring a few interruptions, you have spent two hundred twenty-seven thousand seven hundred and sixty hours in that unit."

She felt dizzy. "What?"

"You were in two hundred—"

"I know that. What does that mean in days or years?"

"How many hours in each of your days?"

She closed her eyes. "Twenty-four."

"How many days in a year?"

"On average, three hundred and sixty-five."

"Just over twenty-six years." The monitor's voice was calm.

It was too much for Ember, she passed out against her better judgement.

She was naked. That was the first thing she noticed. The light covering on her just barely covered the tone of her skin. She tucked the sheet under her arms and cleared her throat. "Monitor?"

"Yes, Ember Velar?"

"Oh, you know my name, great."

"Yes. It was in your file. What do you need, Ember Velar?"

"Um . . . clothing first and then can you tell me how long I was asleep?"

"Twenty-six years on your measuring unit. Your clothing is in the cupboard to your left."

She swallowed. "Right. Right."

She got out of bed, and her body felt better. It was definitely under her control again. She glanced at the port site on her arm and closed her eyes. "How long was I out this time?"

"Six hours. We have regenerative technology powered by the star."

Ember sighed and opened the cupboard. "This isn't a suit."

"You do not need your suit right now. Be comfortable, and you will have the run of the station."

She slid the blue and silver gown off the hanger and slipped it over her head. The robe was encrusted with small gemstones, and it hung open. The gown went to her toes, so only her head and the tips of her fingers were visible.

"Are there any shoes?"

"They are not necessary for the areas you are allowed until you complete your recovery."

She lifted the hem of the gown and wiggled her toes. "I thought you said I was healed."

"You are, but you have no stamina. You need to walk slowly in the light until you are able to go on to the next level."

"The light?"

"The light of Polarium. The star's light is what all of the healing equipment is based on. The frequency is what does the healing, but it is also what rips the holes in space."

Ember was moving around the room and looking for the exit. "What?"

"That is what this base is. I monitor and locate the holes to other dimensions and alert Polarium. The star's Avatar pushes the wrecked ships back through the holes and closes the rifts."

"What is . . . how can someone . . . how do they even form?"

The monitor was only too happy to fill in the blanks. "Polarium is a nexus point in space and time. You can see it from a thousand worlds, each in a different universe. Sometimes, there are stresses in that universe that tear a hole in the ether. He patches the ether and seals the breach so that realities don't collide."

"The Avatar?" Avatars had been a whisper of information in the files she had been raiding.

The monitor paused. "You have not met the Avatar of your world?"

"We don't have one."

"Odd. The file says you are from Terra. Terra is a sentient world."

Ember wished that she had a place to stare. "I don't understand."

"Your world is alive. It has been making matches for its daughters throughout the cosmos."

She turned slowly in place. "How do you even know that?"

"Polarium is sentient. Polarium is linked to Terra, I am linked to Polarium. You are a child of Terra, offered to Polarium. He has offered you to his Avatar, but Cross is interested. He can't see you when he looks at you."

She leaned against the wall and tried to fade into it.

"That is the situation he has a problem with. When he isn't using Polarium's energy he uses his own senses. His senses can't see you."

She blinked. "Seriously?"

"Yes. Your talents operate on a frequency that is difficult for the Rehalik to perceive."

She didn't want to ask what that was. She moved along the wall of the room and finally triggered a door. She stumbled out of the medical unit and into bright and blazing light.

"The light of Polarium floods this level at this time. Your eyes were adjusted while you were being repaired. You should be able to see in a moment. Right now, you are fighting reflexes. Let your eyes adapt."

Ember squinted, and though the light level should have turned her eyes into black cinders, she could see. "Why am I trusting a disembodied voice?"

"You don't have anything else."

That was true. If he was right about how long she had been in stasis, her daughter would have had the letter for ten years already. She would be twenty-eight. Numb, Ember walked to the panel letting in the light. Her daughter would be older than she was.

She stared out at the stars, the wreckage and the darker than dark marks in space.

"Ember Velar, you are crying."

"My daughter grew up, and I didn't know anything about it. I wasn't there."

The monitor was silent for a moment. "I didn't know you had a daughter."

She sniffled. "Wasn't it in my file?"

"None of the other Volunteers had children. Why were you different?"

She hiccuped. "I don't know."

She stared into the light, and she wanted nothing more than to be like it. She wanted to be bright, cold and anonymous.

"The bot will take you to your quarters, Ember Velar. You need a meal and some rest."

"I have been asleep for twenty-six years. I have slept enough."

"Changes have occurred to your biology that require time to integrate."

She was still numb. "There were changes made?"

"It was in your contract. Changes for adaptation were allowed."

Ember nodded. The bot rolled up, and it bowed before rolling along a path, pausing when she didn't immediately follow.

"Monitor?"

"Yes, Ember Velor?"

"How do you know about my contract?" Ember took slow steps after the bot, and it matched her speed as she followed it.

"I know it is difficult to accept, but you were requested by this station. The Avatar cannot do his work alone and having a companion from a receptive species is highly desirable."

She stumbled and when she straightened she asked, "Right. Do you have a communication's array?"

"I do."

"Can you contact the Alliance?"

"Of course, but you are not leaving."

She chuckled. "I have gathered that. No, I want to know if my daughter made it to the stars."

"I will ask Polarium. If it agrees, I will send the request for information."

Ember nodded. "It is a start. Thank you, monitor."

"You are welcome, Ember Velar. Rest well."

She chuckled and followed the robot until it paused next

to an open door. A meal was waiting for her in a dispenser, and the bed looked incredibly inviting.

She ate the oatmeal-like substance and then headed to bed. She didn't even bother to get undressed. Natural sleep awaited her.

CHAPTER FOUR

Cross walked through the station and headed for the control center. "Monitor, do we have increased activity?"

"No, Avatar. There is a two percent decrease in tears."

Cross nodded. "If you say so. How is our guest doing?"

"She is awake, aware, and upset."

Cross chuckled. "You told her that she was a mail-order bride for a celestial being?"

"Not in those words. She is unhappy."

Cross opened the control center and sat in the command seat. He linked his mind with that of the station, and he saw what the orbital body saw.

The rifts were still appearing, but not at an accelerated rate. It was good. Despite Polarium boosting his energy, Cross got tired.

"Where did you put her?"

"She is on the central deck, near the main lift. Right now, she is sleeping."

Cross chuckled. "You would think she has had enough rest."

"She is being altered. It is tiring."

"Altered?" Cross raised his brows. "What are you doing to her?"

Making her closer to a Rehalik. You cannot do the work here alone anymore, and I am not getting less powerful. I tear reality apart, and you put it back together. You cannot continue alone.

Cross was astounded. "You ordered a second Avatar?"

Of course. Your body can barely contain me. Hers has already had a living being inside it.

"What?"

Monitor filled in. "She has had a child. Her body is used to alteration and containment. Polarium chose her because of that."

Cross was still shocked. "Where is her child?"

I did not ask, but it was healthy and alive when she went into the pod.

Monitor spoke, "The files that were transported with her indicate that her child was taken from her and she exhausted her finances to try and get her back. She then enrolled in the Volunteer program."

Cross blinked. "That is all in there?"

"The Ontex who prepared the report was very specific as to Ember Velar's motivations." Monitor was clear.

Cross listened to the tone and chuckled. "One day with her and you are already on her side. It seems she makes friends wherever she goes."

"I am a disembodied voice. I am hardly a friend." Monitor sounded defensive.

Cross grinned. "I have never heard you call yourself that before and I have known you for nine decades."

Monitor was silent.

Do not tease him. I had him built to help us, not to entertain you.

Cross nodded at the voice in his head. "Right. Now, where is she?"

He spun through the internal cams and found her quarters. Oddly enough, Monitor had placed her right next to him.

The woman didn't have the glowing grey cast of a Rehalik female, but her curves were all in the correct place and proportion. She had fallen asleep in her clothing, but the fabric outlined every part of her.

"Hm, I am guessing that I should have gotten to her

sooner. It seems a shame to think that she was floating around in the wreckage for fifteen years."

Monitor was silent.

"Oh, you didn't tell her that. Funny, you are usually so forthcoming with information."

Monitor stated softly, "I would like permission to send a contact burst to the Alliance."

Cross felt Polarium push forward. *"Why?"*

"Ember Velar wishes to know if her daughter made it to the Alliance."

Authorization is granted for all communications regarding Ember Velar and her daughter. If contact can be made, we will facilitate it.

Monitor answered, "Understood. I have sent the information request."

Cross's attention kept being drawn by the image of the woman in a deep and dreamless sleep. Her hair was up in a tie, but it had done some growing when she woke. It formed a rich halo around her features. Her ears were barely visible, but they appeared to be round on the upper arch. Huh. Different.

Monitor asked, "Avatar, why are you enlarging the screen so that only her ear is visible?"

"I feel that looking at her now will get me used to her odd features," Cross muttered. The scanner moved across her forehead, down her nose, and across her cheeks. Her lips were soft in appearance and a darker shade than the rest of her skin.

You will meet her soon enough. Right now, her tolerance to radiation is not what it needs to be. You must be patient. Meeting you now would injure her.

"Is she that sensitive?"

Her species is. Their skin boils, and cells break. Give her some time to grow into the alterations that have been instituted into her body. Monitor says that her eyes are already adapting, so the rest of the corrective measures should come along soon. Monitor will monitor her, and in less than ten days she should be able to withstand a meeting.

Cross looked down at his hands and the faint glow that he emitted. "Okay, I see your point."

Monitor spoke, "Leave her with me, and she will soon be ready for a face to face meeting, but I believe that information from the Alliance would do wonders for her mood."

Cross asked, "She's moody?"

"She has just learned that physically, her daughter is older than she is. That must be unsettling."

Cross nodded. "I can see that. We can't all be selected because we can withstand radiation. She was chosen for the ability to be transformed into something that can."

Monitor answered. "Precisely. And she was chosen with the potential of an Avatar in mind."

Cross resumed normal viewing of her room, and he tried to guess how tall she was. The pod had given him no clear view, and she was a different colour now. "What happened to her skin tone? She used to be blue."

"She takes on the colouration of her surroundings. She was in blue gel, she became blue gel."

Cross looked at the sleeping woman in surprise. "Why can I see her now?"

Monitor responded. "The robe she is wearing has active crystals that vibrate at a complementary frequency. She will remain visible to you as long as she is wearing it. That will last until her suit is ready."

Cross paused. "You are that confident?"

I ordered the suit. She will have it the moment that I take up residence in her.

"You don't mean that she will be your Avatar?"

Of course, she will. You both will. I pledged to have you remain as my Avatar until you chose to retire, or until your body can no longer contain me.

Cross was conflicted. "She isn't even the right species for you."

Her mind is close enough, her body has the correct frequency. I simply need to bolster her cellular structure, and then I can move in.

"She signed up for that?"

She agreed to any necessary alterations, so I am altering her.

The tone of the star didn't brook any disagreement. Cross had been put in his place for now. He was going to keep an eye on the new arrival, and if Polarium stepped over the line, Cross would take measures. He didn't know what they would be, but he would think of something.

I would expect no less.

Ember got up and grimaced at the room around her. She was hungry again.

She stretched up, aiming for the ceiling with her fingertips. Her clothing was surprisingly unwrinkled.

The food dispenser chimed, and the monitor said, "Good rising to you, Ember Velar."

"Call me Ember, please."

"Ember."

"Thank you. Good . . . uh . . . rising to you."

Monitor laughed. "I am always here, Ember. Your meal is ready. Once you have eaten, the Avatar will depart, and you can enter the com center."

"Why do I have to wait?" She pulled out the tray of dishes and sat down to start eating.

"The Avatar is highly radioactive. You are not resistant to the radiation, yet."

"Yet?" She mumbled it around a mouthful of something that was close to oatmeal.

"Because of our proximity, coding has been installed in your cells that will increase your body's ability to process the radiation."

Ember flexed her hand. "I don't feel very different."

"You won't. That is the design. It is supposed to be unobtrusive in execution. In a few days, you will be able to withstand the energy output of a star at close range."

As Ember continued to move her left hand, a slight sheen moved across her skin.

"Is the shine part of the process?"

"No, you need a bath. It is residue from the pod."

Ember coughed as she laughed. "Right. So, the bathroom is where?"

"The main bathing facilities are on the level below, but I think that the bath that is located in the left wall behind your bed should be suitable."

She laughed. "I am taking the hint. So, do I get a change of clothing?"

A wall panel moved to let a wardrobe slide forward. "Choose what you like."

She finished her food and stuck it back in the slot. The tray was pulled in, and it went wherever dirty dishes on a space station went.

Ember found the bathroom, and after asking the monitor for a few pointers on how to manage the plumbing, she went for a quick shower to get the coating from her skin.

Damp and clean, she wandered into her room and opened the wardrobe. There were versions of the robe and gown in a variety of vivid colours. She picked a combination in ruby red.

"You look lovely. Now, the Avatar has departed, so you are clear to view the com center."

"Oh, hooray."

She blinked at the sound of sarcasm coming from her own mouth.

In a more polite tone, she asked, "Monitor, what can I

learn at the com center?"

"You can learn what we do. We are here to protect hundreds of universes. You are going to join us in our efforts."

Ember blinked. "That is kinda pushy."

"I am aware, but another Avatar was desperately needed, and you were a perfect fit. The more training that we can put you through before Polarium joins with you, the faster you will gain control over your skills."

"Polarium will what?"

"Follow the bot to the com center. I will explain it there."

She swallowed nervously and did as the monitor asked. It wasn't like she had anything else to do.

CHAPTER FIVE

Three days of staring at the projection all around her was enough. Ember got out of the command chair and left the com center without saying a word to the monitor.

She walked to the end of her allowed path and stared out at the stars. She pressed her hands to the force shield that kept the atmosphere in place, and she watched the flickering light of the Avatar of Polarium move in the quadrant nearest the base.

It had taken the monitor two days to convince her that she was needed. The last day was her figuring out where she was going to start.

"Monitor, when does the Avatar return?"

"He will be here in a few hours. Why?"

"Because I believe I am ready now, but I am going to lose my nerve."

"I will send the message to Polarium."

She nodded and continued to watch the miniscule figure against the huge bulk of the swirling star.

Her skin was coated with a soft gold sheen. The colour was now permanent, and it would allow the star to provide her with life support when she left the station. It was one of the changes that had been made to her body. The other changes were far less visible, but she could feel them.

The ports had all been removed from her body. Even if she wanted to, there was no way to get back into the pod now. The needles would bend against her skin. She had tried it with a fork.

Monitor had sent a message to the Alliance, but there hadn't been a response yet. There was no word to let her know if her daughter had made it to the stars.

Ember kept her hands pressed against the clear barrier, and she waited. She waited for any bit of information that would change what was happening right now. Right now, she was in between everything, and she was tired of it.

"Polarium wishes you to go to level fifty and wait at the viewing area closest to the star."

Ember smiled. "Good."

She turned her back on the star and walked toward the lift. Whatever was going to happen, it would be a step in a direction she had never imagined.

She was at the point and waiting, facing the star. Nothing happened for ten minutes, so she asked, "Monitor, what now?"

There was no answer from the station. A bright ball of white came out of the star, and it was heading directly toward her.

Ember exhaled slowly and pressed her hands against the surface of the barrier once again. She leaned into the approach and kept her breathing even.

"You are either very brave or very stupid." A masculine voice spoke from behind her.

She turned to see who was talking and the rush of white energy struck her. The impact sent her spinning across the width of the station.

Fire was all around her. She could see it, hear it and feel it coursing through her veins. It skated along her skin and burned in her gut.

You were not quite ready for this, but you are close enough. I am Polarium, and you are my Avatar.

She tried not to scream, and the fire soon merged and became part of her completely.

Ember felt him moving through her mind, turning over

her thoughts and memories. When she touched his con-sciousness, she saw millions of years. It was too much for her overtaxed body. She let her mind go black.

There was darkness in front of her when she opened her eyes. Transparent, shimmering darkness.

I am glad you have joined me. Don't try and take control of your body. You don't know how to use my energies yet, and we need to take care of this rift.

She watched as her own hands stretched outward and a pulse of power was sent out to seal the hole in space. The cascade started as a solid jolt that changed into a pulse matching the frequency of the universe below.

If Ember stared long enough, she could see other planets, other stars, and if someone was out there, they could see her.

The edges of space thickened and the distant universe faded under the repair.

Well done. You haven't panicked, and you have allowed me full access to your motions. We shall return to the station, and you may ask me questions there.

Um, thank you. The form of propulsion that the star used wasn't anything that she could quantify. It wrapped energy around her and moved through space like a wave of radiation.

You will be able to control these methods of transport as well. Even solid light teleportation will be available to you in time.

That sounds intriguing.

You can visit a thousand universes, and millions of planets, without putting your body at risk.

Can you just get me into a place where there is something to breathe? I know that I don't need to right now, but I really want to.

She felt an amused ripple in her mind, and the station got closer at an incredible rate.

When they were fifty meters from the station window,

she closed her eyes and felt a jelly-like touch wrap around her before she was in the climate-controlled area.

You can breathe now.

She inhaled deeply, her body didn't react. It was perfectly fine. It was her mind that was relieved.

You are adapting well. Your body is nearly complete.

She looked down. She was wearing the same ruby gown and robe she had been wearing when Polarium had struck her.

"Is this how you got your other Avatar?" She flipped out the robe, and she glanced around the wide open space.

Cross was traded to me. His folk came through on a ship, and I was in a destroying mood. They begged me and offered him to me, so I accepted him.

She was taken aback. "Ships come through?"

Cross came in, and he answered her question. "Of course. That is why Polarium needs us. He needs us to communicate for him. If you check, you can speak nine hundred languages now."

"How would I check—" She paused when she realized she wasn't speaking English and hadn't been speaking it since she arrived. "Oh."

Cross nodded. "He has been in your mind for a while, and your pod was programmed for Alliance languages. You have been learning for decades."

Ember looked at him as he approached and took in the silvery cast to his face, the shades in his hair and the fact that he was quite a bit taller than she had first guessed.

Six-foot-eight or nine would be her current estimate of his height. His shoulders were wider than hers by half her body width. He was in a suit that mimicked her initial bodysuit in the pod, but his had heavy bands of metal that ran through it. The patterns didn't have any meaning for her, but the blazing star icon on both of his shoulders definitely looked like Polarium.

"Hello. I am Ember." It was all she could think to do. She extended her hand to him.

He grinned and stepped toward her, putting his hands on her arms and pulling her into his embrace. He kissed her on both cheeks and once on the forehead. "Welcome, Ember."

The radiation in her body had nothing to do with the sudden surge of heat to her face. When he stepped back, she kept very still.

"So, you have not yet gotten your suit?" He cocked his head.

Ember swallowed as a wave of power took her mind over. *"I am still deciding on what she will wear as my Avatar. There are a number of options open with her gender. Her body may make it less acrimonious when it comes to dealing with lost ships. Look at this form. Isn't it distracting?"*

Ember was mortified as Cross looked her over. He nodded "She does have an elegant frame. It would make a difference in getting the folk back where they belong. Many cultures perceive a woman as less threatening."

"Whether that is true or not. Excellent. See? She is providing options we did not have before her decanting."

The words were coming out of her mouth, but they had nothing to do with her thoughts. Polarium was working through her and talking about her as if she was a hostess on an aircraft.

Cross chuckled. "I can see that she is not too pleased to be used as a conduit. Ember, be at ease. He means well."

She had control of herself at last. "I understand the urgency of this situation and the importance of it. I just don't want to be flying around in a gown and robe without underwear."

Cross laughed. "Right. Come this way. I will take you to your appropriate garb."

Ember looked at him and the knowing look in his eyes. "He had you flying around naked, didn't he?"

Cross extended his arm to her, and she took it, walking

slowly with him across the expanse and toward a flickering image in the center of the space.

"Only for the first two decades. After that, I put my foot down."

She giggled, and a door opened in front of them. Through the opening in the electric field, she could see a female-figured bodysuit suspended in a blue-lit column. It was beautiful, and she sighed when she saw there was a floor-length sleeveless robe to match.

"Thankfully, he saw the sensibility in giving you a radiation resistant suit on day one." Cross pulled her forward.

Ember walked up to the suit that was decorated in designs of crimson, blue and shocks of gold. The base was the same glowing colour as Polarium, but the patterns on the reinforced seams of the suit were incredible.

"Wow. That is a work of art."

"Indeed. It is yours. You can try it on." Cross hung back.

She glanced at him. "Are you sure that it's mine?"

He grinned. "It definitely isn't mine. That cut is all wrong for me."

Ember turned back to the suit, and when she reached for it, it reached back. It was an effort to climb into it, and Cross had to turn away as he was in danger of choking on his laughter as she pulled it on under her gown and then shimmied it upward in a move she learned in high school. It was amazing to think that a move she had learned in a locker room had served her in a distant part of the universe.

CHAPTER SIX

Ember stood in the shuttle bay of the Hycroth ship, and she looked at the tentacled aliens that she had to work with. "Greetings from Polarium. I am here as the Avatar of the star in order to help you back to your own universe."

The captain stepped forward and cocked his bulgy head. "Where are we?"

"You have flown through a hole in space. We wish to put you back where you belong."

One of the subordinates came forward. "What are you?"

"I am a being of this universe, I also speak for the star. We need you to cut all engines, keep life support to a minimum, and hang on."

The captain stared at her. "Who are you to tell us this?"

"*I am an Avatar of Polarium. I am the voice of the star, and if you do not follow my direction, you will fall into an endless orbit that will only end in your destruction. You have a choice. Send a signal if you are prepared to comply, and you can go home.*"

Ember watched as Polarium lifted off the deck plates and he flew her back toward the door to the shuttle bay. The part that would truly disturb the aliens was Polarium phasing her through the hull. That was the reason for the suit. Not just any fabric could pass through matter. It took a special designer to make a suit like that. It was one of Polarium's passions. He loved dressing his dolls up.

Ember took over control of her body once they were out of the ship. She flew a distance away and then turned to watch the ship.

She slowly twirled and twisted around as she waited.

When the ship slowly powered down, she grinned. Polarium summoned Cross, and Ember moved to place her hands next to the ship's hull. It wasn't a push, so much as she was positioning herself between the gravity of the star and the hull. With Polarium pulling the strings, she had enough energy to keep the two things apart.

The glowing bolt that was Cross flew up and pushed against the ship. He moved it, and once it was in motion, she joined him. They didn't need to speak. Polarium moved them both into the right position for the manoeuvre.

With the propulsion off, they could move the ship easily as long as Polarium gave them the barrier to push against.

Once the ship was moving, she stopped pushing and started to weave lines of energy on either side of the tear. When Cross was on her side, and the ship was on the other, she pulled at the lines of power and sealed the hole, shutting off the light from the other universe.

Cross flew up to her and smiled. He waved, did a slow arc and headed off to another rift.

There were two other float-ins that Ember had to attend to and one of them was heading right for the star. She flew off to get in front of it while Polarium sent a signal via their com system.

It was odd to listen to a conversation in another language that didn't seem to be made of anything other than deep gurgles.

Polarium's direct conversation using their ship's systems seemed to be enough to get them to cooperate. They shut down and prepared for the push.

She flew toward the ship on waves of radiation and extended her hands toward the hull. She saw the crackle of energy before she felt it, and it coursed through her with no effect.

That was very impolite.

Ember didn't comment. She shoved hard and got the ship moving. When the weapons array pointed toward her, Polarium gave her the power, but it was her body that redirected the energy back at the ship. The rear of the vessel exploded, and interior atmosphere streamed out. The ship picked up speed and vented whatever they breathed. The ship shot through the tear, and she closed the energy rip behind them. They could limp home in their own universe.

She flexed her hands and looked down at the scorch marks on her abdomen. *Thanks for the suit, Polarium.*

This is an occupational hazard. Not everyone who falls through the rift is prepared to return home. It is to everyone's benefit that we send them back where they came from.

Can the suit be fixed? She lazily turned away from the closed patch in space and propelled herself back to the station. It was almost easy to match her velocity and trajectory now that she had a few weeks of practice.

There are six new suits waiting for you.

She passed through the energy seal on deck fifty. "Wonderful. I am glad to see that you are thinking ahead."

"Was that addressed to me, Ember?" Monitor murmured in an amused tone.

"No, I was muttering to Polarium. How are you today?"

"I need you down at the com station." Monitor was serious.

Ember shrugged and headed for the lift. "On my way."

Exploring the station took up her spare time, but there was nothing like wandering into the command area to see the displays and projections of the local rifts and distant stars. Somewhere, out there, was Earth.

"Okay, I am here, Monitor. What did you need to show me?"

"Take the chair. I have gotten a response from the recruitment branch of the Alliance."

She was lowering herself when she heard that, and she

landed with a thud. "You did?"

"We did. The information is interesting, and I had to use genetic matches to find your daughter, but between the archive and the genes, I believe we have located your offspring."

"Show me, please."

A woman's face was suddenly on the screen, and Ember gasped. She covered her mouth with her hand, and she looked at the young lady who had a wry smile and an intelligent twinkle in her eyes. Ember never dreamed that her daughter would share so many of her features.

"What is her name?"

"Ember, I would like to introduce you to Citadel Specialist, Margo Amber Leclerk. She is stationed at Citadel Balen and is working toward taking an administrative position of her own."

She listened to Monitor's voice, but she was locked into staring at her daughter's face.

She whispered, "When did she enroll in the program?"

His voice was soft. "She enrolled when she was fourteen and left when she was eighteen years and one day."

Ember blinked. "Was she unhappy?"

"I am sure that I don't know, but there are sealed correspondences with you. I have the files, but it will take your authorization to open them."

She blinked rapidly. "There are messages for me?"

"Eighty-four to be precise."

She giggled and sobbed through her fingers. "Eighty-four?"

"She has recorded one message for you per Terran month or every thirty days. The Alliance has kept them in an archive until the day you ask for them."

Ember lowered her hand and gripped the arms of the command chair. "Where does she think I have been?"

"There is a note in your file about the stasis pod. It kept sending a ping when it paused for maintenance. The Alliance knew you were alive. Eventually, each ping reached a relay station that could pass it on."

"Even through the ships that were carrying me?"

Monitor let out what passed for a chuckle. "It is a very sophisticated pod."

She wrinkled her nose and then paused. "Can I send my daughter a message?"

"Of course, but you might want to listen to her messages first."

"Can I? Do I have to do it here?"

Monitor said, "Unfortunately this is the best place to view them. Once you have watched a letter, you can view it at your leisure in your quarters, but for the first viewing, seeing her holographic projection at full size is your best option."

Polarium, do I have time to watch a few of them now?

The voice in her head sounded calm and concerned. *I insist that you do. I look forward to seeing your offspring.*

"Right. Monitor, I have authorization from Polarium, so can you show me the first letter?"

"I am delighted. File one . . ."

"Hiya, Mom. Damn, that feels weird. Right. Mom. Well, since you are out here in space somewhere, I thought I would try and get in touch. My name is Margo Amber Leclerk, but I am guessing you know that. I used to be mad at you, but then I looked into you, and the more I looked, the more I understood that you did what you could until you had nothing left to fight with. Your letter just confirmed it."

Ember felt the tear trickle down her cheek. Her daughter was a glorious eighteen. Her hair was a few shades lighter than Ember's, but otherwise, the resemblance was unmistakable.

"I have enrolled in the Volunteer program and have actually met the Earth's Avatar. Can you imagine it? There is really a woman who contains the thoughts and will of the planet under our feet."

Margo shifted from side to side and then she smiled. "I guess I hope that I can see you one day, even though the Alliance officers say that you have been missing but are known to be alive. I hope you are somewhere safe right now and that you are comfortable. Talk to you soon."

The projection went blank, and Ember wiped her tears away. When she was under her own control again, she looked up and smiled. "Can I see more?"

Monitor responded by dimming the lights and projecting an image of Margo in a body suit. She waved. "Hi, Mom."

Ember sat back and watched her daughter tell her about her first month of basic training. Ember laughed at some of the events described and wanted to punch some other new Volunteers for being rude to her little girl.

Watching the letters of the first two years made her laugh, cry and gave her an incredible urge to skip to the end. Monitor refused to do it, though. He was very linear when it came to delivering the mail.

She wished that she had popcorn, and she could feel Polarium watching from behind her eyes. He felt affection for the creatures living in his star system, but it was nothing like this. This was a moment in her life that she would cherish always. Her daughter had called her *Mom* for the first time ever.

CHAPTER SEVEN

The letters became a treat for her when she wasn't working to keep the space around Polarium clear. When Ember watched the last one, she stood in front of her daughter's image.

The robes of a Citadel Specialist swung slightly as she stood in the center of the projection.

"Hi, Mom. My friends here on Balen think I am nuts for talking to you, but that is just one of my many loveable characteristics." Margo grinned.

"I have gotten a message that you have come out of the stasis pod. Damn. That is one beauty sleep that I don't envy. I hope you came out of it okay. It was a long time to be under."

Ember muttered, "You're telling me."

"I know I mentioned earlier that I have a boyfriend, but I didn't get into specifics. He's Azon, a specialist in aerial combat and yes, that means he can fly." Margo grinned. "He isn't superman, but he is a dark purple-blue. He is fully behind my letters to you, even if they are just messages."

Ember grinned and then scowled. "Monitor, when this is over, I want specs on her Azon."

"That is classified information, Ember."

"I do not care." She crossed her arms and paid attention to Margo's letter again.

"I can't believe that blending in could be a talent, but since I have been on a few missions after my training, I now know that being part of the background can save lives."

Margo hugged herself. "I never imagined that I could make any kind of difference, but here I am, disappearing for a living and loving it."

Ember smiled. "I always liked it myself."

"Well, I leave tomorrow on a mission, so I will talk to you in a month. Hugs, Mom. Thanks for listening." Margo waved, and the platform went dark.

Ember sighed. It had been three weeks since the first file had been shown to her, and now she was all caught up.

Polarium, are we able to send a message to her?

Of course, Ember. I would not have allowed you to get the information if I wasn't going to allow communication.

Ember got out of the chair and stalked out and into her quarters. She left the door open while she went through her wardrobe. She wanted to make a good impression.

Cross called out from the doorway. "What are you looking for?"

Ember glanced back at him and winced at the scorch marks and damage to his suit. "I am looking for something that says I am mature and responsible. What happened to you?"

"Dual asteroid collision. I got pinned in between until they slowed to a halt."

She blinked at him. "Why didn't Polarium send me out?"

"The same reason he didn't send me when you were dealing with the Jurcorans. You could handle it."

She wrinkled her nose. "They were particularly unpleasant and grabby."

"And yet, you were left on your own. I would gladly have torn the ship apart, but they were not dangerous, only insecure. You handled them, and they made it home." Cross wandered inside her quarters. He reached past her into the wardrobe and pulled out a vivid blue robe. "If you don't want to wear your very stunning suit and robe, I would put this on over the suit. The suit is how you live now, so it is the best representative of your station."

He was close to her. Extremely close.

Ember pushed all thoughts of her ex aside and leaned up to kiss him.

Cross didn't push her away, but he didn't pull her close. When she ended the kiss, he smiled down at her, with Polarium glowing in his eyes.

"So, that was not wanted?" She didn't look away. With only the two of them on the station, they didn't have a lot of space for shunning.

He handed her her robe and pulled her to him by the shoulders. "I didn't want to drop your clothing."

The kiss he gave her curled her toes and made her wish that he wasn't wearing his battered suit. When he leaned back, he asked, "Was that unwanted?"

She licked her lips, and his eyes continued shining bright with the mind of the star riding behind them. "It was definitely wanted and very appreciated."

"It is the beginning of a courtship for your people, yes?"

She nodded. "We have already done the shared meals and discussions of our past, so it is the next phase. Yes."

He smiled. "Good. What comes after this?"

"Bodily contact and eventually sex."

"Sex?"

"Intercourse." She punched him in the arm when she saw he was snickering. "Don't make me break out the euphemisms. What do your folk call it?"

He gave her a serious look. "Summoning the soul."

She blinked. "I have never had that particular experience."

He stroked her cheek. "I will be delighted to demonstrate when the time is right."

She didn't want to shiver at his comment, but she did.

Ember cleared her throat. "I think you are right and I

should just put on a new suit and robe. It is what I am now."

"And so much more. She will be proud to call you her mother."

Ember felt a lightening of her spirit. "She already does."

She made sure her hair was straight and over one shoulder. Her robes were smooth and hanging evenly, and she was wearing a new bodysuit.

Monitor was waiting for her authorization.

She took a deep breath. "Okay, right. I am good. Proceed, Monitor."

"Recording."

There was a dot set up for her to look at, so she smiled. "Hello, Margo. My name is Ember Velar, and I am your mother."

The exhalation was heartfelt. "I have been waiting years to do that."

"I have been waiting for years for this moment, but frankly, I thought I would look older when you were this age. Life never turns out the way we plan."

She sighed and then smiled. "I am a stellar Avatar. My star is Polarium, and if you are interested, he has the ability to help me do a long-range projection to talk to you, even if it is unlikely we will ever meet."

"I was young when I had you, and too young to fight to keep you. While I wish things were different, I hope that your upbringing was good, safe and comfortable. You seem very put together with none of the issues I was worried about being inherited."

"My ticket to the stars was my ability to blend in, but here it has been used to allow my genetics to be warped in order to let Polarium settle in. I think I am too radioactive for us to ever have contact, but know that I love you, I loved you when I carried you, and I love you now. Talk to you soon. If you want to know anything, just ask."

The light flickered, and she let the tears come.

Monitor remained uncharacteristically quiet. When she finished sobbing, she stood up and wiped her cheeks. "Any new tears, Monitor?"

"There are six today. Small ones."

"I should get to it then."

"It might help distract you, Ember."

She nodded. "Off I go."

"Wait, you need the coordinates."

Blushing, she stopped in her tracks. "Right."

She settled in the com chair and got the locations. They were farther away than she had ventured so far, but she really needed something to do.

Polarium was willing to help, and he kept quiet as she ran up to level fifty and walked out through the energy shield.

She flew through space at a speed that wasn't even possible back on Earth with a spaceship, but the area was full of the waves of radiation that Polarium put out and she was able to surf them to her destination.

The technique you use for using strands of energy is a definite time and power saver.

She chuckled softly. *When I was pregnant, I made dolls for my daughter. I couldn't do much, but I could sew, so I did. All the dolls but one were donated to charity when they took her away.*

What happened to the last doll?

She finished webbing one of the tears, and she yanked on the stitching. *I sent it with my baby. I don't know if they kept it.*

How many dolls did you sew?

Seventy-five, from basic to elaborate.

Is that good?

She laughed silently and sealed the tear. *It was good for me. I taught myself a skill and used it for the one I loved.*

I understand. These rifts and the dead didn't bother me until someone came to tell me that it was having larger ramifications.

My little portion of space was tearing apart planets simply because I didn't care to learn how to fix it. So, now I have Avatars to help me fix it, but no one in those worlds will ever know how much effort it took to make them safe again.

A lot of effort and you will never know if anyone noticed.

Exactly.

Ember smiled and propelled herself to the next rift. It was weird to think that she had anything in common with a giant ball of gas and energy. She supposed weirder things had happened, but she couldn't think of an example.

Chapter Eight

"Monitor, are there any new letters?" Ember was wearing one of the gowns and robes as she worked on growing some plants in the green space.

"No, Ember. It has only been a week. It takes a while to send the signals through the relays."

"Is there any way to know if she got my recording?"

"There is no interference on our com pathways. She would have the file relayed to her."

Ember dug a hole and planted one of the special seeds that Polarium had Cross bring to her. "I hate waiting."

"Polarium can teach you about waiting. He is a master of simply being himself until there was someone else."

Ember covered the seed and watered it. "That is a lie. He ordered me like I came from a catalogue and then had to wait until I got here."

"Yes, and he didn't want to wait, but the ships could only fly so fast."

She chuckled. "Well, I am glad I made it. Not sure I am a fan of the ship being shredded."

"They were refusing to part with you, and the ship glided in too close to an open rift. Their ship was torn to pieces and Cross had to cut your pod free. He was busy, so he left you there until he could come and reclaim you."

"Or until the pod died."

"The pod was set to absorb ambient radiation, you had the energy you needed."

"Until I didn't." She snorted.

Cross's voice came at her from around the corner. "Polarium set a timer on your pod. If I went too long without collecting you, the pod would send out a signal that we wouldn't be able to ignore."

She glanced over, and he leaned around the corner. "Flattering."

"It was what happened then, this is now. Now, what are you doing?"

She looked around the green space at all the small mounds of dirt. "I am planting a tree for each year of Margo's life. It will be a reminder for me, and eventually, this entire area will be filled with trees."

Cross looked at the seeds and appeared surprised. "Where did you get those?"

"Monitor had supply send them up. Why?"

He crouched and prodded the seeds with a fingertip. "They are from my home world. Every young man gets a bag of seeds, and as he travels, he plants one seed for every child he begins."

She blinked. "Wow."

"We do not have a high survival rate, so the plants and their fruit help keep our biological balance. They reset us."

"Do you have a lot of children?"

He shook his head. "We are also not prolific breeders. That is why we travel, we try and seed our kind in the stars in an effort to find a species that has a higher success rate. Our own couples cannot bring a child into the world together."

"That is horrible."

He looked up from the seeds. "That is why we travel the stars. Once a woman gets pregnant, or a man manages to find a partner, the child that they raise is spoiled and taken care of by the entire community."

"That is a lot of interesting social structure." She smiled

slightly and brushed the dirt off her hands.

"You are away from your contained world now. Different cultures have different issues, and it colours the way we deal with the universe around us. Survival is the key issue for most species and mine was no exception."

Ember looked at him, and he was wearing a serious expression. "Wait, so am I doing something horrible by using these seeds?"

"No. They are also used to make gardens when we homestead. As we are currently not going anywhere, I think this is very appropriate for our home."

She glanced around her and nodded. "It is starting to feel like home. We have a butler and a parent living with us."

Cross smiled wryly, "In us."

"That too." She rose to her feet. "Monitor, can you activate a watering cycle?"

"Of course, Ember."

A series of small nozzles appeared at ground level, and the soft mist that emerged clung to the soil before it began to dampen the ground.

She looked at Cross, and he stood straight. "I just have to wash up. Would you like to have dinner again?"

He nodded. "I would. I would also like to look at the stars with you."

Ember blinked, and she nodded shyly. "That sounds pleasant."

He chuckled. "You are hard on my ego."

She shrugged and headed for the door. "I am learning as I go."

"You have mastered keeping me in my place."

"I needed a hobby." She giggled as she left level thirty and used the open span in the center of the level to levitate herself to the fortieth floor. From there, she headed to her room, washed her hands and brushed her hair. Date night was becoming one of her favourite moments on the station. If she could get her nerve up, she was going to try to summon his soul tonight.

Ember walked out of her quarters, and she met Cross on the way to the dining hall.

"I haven't asked Polarium, but why is this station so big?"

Cross chuckled. "I asked. It fell through one of the rifts. Monitor came with it, so Polarium reprogrammed it for his Avatar. It makes a nice home base and the bots that are available keep things clean and functioning. They were programmed for our needs."

"So, he knew he was going to be getting an Avatar?"

"He had one before me, but when you don't have a place to rest and recharge, it drives you mad. Komil begged for death, and eventually, Polarium let him go."

Cross held her chair for her and stroked her shoulders before he walked around and took his seat.

"So, that is our way to quit? Polarium works us until we die?"

Cross shook his head as a bot pulled up with their meals. "No, we are Avatars now. We are no longer the species that we were born to. We will work for Polarium, we save lives and keep folk from getting lost, and we will remain together as long as Polarium maintains us."

She nodded. "Together?"

He took her hand and rubbed his thumb along her palm. "Together. We make a good team. He was not wrong about that."

She blushed. "I would have to agree. You have skills and practices that I could never duplicate."

"You have a light touch that doesn't cause bleed through in the energy lines."

Ember chuckled. Their compliments were getting weirdly specific.

She got up, walked around the table and sat in his lap. She smiled. "Keep talking."

He laughed and leaned in to kiss her, and their meal was left on the table.

He summoned her soul twice, and they were spooning on the floor, watching the stars through the force screen.

He measured her hand against his and smiled when she wiggled her fingers. "You are very loud."

She chuckled. "There was no one here to hear it but you."

Cross smiled happily. "I am a devoted audience for your song."

She laughed with a blush on her cheeks. "I am glad you could work out the difference in biology."

"It only took me a moment. You feel wonderful."

She blushed again.

They lay together for hours, her robe over top of them and the rotation of the station showing them their star before it rotated out to the empty expanse that led to other tiny stars in the distance.

It was a pretty good night when she looked at it from outside her situation, and from inside her own mind, she thought it was amazing.

CHAPTER NINE

Ember was tired. She stomped across level fifty, and she glared around her when she heard Monitor's voice.

"Ember, you have a letter."

Her mood swung from grim to hopeful so fast she felt her brain snap. "I do?"

"You do."

She sprinted to the com center and slid into the chair. "Play it."

"Yes, Avatar."

She wrinkled her nose, and to her shock, it wasn't Margo. The woman had long dark hair, was wearing Master's robes and there was a raptor of some kind on her shoulder.

"Avatar Ember, my name is Veera. I am the head of Citadel Balen. I am contacting you to let you know that your daughter is en-route to you. Please notify the Citadel when she arrives."

She kept talking, but Monitor interrupted. "Ember, there is a ship approaching."

Ember looked around. "Is it . . ."

"There is an Azon vessel on a slow approach. They are hailing the station. Should I answer?"

"Yes!" She slammed her hands down on the arms of the chair, got up and ran for the door before she remembered that she could fly.

Cross was coming in as she flew past. He called out a query, but it was Monitor who had to fill him in. Ember had a ship to meet.

She paced back and forth, waiting for the ship to extend a docking bridge. Cross came up behind her and wrapped his arms around her. He pressed a kiss to her temple. "If she is on this vessel, you will only have to wait a few minutes."

"Are you holding in your radiation?"

He laughed. "I am. Are you?"

"Oh, shit." She quickly pulled back all the power that her excitement was radiating.

Cross's arms were still moving with his silent chuckle when the ship docked, and the seal was made.

Ember's palms were sweaty. Four figures in military suits came toward them and paused at the entryway.

Cross leaned down, "You have to open the gate by command or touch."

She nodded and stepped out of his embrace, pressing her palm to the glowing section of the wall. The door opened, and the four travellers stepped in.

Ember stood next to Cross, and she watched as the newcomers took scans before removing their headgear.

Ember looked into the eyes that were so much like her own. She wanted to cry. Instead, she inclined her head. "Hello, Margo."

Her daughter gasped and covered her mouth with her hand. Ember blinked at the familiarity of the gesture.

The purple-blue Azon next to her supported her with a hand under her arm. Ember smiled. "You must be the flyer."

He blinked. "Kabro in Korzik. Citadel Specialist."

"I am Avatar Ember-Polarium. This is my mate, Avatar Cross-Polarium."

The bow that she got from the Azon and the two escorts that had come with them was profound.

Ember blushed.

Margo was staring. "I can't believe . . . you look younger than me."

Cross cleared his throat. "Technically, she is. The pod had a temporal restriction that kept her the same age that she went in with, aside from a few days of maintenance."

Margo reached out and then curled her fingers back.

Ember nodded with a lump in her throat. "May I give you a hug?"

Margo nodded and surged forward, grabbing Ember as if she never wanted to let go. Ember felt the same and held on, trying to absorb every moment of her daughter's life in that one contact.

When they parted, Ember stroked Margo's hair away from her forehead, and the other woman laughed.

Ember smiled. "What?"

"That is the same thing I do to my son. His hair sticks up everywhere."

Ember's knees buckled. "I am a grandmother?"

Margo grinned. "Yeah. I thought you knew."

Ember shook her head. "It has been over a year since I got a letter."

I got the letters. I ordered Monitor to keep them aside. This was my surprise for you.

Ember was speechless. "You were invited."

Margo suddenly looked unsure. "I thought we were."

Ember blinked as she realized what Margo was thinking. "No, I want you here. I am so happy to have you here, but the star invited you on my behalf and kept it from me."

Kabro caught on. "The stellar presence took over her body and kept her mind out of it. There are two people living in your mother's body. She is only one of them."

He touched his wife's shoulder.

The small touch seemed to wake Margo. "Right. That was described, I just thought you would be looking forward to this as long as I was."

"Oh, honey, I have been looking forward to this since the day we were separated. Never think for an instant that I didn't have you in my thoughts. Even Polarium got tired of hearing about you, so he started to give me more personal time."

Cross chuckled. "Polarium loves those who live in his domain, but Ember's obsession with you gives him a headache, and he doesn't have a head."

Margo chuckled.

Ember looked at the men behind the couple. "Not to be rude, but who are they?"

Margo blinked. "Oh, right. These are two Citadel members who have interest in stellar Avatars and living stars. They want to ask you questions. Your star approved them coming."

I did. There are more of my kind waking and even more in need of a way to communicate. If the Citadel can run an Avatar recruitment, we could have Avatars who come to us of their own free will.

Ember answered him silently, *Instead of mail ordering them like a talking toaster.*

Precisely.

Ember nodded. "Of course. I have just been briefed, if you would like to follow me to the observation deck, I can answer any questions you have."

Cross put his arm around her shoulder, and he pressed a kiss to her cheek. "I will take them. You spend time with your daughter."

Ember smiled at him and watched him take the other two of their guests off to learn the ways of stars with bodies.

She turned back to Margo and Kabro. "Would you like to see the gardens?"

Margo grinned. "Please. I didn't think you could grow much with this level of ambient radiation."

Ember began to walk toward the lift. "They are shielded."

Kabro looked around. "I am guessing that they would have to be."

She took them to the gardens, and she smiled when she saw Margo's mouth open. "There are so many of them."

Ember walked to the plants she called *Cross's trees*. "I planted one for every year of your life that I missed. I guess I can stop planting now."

"What are the small bushes everywhere?"

"Ah, I planted one of those low bushes for every month I have been on the station. I am going to have to stop soon, I am running out of room." Ember laughed and touched one of the little fire-red bushes.

"How long have you been here?"

"Just over two years. There are twenty-five little shrubs all doing their thing for oxygen creation and atmosphere scrubbing."

Kabro looked around. "It seems like more than that."

"Each original plant reproduces itself every three months. I have to keep drying and pulverizing them before I put them into the recycler or they gum up the works."

Kabro was intensely interested in the plants, and Margo smiled and said, "His family has greenhouses."

Ember answered what she could and had Monitor answer what she couldn't.

Ember wandered over to where Margo was admiring a bloom. "You said you had a child?"

"Yes. A son. He's on the warship."

Ember fought the urge to get her ass into that ship right away. She cleared her throat. "Can I meet him?"

Margo bit her lip. "You would have to come on board. He isn't radiation resistant, nor could we find a suit in his size."

Ember nodded. "Of course."

"If you let us get the halls cleared, you can come and meet him if he is in a containment shell."

Ember smiled. "I would like that."

"We are staying here for the week as long as our shielding

holds out, so we have a date."

Over the next week, Ember learned about the family that had adopted Margo, their lives, their comfort, and their determination that she not feel confined. They gave her the confidence and competence to be free, and she used it.

Ember brushed at her bodysuit and her robes on the last day that the warship was docked.

Cross was already up and speaking to the representatives of the Citadel. Ember was going over to the warship to meet her grandson.

She walked up to the connected pathway and opened the door. The walkway out across empty space should have freaked her out if she hadn't spent the last two years fighting tears in the universe.

The door to the ship was waiting, and they had a proper airlock. Ember was rarely invited onto the ships that she boarded, so it was a bit of a surprise to see the command crew there and bowing to her. As she passed, she noted a few curious glances and at least two recording devices. It was a good thing she had brushed her hair. This was a historic moment for someone.

Margo looked so happy and relaxed, she grabbed Ember's hand and hauled her through the ship to an area that had private quarters in it. Margo opened the door with a flourish.

"Ember Velar, may I present to you your grandson, Embiru. Wait, where the hell is he?" Margo looked at the large shielded pod in the center of the room, and Ember laughed.

"He is in the center, chewing on something. He is using a blending technique." Ember smiled. "You did the same. You only appeared on half the ultrasounds I had. They were panicking and thought I had hysterical pregnancy while you were just playing peekaboo."

Margo sighed and glanced at her. "Do you have your radiation tamped down?"

"I am holding it in."

"Good." Without any warning, Margo flipped the pod open and reached for her son. The child was scooped up, and the next moment, he was in Ember's arms.

Ember blinked. "You said his name was . . ."

"Embiru. It was my tribute to you as I had just gotten your letter before he was born. Knowing that you were out here facing the same stuff that I was, brought me closer to you than I thought possible."

Ember smiled. "Embiru. I am pleased to meet you. I am your grandma Ember. What is that you are holding?"

Margo reached out and brushed Embiru's hair from his forehead. "When I was growing up, there were pictures of me holding this doll. My parents kept it, and when I left for the stars, I took it with me. When I was a teenager, my mom told me that my birth mom had made the doll and I screamed when they tried to take it away, so they let me keep it."

Ember blinked at the little grey, scruffy dolly. "I did make one for you. It had a little petticoat, stitched eyes, and hair that was embroidered in place so no baby would choke on it."

"Embiru was born with his fangs starting, so he has been rough on it. We both love it though. He sleeps with it every night."

Embiru looked up at Ember with the doll stuffed in his mouth and his giant green-gold eyes bright. He looked like a little blue lion and his grandma's heart just melted.

"I am very glad to meet you, little dude."

He took his mouth off the doll and gave her a wide and predatorially toothy grin.

Margo chuckled. "Thankfully, bottle feeding is accepted by Kabro's family of Azon."

Ember laughed. "I can see why that would be a good idea."

She was going to say more when she felt a disturbance in the ship.

She kissed Embiru, hugged Margo, and whispered, "I am going to keep in touch, but for now, I have to work."

She left Margo's quarters and ran for the shuttle bay. She wasn't going to make it in time.

Turn left and jump. We can leave via the stargazer dome.

Righto. Ember bolted past a number of crew members who flattened back to get out of her way. The collision alarm was sounding.

Ember jumped, wrapped herself in star fire and passed through the shielded window on the observation deck.

The problem was apparent. A war had spilled into Polarium's realm, and a ship was heading straight for the Azon cruiser.

Ember sped up and formed a ball of power in front of her hands. It acted as a cushion as she pushed as hard and fast as she could. The spread of power kept her from breaking through the ship and slowly stopped the vessel a few hundred yards from the Azon ship.

Once it was stopped, she got it moving again. Cross was dealing with other vessels, and she pushed the ship back through the hole where other embattled ships were fighting.

Ember didn't care about the other ships right then. It was enough to keep Margo and Embiru safe, along with Kabro if she had to stretch her protection.

She shoved the ship back through the portal and wove pieces of space back together as Cross did the same with his burdens. When the ships were through, she sealed the rift and turned back to look at the station.

Polarium, is anyone injured?

No, but they are leaving. Their shields took a jolt when you passed through them. It isn't safe for their personnel here.

Right. Glad I said goodbye.

Your daughter is impressive. Very much your genetic inheritor.

Ember was ridiculously pleased by that. *Thank you.*

Cross came up beside her and wrapped his arm around her waist. He got her back to the station, and he held her while she sobbed.

His surprise when she looked up was apparent. "I thought you were upset."

"I was, but I got to see and hold my family for the first time ever. No explosion or invading army is going to take that away from me."

Cross narrowed his eyes. "You are a very strange woman. I like it."

She laughed and hugged him, planning her next letter to her daughter and her first to her grandson. They were going to have adventures in the Citadel, and even long distance, she was going to be part of their lives.

AUTHOR'S NOTE

By the end of this book, it has been over 20 years since the first Terran stepped into space.

The Citadel is gobbling up Terrans as fast as we can produce them, and many of them don't mind the physical changes that they are asked to engage in.

So, this is the first step in a new direction of Citadels, Guardians, and Peacekeepers. I haven't named the new series yet, but I will in the next month or so.

Thanks for reading,

Viola Grace

About Viola Grace

Viola Grace (aka Zenina Masters) is a Canadian sci-fi/paranormal romance writer with ambitions to keep writing for the rest of her life. She specializes in short stories because the thrill of discovery, of all those firsts, is what keeps her writing.

An artist who enjoys a story that catches you up, whirls you around and sets you down with a smile on your face is all she endeavours to be. She prefers to leave the drama to those who are better suited to it, she always goes for the cheap laugh.

THE LION'S STOWAWAY
BY
GABRIELLA BRADLEY & TARYN JAMESON

CHAPTER ONE

Isabella looked at the two small duffel bags on her bed. Travis and Hannah had warned her to be very careful what she packed — her iPad that held all their family photos, some memorabilia, two pairs of jeans, four t-shirts, underwear, a jacket, running shoes, and two sweaters. That was all she could fit in. Hannah would make sure she'd pack enough shampoo and other necessities for the two of them in her own luggage, but Isabella was so much shorter than her sister and thinner. Sharing their clothes wouldn't work. She sighed, anxiously cracking her knuckles while pacing back and forth.

Her mother peeked around the corner of the door. "Nervous, honey?" she asked, then stepped into the room.

"Yes. I don't know why you're making me do this. It's scaring the shit out of me."

"Izzy, you know why. We've gone over this so many times. There is no future for you here. You'll at least be with your sister, think about that." Her mother's eyes pooled, tears threatening to spill.

"The thought that I'll never see you and Dad again is killing me. Never mind the idea of sleeping for how many years? What if something goes wrong? What if we're caught?"

"We're not going to get caught, Izzy." Hannah had followed their mother into the room. She took Isabella in her arms. "Hon, you and I will be together and get to live to a ripe old age. Think about that instead of dwelling on morbid stuff. Come downstairs, Izzy, dinner is waiting."

Isabella let her sister pull her out of the bedroom. "Aren't you upset at all about leaving Mom and Dad behind? Fuck, Hannah, we'll be a couple of hundred years old by the time we get to that planet. Our parents will be long gone."

"At the rate food rations are getting smaller and smaller, many people will die of starvation and subsequent disease, especially the elderly and babies. If we stayed here, our parents would probably be gone long before us, and we'd be lucky to live to thirty."

"You can't force me to go," Isabella said stubbornly. "Hi, Travis."

"Mom and Dad used all their savings, sold whatever they could, and took out a second mortgage on the house to make it possible. You're coming along. Stop behaving like a kid." Hannah frowned at her sister as she sat at the table.

"Damn it, I *am* still a kid. I wouldn't call seventeen grown up."

"Grown up enough when you want to be, and you'll be eighteen in a couple of months. The day after tomorrow you'll be on that ship with us. Now eat and stop sulking."

"You guys all forget I was fifteen when this decision was made, hardly adult enough to know better."

"You knew better when it suited you," Hannah retorted.

Isabella toyed with her food. If one could even call it that. Her mother had done her best to make the most out of the dried potato flakes and meager dried vegetables, and a rare treat, some kind of meat out of a can, but it still tasted like cardboard, and the meat tasted awful. She toyed with it. Maybe it was dog or cat food. Although most people couldn't afford to have a pet, so even food for animals was scarce. Unless you were rich. "Dad, say something." She looked at her father for help.

He shook his head. "We're doing what we feel is best.

Hannah was fortunate that they accepted her into the relocation program. Lord knows when they'll be ready to send more people. It took them forever to build the ships for this mission. We'll be long gone when the next lot goes out. That's if there is going to be another relocation mission and if there are even any young people left to send."

Her mother chimed in. "Honey, how do you think we feel that our children are leaving us? It's breaking our hearts, but at the same time we're happy you'll both have a future, one you would not have here on Earth."

"Do you know how many applicants they rejected for the program? There are tons that would give anything for the opportunity to leave this hellhole. We've been fortunate to have grown up in a house at least. Look at all the people living on the streets," Hannah snapped.

"A house we've been forced to share with family and strangers. Where are they tonight?"

Her father was quick to chastise her. "Where is your sense of charity? They were homeless. If it weren't for your two cousins, none of this would be possible. They've sacrificed a lot for you and risk losing their jobs if caught. Lucas and Jeff have to work overtime, and Harriet and Joe, our closest friends I might remind you, went out for the evening so we could have privacy tonight."

"You've got one more day. Make the most of tomorrow, little sister. Tomorrow night you'll be in stasis," Hannah said.

"What time are you picking me up?"

Travis had been quiet during Isabella's little tantrum. "Around ten. We have to attend the farewell dinner first. Make sure you're ready and don't do anything silly."

"Like what?"

"Enough!" Her father raised his voice. "Let's try and enjoy this evening. This is the last time Hannah and Travis will be having dinner with us as a family."

After Hannah and Travis left, Isabella said goodnight and went back to her room. The two bags were mostly packed. Travis had told her they would fit beside her feet in the stasis unit.

She got undressed, threw the bags to the floor, and decided to try to sleep. But sleep wouldn't come. The thought of being put in a coffin-like contraption terrified her. What if she never woke up? What if, when and if she woke up, her brain was dead? Sure, they had tested the units successfully using animals, but she was looking at hundreds of years. What could all happen to one's body if you're frozen in time for so long? And if they got caught, what then? Lucas and Jeff would lose their jobs and get thrown in jail, and Hannah and Travis would lose their chance at a new life and join their cousins in prison. Probably for life. They had gone over the plan so many times, but tomorrow night that plan was going to become a reality. The destination planet was called Thauro—a distant planet in the Angoro system, a faraway universe. What would they find there? If they survived the journey, of course . . . Hannah had told her the planet was uninhabited, but hell, there could be weird creatures, monsters . . .

Eventually, she drifted off, but her sleep was plagued by dreams of aliens and creepy beasts.

The next morning, she woke up before anyone else, and like every day, she put on her sweats to go for her daily run. This morning she jogged longer than usual, drinking in final glances of the surroundings she'd grown up in. Finally, she stopped for a rest and to quench her thirst. Screwing up her nose at the tainted water, she took a long drink. Each time their water restrictions allowed it, her mother filled a lot of empty bottles with water she boiled religiously, but of course that did not make it clear. Even the bottled water they got with their rations didn't taste good and wasn't crystal clear, as water should be, she'd been taught.

Gazing out at the ocean, she wondered if Thauro would have oceans and beaches. She sat for a long time just staring at the murky waves, then at the garbage-littered beach, the dirty sand, and the homeless people that slept there. Her parents were right. There was no future on Earth. A thick layer of smog hid the sun. The air was foul. A lot of people with weak lungs suffered from the lack of clean oxygen. Her heart and mind were filled with regret at her behavior of the night before. She knew it was hard on her parents to see their only two children leave for good. She really had behaved like a little kid. Her parents, her two cousins, Hannah, and Travis, they were all taking a huge risk for her. It had been a toss between her cousins and her. Only one of them could go. They had drawn straws, and she'd been the lucky one to pull the shortest.

Hannah had spent every free moment she'd had teaching Isabella everything she learned, survival skills and how to defend herself. She had taken her to a shooting range and taught her fencing. They'd spent hours in the public swimming pool, training there . . .

Determined to apologize to her parents, and that evening to Hannah and Travis, she jogged back to her home. She would make the most of her last day.

CHAPTER TWO

Isabella ran to open the door for Travis and Hannah. "You guys are early."

"Yes. Some of the others have gone on to party at a bar, but we left right after the dinner. I want to spend a little bit of time with Mom and Dad," Hannah said and handed her mother a small package. "I managed to sneak some of the food out for you. There's ham in there."

Isabella saw the tears in her mother's eyes as she sniffed the package. "Ham? Oh, my . . . I haven't tasted ham since I was very young."

Travis scrutinized Isabella's clothing. "Are you packed and ready, Izzy? You're not wearing your spacesuit. Remember, when you wake up, you need to blend in with the rest of the crew."

"Yes, I know. But what are they going to do? Send me back to Earth on my own? Throw us in a non-existent jail? I was about to go upstairs to put it on. I'll do it right now." Isabella ran up the stairs two treads at a time.

After she struggled into the tight suit, putting on her jeans and a long-sleeved shirt on over it, she checked her drawers. She took one last look around her room, then grabbed her purse and the two bags and went back down. Leaving the bags near the front door, she headed to the kitchen. She threw her purse on the table in front of her mother. "Mom, you always liked this purse. There's money in there you can have. It won't be any good where I'm going."

That caused her mother's tears to flow again. Her father

was very quiet. The only evidence that he was emotional was the grim set of his lips. Studying them both for a few minutes, she imprinted their faces in her mind and fingered the gold locket resting on her chest, the one that held their photo and Hannah's.

"It's getting close to ten. We should load up and leave," Travis said. He got up and left the dining room, giving the family some alone time to say their goodbyes.

Isabella thought her mother would never let go of her. Finally, she tilted Isabella's chin and smiled through her tears. "You be good, you hear? Listen to your big sister. And wear this. It will protect you." Her mother pushed something into her hand. When she looked at what lay in her palm, she almost choked up. It was her mother's gold chain and cross.

A tight hug and a kiss from her father, who also tried to smile, then she hurried out of the kitchen and to the door, trying to pretend she was just going on a long overseas vacation.

Travis had the trunk open, the baggage waiting on the driveway to go in after her. "Okay, midget, get in."

She heaved a sigh. They had to smuggle her in that way. She pulled the gold chain and cross over her head, then got into the very back of the trunk. Curling up, she waited for Travis to cover her with a blanket, then closed her eyes after he put the baggage back and closed the trunk.

Hannah had already put her two small bags inside her and Travis' suitcases. Isabella heard her mother's voice, then Hannah calling another goodbye. Too soon, the car doors slammed, and Travis started the car.

Goodbye, house . . . goodbye, street . . . goodbye, Mom and Dad . . . She fought against the tears that threatened and instead concentrated on what lay ahead.

Lucas and Jeff had explained everything to her. The cargo would be loaded that evening and during the night. Months ago, they had stolen one of the extra stasis units NASA kept in storage, just in case another unit failed, and her cousins had built a metal crate around it. It would look just like many of the other metal crates of all shapes and sizes to be loaded into the cargo bay.

Jeff, her brilliant computer technician cousin, had managed to redirect wiring from the mainframe computers to the cargo bay. There would be small holes in her metal box for the wiring to go through to attach to the stasis unit. Her unit would work exactly the same as the thirty-two units in the hibernation chamber. The system was already live and operational. They would put her in stasis that night.

Jeff had also programmed the mainframe computer, so it wouldn't show an extra unit. Take-off was automated, as was everything else. All the travelers would be asleep when the ship took off.

The drive seemed to take forever, though they didn't have that far to go. The car doors opening and closing startled her. When Jeff opened the trunk and finally removed the blanket from her, she quickly scrambled out. "Boy, that was a taste of claustrophobia. I'm glad I'll be knocked out while in my coffin. How fast do you go to sleep?"

"As soon as Jeff hooks up the computer. You'll feel a small prick in your neck, and in seconds you'll be out like a light," Hannah assured her. "If you're even awake. I've got a sedative for you to take before we put you in the unit. It's a potent one."

"What if they stick other crates and boxes on top of mine?"

Travis chuckled. "Yours is marked clearly that it contains fragile computer equipment and has *do not block* marked on it. Jeff will make sure it's in the right place where he installed the wiring. Stop worrying."

"I can't help it. You guys will be safe in the hibernation chamber. How would you feel if it were you getting shoved into the cargo bay?"

"I'd worry, just like you. The crate is in my room. Once we have you in the unit, Jeff and Lucas will come to get you. Hannah and I can't go into the cargo bay," Travis told her while they walked into the building.

When they were in Travis' room, Isabella looked at the tall metal box standing upright in a corner. "That's it?"

"Yup." His phone buzzed. "It's a text message from Lucas. They're ready to come and get you as soon as we give the go-ahead."

"Won't it look odd, them walking around the building, wheeling a dolly with a crate on it?"

Hannah shook her head. "All the crews are either at the bar or with their friends or families. We have to hurry. Everyone is supposed to be back by midnight. Here, take this." She handed Isabella a white capsule and a bottle of water. "Do you need to use the bathroom?"

"No. I'm good." She swallowed the pill and gulped down some water.

Travis moved the crate away from the wall and, with effort, lowered it to the floor. "This thing weighs a ton."

"Izzy, the lid has internal clasps that will lock automatically when we attach it properly. Travis will show you," Hannah said.

Isabella shivered when Travis removed the lid. The unit really did resemble a coffin, with half of the domed lid made of thick transparent plastic. It was open.

"Izzy, look at the locks. There is a little lever just above your head on the inside of the crate. I've put a small flashlight next to your head. When the computer brings you out of stasis, the dome will slide back automatically. Then just pull that lever and push up on the lid. It's not that heavy. After you wake up, you might experience some dizziness, maybe some nausea. Be sure to immediately drink plenty of water." Travis pointed to the lever.

Hannah embraced her sister. "Take your jeans and shirt off. Time to go to sleep, baby girl. After we land on Thauro, Travis and I will come and get you as soon as we can."

Isabella was already experiencing the effects of the sedative and beginning to feel terribly sleepy. She took her jeans and shirt off and with Hannah's help climbed into the unit. She hardly heard them putting the lid back on the crate. Within seconds, her eyelids drooped, everything went foggy, and she felt herself sliding into dreamland.

Isabella opened her eyes to inky darkness. Disoriented for a few moments, she tried to sit up, but couldn't. Her head hit something hard. Then she remembered. Stasis. The computer had woken her. "I guess we've already arrived," she mumbled. It seemed like only yesterday that Travis had put her inside the unit. Her mouth was really dry. With a soft whizzing sound, the transparent lid slid back. Thank God.

"Water. Travis told me I need to drink."

She felt for the bottle of water Travis had placed next to her, and after locating it, she took the cap off and drank deeply. Now she had to get the lid off the crate. She groped for the flashlight and shone it behind her. Twisting her head, she reached for the lever and yanked it. It was stuck. Just as she began to panic and really wrenched it, she heard the locks click. She pushed hard, but it wouldn't budge. Somehow, she managed to get her legs out from the bottom of the unit. Raising her feet, she kicked the crate lid hard several times. The top shifted and moved. One more hard push and the lid popped open, swerved to the side, and fell to the floor of the cargo bay. She thought she'd hear the clattering of metal on metal, but for some reason, the lid hadn't made a sound when it landed.

She'd expected to wake up in the dark cargo bay, but instead, bright sunlight shone down on her. It was so brilliant, she had to shield her eyes for a bit. When she took her hand away, she saw a blue sky and two suns. Grasping the sides of the unit, she pulled herself up and slithered upward, then climbed out of the crate onto a mossy ground. A wave of dizziness attacked her, and her stomach churned, so she plopped down and leaned against the crate.

After her stomach settled and her eyes cleared, she gazed at her surroundings. White lacy leaves resembling a bride's veil poured to the ground from huge trees. Light and dark green bark covered the trunks, some of them almost blue. At the base of the trunks, thick foliage spread out in an array of colors with strange, feathery leaves resembling a peacock's tail but with more colors. Flowers carpeted the ground in a myriad of hues. Several birds stepped among the flowers — they were graceful like ballet dancers, sort of like flamingos. These birds were white with a marble effect of pale blue and pink and they had four graceful legs. The scene was surreal, almost ethereal in beauty. It didn't look like the images Hannah and Travis had shown her of Thauro, pictures sent back by the space probe NASA had launched quite a few years ago.

Isabella tried standing again. This time she was steady on her feet. She took a step, then another, startling the birds that soared up, squawking at the intruder. She was wobbly at first, but she soon found her footing. "Okay, this is fucking weird. Not a sign of the ship or anyone. And why is my crate sitting by itself in a forest? Shouldn't I still be in the cargo bay?" Had the ship crashed? If it had, why wasn't her crate damaged? *Am I dead?* Surely not. She didn't feel like she had died. And if she was alive, where were the others?

She decided to investigate. She screwed the top off the flashlight and used the edge to mark tree trunks, so if she needed to, she could find her way back to the crate.

She trudged through the forest, paying close attention to her surroundings. There had to be something. Debris from the ship, other crates that may have dropped from the cargo bay, other luggage—anything. *People? Please, let me find someone?* Her stomach growled. Damn, she would have to find food and water soon. All the water she had was the nearly empty bottle she had left in her crate.

"Oh, Hannah. What am I supposed to do now? Where the hell are you?" Fear for her sister wrenched at her heart. God, she hoped nothing had happened to her. The fact that her crate was sitting forlorn in a forest was not a good sign.

Frustrated, she walked a little further. The forest seemed endless. Shielding her eyes from the bright rays of the suns, she gazed at the sky to see if she could determine what time it could be. Judging by the position of the suns, it had to be getting late, but it was hard to tell. Unlike Earth, there was no smog covering their light. Images of alien monsters filled her mind. Her body shuddered. She had no weapon. There was no way in hell she wanted to be out in the open after dark. She turned around and followed the markings she had made on the trees back to her crate.

Once she reached it, she climbed in, stepped into the unit, and bending low, rummaged for the bottle of water. She would have to find a stream soon, or she would die from dehydration. Her foot tangled, causing her to stumble forward into the stasis unit. Steadying herself using her hands, she felt a bag. She thought it was one of hers. She reached down and grabbed what felt like a smaller duffel bag.

Feeling claustrophobic, she heaved herself back out, dropped to the ground, and sat in front of the crate, leaning her back against the metal side. She pulled the bag back into her lap. It wasn't one of hers. Travis or Hannah must have put it in the unit for her. She unzipped it and looked inside. Wrapped in a small blanket were six bottles of water and ten protein bars.

She grabbed a bar, ripped the package open, and took a bite. It was nasty, but she was starving. She chewed, swallowed, then took a drink from her half-empty bottle. She poked around in the bag to see if there was anything else inside. Beneath the blanket, she spied a folded piece of paper. She took it out and unfolded it, gazing at Hannah's familiar writing.

Izzy, I imagine we will be hungry enough to chew off our fingers when we wake from stasis. Travis and I saved some of the protein bars and water from our rations. This should tide you over until we can get to you. See you when we land.

I love you, baby girl. Hannah.

Tears streamed down her cheeks as she folded the note back up and stuck it in the bag. She wiped her face on her sleeve and leaned her head back against the crate, memories of her sister flowing through her mind. She reached for the locket around her neck and opened it, then touched the small likeness of her parents on one side and her sister on the other.

Isabella sighed. "God, Hannah. I miss you. I don't know what the hell I am going to do. I need to find you and the others."

CHAPTER THREE

Isabella rubbed her eyes and opened them. It was night. She must have fallen asleep. The effects of being in stasis for God knew how many years was still playing havoc with her body. She gazed up at the sky. It amazed her how clear it was. She could see the stars, and there were four moons and the largest star she'd ever seen. Well, it wasn't that often that on Earth one could even see the stars, but the few times it had been possible, they'd been very faint. Was this the same as the North Star her parents had told her about when she was young? The light of the moons shining on the lacy leaves of the trees caused them to glow softly. A brilliant beam from the big star seemed to light up something far away.

The glint in the distance caught her attention. She grabbed her flashlight, but she didn't really need it. The moons and the reflected light from the trees illuminated the forest. She stood and hastily made her way to the shining object. To her surprise, it was a small storage crate from the Initiation Two, although it was bent and broken, the lid ripped in half. The contents had spilled to the ground.

She giggled. She could hardly believe what she was seeing. The ground was littered with rations and bags of juice. The food was freeze-dried and normally sent with astronauts on space missions. She ran back to her crate and dumped the contents of the duffel bag, then grabbed the blanket. She could tie it closed and carry more of the food back with her to the crate.

Once back at the busted crate, she crammed as much of the food and fruit juice into the duffel bag as she could and zipped it shut. She spread the blanket onto the ground and loaded it up as well, then grabbed two corners and tied them into a knot, repeating the same with the other two. She heaved the duffel bag onto her shoulder and grasped the blanket by the center knots. Gazing up at the night sky, she thanked the powers that be for the supplies she'd found.

From the corner of her eye, she saw a bright flare. Turning around, she looked at the sky. That star was sure huge. It was radiant in its beauty and outshone the other stars in the darkened sky. An omen? Good, she hoped, because she was trapped on an alien planet, seemingly alone, and it scared the crap out of her.

She returned to her crate and dropped the duffel bag and loaded blanket to the ground. She unzipped the bag and grabbed a packet of the freeze-dried food and a bottle of water. She quickly ate and drank, then put her findings inside the crate. Who knew if there were animals here. She'd hate to wake up to find it all gone. After picking up the crate's lid and placing it halfway across, she heaved herself back into the crate and crawled into the stasis unit. She had to get some sleep. She would explore more in the morning. Maybe she would find other cargo and locate the ship. It had to have crashed. Had everyone survived? For now, she shoved the unsettling thought from her mind. Carefully, she drew the lid of the crate to cover her. She couldn't take any chances of some animal finding her. Leaving just a crack open for oxygen, she settled down to try to sleep.

As soon as she closed her eyes, she couldn't help thinking about her nightmares. Alien creatures had plagued her dreams for months while she had prepared to go into stasis. She opened her eyes, pushed the lid back a bit, and gazed at the sky. There it was. That star. The warmth of its bright yellowish rays soothed her like a mother's caress. Her eyes drifted shut, sleep starting to overtake her. A faraway whisper. Was she dreaming? *Do not worry, child. You are safe until he finds you.*

After she woke up the next morning, she ate something first and drank a bottle of water, then decided to explore and try to find the ship. She'd walked for a long time when she heard the gurgling sound of a river or stream. Isabella stopped walking and wiped the perspiration off her face. She gazed around the forest. She had been following the sound of the babbling water. Somewhere close was a creek or something. There had to be. She couldn't be hearing things.

A sparkling light on the ground caught her eye. It was a flower, the color of gold and shaped like a star. Another, then another after that. There was a whole path of them. Something, a gut feeling, urged her to follow them. The path didn't lead far. She came to an opening in the trees, and she saw the stream, the bank littered with the star-shaped flowers.

She couldn't believe her luck! She rushed to the water. It was crystal clear. She didn't care if it would make her sick — it had to taste a hell of a lot better than the bottled water she had with her. She kneeled and cupped her hands, then took a long drink. It was sweet and crisp and tasted so clean. She had never had anything like it. She pulled an empty bottle out of her bag and filled it with the fresh-tasting liquid.

She stood up and followed the flowers up the stream a way. The stream widened. It looked more like a narrow river now. The flowers grew away from the water and back to the tree line. The trees were huge, like the sequoia trees in California of which she had seen pictures. One looked as though it had been hollowed out, or maybe it just grew that way. She rushed to it and cautiously peered inside to make sure there wasn't some animal hibernating in it, then stepped inside. She couldn't believe her eyes. The space within was bigger than her bedroom and would keep her safe from the elements much better than the open crate.

She made her way back to the crate and gathered up her supplies. She had found both of her bags of clothes after she had woken up. She couldn't wait to wash herself and change out of the spacesuit. She slung the three bags onto her shoulders, grabbed the filled tablecloth, and took everything to the tree. By the time she had dropped the bags in front of it, she was starved.

She plopped down on the ground, grabbed a protein bar, and demolished it. It tasted like cardboard. This freeze-dried food wasn't much of a step up. She had to find fresh food. Soon. She dared not try any of the berries she'd seen or roots. Hell, they could be poisonous. This forest was like a fairytale. Surely there'd be fruit trees somewhere?

She had nothing for survival. A knife would come in handy . . . and string. If she had some twine or something to tie to a stick or a way to make a spear, she might be able to fish. She grimaced. She didn't know how to start a fire without matches or a lighter, and no way was she going to eat raw fish. Did they even have fish on this planet? The stream had been very clear, and she'd not seen any movement in the water.

A light breeze blew, and the aroma of roasting meat filled the air. Her mouth watered. She stood up and gazed at the sky. The suns were still high. She should have plenty of time to explore. She had to find the source of the delicious smell. It could be the others from the Initiation Two. They'd made camp somewhere and were roasting something over a camp fire.

She started forward, back to the stream. The star-shaped flowers bloomed a trail down the bank. Then both the stream and the flowers disappeared beyond the tree line.

She followed the flowers. Now and then small furry animals darted from her path. They sort of resembled rabbits. Flocks of strange colorful birds scattered as she disturbed their peace. At least if she kept to the flowers and the stream, she wouldn't get lost. The forest had to be huge. She hadn't come across any more crates or debris from the Initiation Two in her explorations. Her heart clenched with pain. *Hannah . . . I miss you.* She shook off the thought of her missing sister. She had to keep strong if she had a hope in hell of surviving this place.

The smell of roasting meat grew stronger, and she could hear a bustle of noise like people were milling around. The sound of voices drifted to her ears. Could it be the people from her ship? She rushed forward and broke through the trees. A wide dirt road, splitting the forest and a small village, was on the other side of a clearing across from her. The stream meandered along the forest line and disappeared back into the trees.

She quickly hid behind a massive trunk and peered at the village. It looked like it was from the Middle Ages. *Have I just found the movie set of The Lord of the Rings? If it weren't for the two suns and the four moons, I'd swear I've traveled back in time. No, this is an alien planet, but it sure as hell isn't Thauro. Hannah told me Thauro was unpopulated.* She saw thatched roofs and stone buildings . . . Old clunky wagons being pulled by horses . . . And the clothing . . . The women were in long dresses and sandals, and the men wore tunics, tights, and tall boots. It all looked so medieval.

Blend in, Isabella. You need to blend in. Yes, she would need to blend in, but how? She would have to steal what she needed. No way in hell was she going to saunter up to that village dressed in a spacesuit or even her jeans and a t-shirt. The people looked medieval, so their way of life and their laws could be the same as the medieval history she'd read.

She shuddered. On Earth, in the Middle Ages, they would stick people in stocks and chains, torture them. Cut off a thief's hand . . . Would they burn her as a witch? The thought chilled her.

Scanning the village, she peered to see if she could spot some type of market. Villages had them, didn't they? She caught sight of some women carrying baskets filled with goods, vegetables, and bread. First, she had to get her hands on their type of clothing. How was she going to do that? *Steal. Okay, so now I'm contemplating becoming a thief and risk getting a hand chopped off . . .*

She decided to wait until the suns went down. If she ran across the clearing now, someone, especially the children playing here and there and sometimes running across the road, would surely spot her as some kind of alien. The people looked normal, much like people on Earth. As hard as she looked, except for their clothing, she saw no difference. All the women had long hair, and so did the men. Fingering her own long, blonde locks, she decided if she could get a hold of their type of clothing, she wouldn't look out of place.

Nightfall took forever. Probably not, but just sitting there spying on the village, it seemed like a very long time. After the suns had set, she ran as fast as she could across the road and the clearing. A dog barked. At least . . . it sounded like a dog. Hiding in the shadows, she crept from one house to the next. How was she going to find clothing? Sniffing, she inhaled the smell of bread baking. *Lord, I'm going to die of hunger just exploring this village.* When she came to the last house, she spotted the small market.

Farmers and their wives were busy packing their goods. She saw a stall with clothing, another with bread. Neither of them had people anywhere near. Maybe the traders had gone to the local pub? Listening to the chatter, she shook her head at their language. None of it sounded familiar. Several of the farmers formed a little group. They chatted for a bit, then strolled out of the market and went to a small building with a sign hanging in front. Maybe it was their pub? The wives followed them. Well, she thought they were wives. Could be daughters or whatever.

Holding on to her bag tight, she scooted to the stalls and made straight for the clothing. Crouching low, she pulled clothes off the table and looked at them quickly. A skirt, some kind of overdress, a blouse. *Damn, I need a pair of sandals.* Daring to straighten a bit, she peered over the table. At the far end were several pairs of sandals. One pair looked like her size. She stuffed her loot into her bag.

Crawling to the next table, she reached up and grabbed a loaf of bread. Into the bag. Dare she explore further? A few people were still packing up their wares. One more table. It was far enough away from the people still there. She was in luck. The table held cheeses and some sort of meat. Groping beneath the netting that covered the food, she grabbed a chunk of cut cheese and several pieces of the meat, then hastily put them into her bag. She looked for an opportunity to sneak away and head back to the forest.

Running as she never had, she almost dove into the forest and sank down behind a tree. Her heart thudded as if it would jump out of her chest. *I'm a thief. Damn, what would Mom and Dad think of this little escapade?* She clasped the cross that hung from her neck, her eyes burning with tears, but she quelled the urge to cry. *Hannah would probably be proud of my intuition and bravery.*

After her heart had settled down and she had her breath back, she slunk into the forest and looked for the path of flowers. The blooms shone brightly in the rays of the moon and the brilliant star, leading her back to the gurgling stream. She followed it, warily watching for animals or unknown creatures until she arrived at her shelter.

The only things she unpacked were the cheese and bread. Oh, but that bread tasted heavenly. She couldn't remember any bread on Earth ever tasting so good. And the cheese . . . It was only for the rich back home. Her parents couldn't afford this delicacy. She felt almost guilty as she bit chunks off the huge piece. She followed her meal with a drink from one of the juice bags. Well, supposedly juice. She'd never tasted real juice. This was colored water with some added sugar. They called it juice.

Feeling quite full and tired from her adventure, she curled up, using the small blanket as a pillow. The weather was at least mild. Vaguely she thought about winter. Were there winters on this planet? But maybe she would have found Hannah by that time. *Be patient. We will watch over you. He will come.*

Again . . . that whisper in her mind. Thinking she was really starting to hallucinate, she drifted off.

CHAPTER FOUR

Isabella woke to the suns blazing down. She quickly relieved herself, then went back to her tree to eat. There was a good amount of bread left and the meat and cheese. This time she decided to try the meat. The strips appeared fine. It smelled and tasted like it had been smoked. She bit into the bread. It wasn't as fresh as the night before, but it still tasted fantastic. "Damn, I really need a knife," she muttered.

Now that her stomach was full, she unpacked the clothing she'd stolen. "A bath first. I'm glad I have at least myself to talk to." Giggling at herself, she took the spacesuit off, then her bra and panties and headed for the stream.

She carefully tested the water with her toes. Relieved to find it was quite tepid, she waded to the middle of the stream, then lay down and let the current flow over her body. It felt so good. Leaning back, she rinsed her hair. No shampoo, but at least it would feel a lot cleaner. She stayed in the water until her skin wrinkled and she began to turn into a prune.

Wading back to the bank, she had no option but to dry herself in the warm rays of the suns. "I wish I had a book to read. Oh, I have my iPad. Stupid. No, if I use that, I'll soon run out of battery life."

She basked in the suns until she felt dry. Raking her fingers through her hair, she stood and went to the tree to try on her new clothes. Clean underwear, her bra, then she tried on the blouse. It was fairly large on her, but she didn't care. Next was the overdress, which actually didn't fit too badly.

The sandals fit perfectly. She tied the straps around her ankles. Wishing for a mirror, she twirled around. "Wait, the metal of the crate. I can see myself in it."

The metal wasn't shiny enough. All she saw was a foggy reflection. Finger-combing her hair, she was glad her hair was curly. She'd always hated it, longed for straighter hair, but at least her unruly curls wouldn't look that bad. She headed for the trail of twinkling flowers and back to the village. Dare she mingle and just walk around freely?

Discovering the skirt had deep pockets, she stuck her hands in them and began to casually stroll across the road and the clearing until she came to the main street. No one took any notice of her.

Could Hannah and the others be in this village? If so, where? She could hardly ask. Soon as she opened her mouth, she'd be pinpointed as a stranger, an alien. She stopped in front of the place that looked like a pub or inn. It reminded her of an old Western bar as depicted in movies. Did she dare look inside?

Pushing against the swinging doors, she entered. The interior was dimly lit. Small tables stood scattered with people drinking or eating at them. There was a bar with stools that were all filled and behind it a bartender. The smell of the food caused her mouth to water, even though she wasn't hungry, having filled up on bread and cheese before she headed out.

Her foot hit something shiny on the floor. She looked down and saw it was a gold coin. Bending, she quickly snatched it up and stuck it in her pocket. She glanced around, but no one seemed to have noticed. There was no sign of Hannah or the crew. She sighed. She'd so hoped to see familiar faces. If they had survived, where could they be? Shaking the thoughts from her head, she fingered the coin in her pocket. *What could a gold coin buy me? Is it real gold?*

A young, pretty, black-haired woman approached her. She was wearing an apron and said something. Maybe a waitress? Isabella just smiled and kept on walking toward the doors. Oh, she felt so lost. Close to the doors was a table just recently abandoned by some customers. She noticed leftover food on plates. Quite a lot of it. She could hardly put it in her pockets. Would anyone notice if she sat and ate some? Did she have the courage? Hell, why not? If they caught her, so be it.

She wasn't that hungry, but hell . . . it smelled so good. Whatever the food was, it tasted heavenly. She chose the plate with the most food on it, then gobbled it down as fast as she could. After she put the fork back on the plate and pushed it aside, she noticed something sticking out beneath it. Four gold coins. It had to be a tip. She left one coin and shoved the other three in her pocket.

Glad she was so close to the doors, she got up and quickly left the pub, feeling guilty about stealing the waitress' tip, then walked as fast as she could to the market.

She strolled casually, inspecting the wares on each stall table and watching how people paid and the change they were given, if any. Some people traded goods, she noticed. Well, she had nothing to trade. All she had was the treasure in her pocket. At a vegetable and fruit stall, she noticed a woman paying with a gold coin. The woman's basket was filled with strange-looking fruit. The farmer handed her change — a handful of silver coins.

Happily, she chose some fruit that resembled peaches and some kind of berries. Pretending to be mute, she pointed to what she wanted and filled her pockets. She gave him a gold coin and received a lot of silver change.

To her delight, she found a table with scissors, knives, swords, and other hardware. She chose a dagger, then with gestures, and holding out a gold coin, looked questioningly at the trader. He took the coin but gave her no change. So now she had two gold coins left and a bunch of small change. A blanket. What if it got cold? No. Her stomach was more important at the moment, and it was quite warm at night. She'd deal with blankets and warmer clothing later. Judging by how hot it got during the day, it had to be summer right now.

The fresh bread made her stop. She still had bread left from the night before, but this smelled freshly baked. She bought another loaf of bread and some cheese. That took care of most of the silver change. At another stall, she bought a basket like the women carried. Quickly, she loaded her purchases into it.

She came close to the stall from where she'd stolen her clothing. Afraid the woman behind the table would recognize her blouse and dress, she swiveled and walked back.

When she got to the road, she had to wait for some wagons. Following them were three men on horseback. They appeared to be soldiers, judging by their weapons and manner of clothing.

After they had all entered the village, she hurried across the road, the clearing, and running through the forest, made for her safe tree.

Once inside, she fished her loot out of the basket and happily bit into the peach-like fruit, moaning in delight. It was fresh and sweet. She had never had anything like it on Earth, had only seen pictures of many of Earth's fruits. The only fruit she had ever tasted was freeze-dried or canned when their parents could afford it. Quite proud of herself, she decided to explore the other side of the forest. Tomorrow she'd go to the market to look for a brush or comb, soap, and a few other necessities.

The snow had finally melted, and the rays from the suns

became a lot warmer. It had been a cold winter, but she had survived it. Isabella had no idea how long she'd been there. According to the scratches on the inside of the tree, she'd lived in her tree for months. And every night before she fell asleep, she heard the whisper. *He is coming soon.*

She blamed it on her isolation and imagination. Each day she went to the village and the market. The villagers were starting to recognize her face and often greeted her. She'd learned the words of their greeting and responded. She had also learned some of the names of the fruit and vegetables, the bread, and the cheese. And she stole like crazy and hadn't been caught yet by the farmers and traders.

The waitress in the pub had caught on to her. But all she did was send Isabella pitying glances and let her eat leftover food customers had abandoned. It was as if the young woman knew Isabella was homeless. The waitress often would come to clear the table, wipe it, and only take half the coins left for her tip. Isabella knew she did it on purpose and hoped one day she could repay the waitress for her kindness. The waitress quite often brought her a glass of juice, too, and occasionally, a glass of milk.

Isabella spent a lot of time inside the pub, just sitting there observing people and listening to the customers. Especially during the cold winter months. She had yet to find anything that looked like matches, so she couldn't light a fire. Though she'd rubbed sticks together, stones, she'd not been able to get a spark. At least she'd been able to buy two warm blankets and some winter clothing.

Heading back on the familiar trail, that she could almost walk blindfolded now, she hummed a tune. That was something she missed. Music.

When she was close to her tree, a sound startled her. It was too loud to be made by one of the little furry creatures she so often saw darting around among the flowers. She stopped. Her heart sped up. She'd seen no other human in the forest since she'd lived there. Not once. The sound came from the direction of the crate.

Standing very still, she held her breath and waited. A crack, then another. Suddenly a huge lion faced her. She dropped her basket, her purchases spilling to the forest floor, screamed, and ran to the nearest tree.

She peeked at the lion from behind the trunk and started hitching up her skirts to tie them in a knot above her knees. "Go away, kitty!"

She hoisted herself onto a branch and started climbing. When she was halfway up the tree, she dared to look down. She couldn't remember. Did lions climb?

"Nice kitty, kitty, kitty." She climbed a couple more limbs but dared not go any higher. The branches were starting to get thin and might break beneath her weight. She leaned forward and peered down at the lion.

"Holy shit! You are one big cat!"

He was the biggest lion she'd ever seen. Their parents had taken them to a zoo when she and Hannah were still little. The lions had awed her and had seemed gigantic. But this one was huge. Of course, he had to be. It was an alien lion.

What in the hell was she going to do? Was it hungry? Was it looking at her for its next meal? She grabbed the piece of smoked meat she had in her pocket, pulled a chunk off it with her teeth and held her hand out. "Look, kitty. Mmm, it's good, see?"

She threw the piece of meat. It landed on the ground a distance from the tree. "Go get it, boy!"

The lion just stood looking up at her. He did not attempt to climb or approach the tree . . . nor did he go after the food. To her consternation, he suddenly growled. Then it appeared as if his bones were popping through his skin.

"Oh, fuck, no!"

It freaked her the hell out. It reminded her of the movie *Thing*. In the movie, an alien made itself look like a dog, but when it showed its true form, it was a grotesque monster.

She couldn't take her eyes away. It was all so crazy. It wasn't a hideous creature he was mutating into. When the transformation was complete, he had become the most gorgeous hunk of male flesh she'd ever seen. She rubbed her eyes and looked again. Was she going insane? *Okay . . . I'm dreaming. There is no way this is real.* She pinched herself. *Wake up, Izzy.*

The man said something in the same foreign language she heard every day in the village.

"Oh no, no!" She shook her head wildly. "That is how the aliens lure you in. They turn into a sexy guy, play all nice with you, then boom! Invasion of the body snatchers! Go away!" she hissed.

But he didn't go away. Instead, he stepped forward and held his hand out. He was offering to help her down. She gazed at him. He had earnest blue eyes, long, wavy, brown hair, a perfect nose, the cutest dimple in his chin, and was dressed in a tunic, pants, and high boots. He motioned for her to climb down from the tree.

Had she merely imagined the lion? Was the shock of meeting a handsome hunk in the forest playing games with her brain? She shook her head to clear it. This guy could have stepped straight out of the movies. And she had to find him in a forest on an alien planet? Suddenly that whisper in her mind. *It is he. Trust him.*

Now she was going totally schizo. She'd wake up inside her tree shortly and discover it was all some weird nightmare.

Several golden star-shaped flowers began to grow on the ground near his feet. Those wonderful flowers that had giv-en her a lifeline to survival her first days on the planet and had sprung up from the snow during the coldest days of winter, giving her solace when she felt so alone.

She cautiously lowered herself to the bottom branch, her dagger in one hand, while she accepted his hand to jump to the ground. She looked up at him. He towered over her. He had broad shoulders, and the muscles of his arms strained his shirt sleeves. And he wasn't just downright hot; he had a kind face and a brilliant smile. "Who are you?" she whispered in a shaky voice.

He shook his head, indicating he didn't understand her. He pointed at his chest. "Tanoth."

"I gather that's your name? Tanoth?" She pointed at herself. "Isabella."

He began to talk, but it was all gibberish to her. Then he reached into his pocket and pulled out what looked like an iPad. He swiped his fingers across the screen and pulled up a picture.

She almost jumped out of her skin. Was that Erica Martinez? She looked closer at the picture. It was Erica but with shorter hair, and she was standing beside a handsome man at what looked like a wedding. "Oh my God! It's Erica! Erica is my friend. Do you know Hannah? Travis? What about Laura?"

He nodded. "Laura, Erica."

Wow. Laura and Erica were here somewhere? But where? "Take me to them? Please?"

Okay. Sign language. She thought for a moment. She pointed at him, then at herself and, bending down, made a walking movement with two fingers. She stood, pointed at him again and herself, then pointed at Erica's image. "Take me to Erica? Laura?"

He smiled and nodded. *Oh my God.* That smile turned her legs to jelly.

"Erica, Laura, Bernie, Julia," he said and nodded again.

"Well, dammit, don't just stand there. Take me to them,"

she almost shouted, happiness flooding her heart that other members of the relocation teams were on the planet. It had to be Thauro. The reports that it was an uninhabited planet, had been wrong. And the pictures she'd seen, must have been taken at another location on the planet.

She allowed him to take her hand and lead her to the crate. Beside it stood a horse. He pointed at the crate, then to her, and said something.

Isabella nodded. "Yes, that's my coffin." That was how she'd come to regard the stasis unit. The ship had crashed, and she'd been dumped into some department of Heaven along with a bunch of foreigners.

Next to the crate stood a small toolkit. He closed it and put it in his saddlebags. After strapping on a sword, he mounted the horse. She was about to yell at him for abandoning her, when he held out his hand and in one swoop lifted her onto the horse to sit in front of him. Her skin prickled with awareness and all she wanted was to lean back against his strong chest. She took a deep breath. It had been so long since she had been this close to anyone, and Tanoth was hot. *All right, hormones. Calm the hell down.*

He began to ride out of the forest and onto the road she'd crossed every day since her arrival. "How far is it?" she asked. But he didn't understand her of course. He spurred the horse into a gallop.

They'd traveled for quite a while when he veered off the road and into a veld of tall grasses. In the distance, she could see a mountain range. He slowed the horse to a trot until they came to a clearing. She gasped. A sleek, smallish spaceship was parked there.

He stopped, then dismounted and held out his hand to help her off the horse. She watched as he led the horse to the ship. A large rear door opened, and he guided the horse into it. Then he motioned her to join him.

Isabella entered the craft, sat in a seat, and strapped herself in. A stern-faced man was stationed at the controls. Tanoth said something that sounded like a command, and the craft took off.

He touched a couple of buttons on one of the consoles, then began speaking. She thought she heard her name. It had to be a radio or communication device because a woman's voice replied. When he had turned off the instrument, he claimed the empty seat beside her.

"All my things. They're in the tree," she told him. "We need to go back to get them."

His face was one question mark, and he held up his hands, then shook his head. He didn't understand. When he patted her on the leg, a surge of electrical impulses shot upward, to her belly, her stomach, her heart. God, what was wrong with her? *Get yourself under control. Remember, he's also a lion, Izzy.*

He pointed at the small window. She looked out and down. Below she saw a city unlike any city she'd ever heard of or seen in fantasy movies. It looked magnificent and nothing like the medieval village she'd been raiding all this time.

The ship surged and began to descend. Still peering through the window, she could see a sprawling manor on a large property. The gardens were gorgeous with so many flowers and tall trees. She braced herself as the ship touched down in what looked like a courtyard. Tanoth took her hand, and just like before, his touch sent bolts of electricity pulsing up her arm, through her veins, causing her stomach to flutter. *Okay, Izzy. You're not going to fall for the first hunk that crosses your path. Especially not one that can turn into a lion and will have you for dinner.*

When the door slid open, the first thing she saw was Erica standing on the landing pad, a man next to her. Isabella almost fell down the steps in her hurry to get to a familiar face. "Erica! Oh my God! I can't believe it. Are we all dead?" she shouted, then fell sobbing into Erica's waiting arms.

Erica's eyes were filled with disbelief. "No, you're not dead, Izzy. But how in the hell did you end up on this planet? You weren't part of the program."

Isabella chewed on her lip, then took a deep breath. No one could get in trouble for it now. "I was a stowaway on the Initiation Two."

Erica brushed her fingers through her curly hair and shook her head. "How is that even possible?"

Isabella hugged Erica again. Was she truly real? "Oh, I can't believe I'm actually talking to someone and a person who can understand me. I'll explain everything. Where is Hannah?"

Erica's eyes darkened and filled with tears. She looked down at her with a troubled expression. "Honey, Hannah didn't make it. There were only seven survivors of the Initiation Two. Travis was one of them. And now you, of course."

Isabella's hand flew to her breast. She had Hannah's note safely tucked away inside her bra, close to her heart. Tears flowed freely. "Are . . . are . . . you sure? I survived . . . and . . . I—"

"Yes, hon. Quite a few of the computers were damaged. The others died instantly without ever waking up. They didn't suffer, Izzy."

"Then how can I still be alive?"

"If you were a stowaway, you must have been hooked up to the same computer that controlled the seven stasis units that survived the crash. When the ship crashed, you automatically came out of stasis. How have you survived all this time?"

The handsome man Isabella recognized from the picture with Erica approached her and pinned a small device to her dress. "This is a translator. Now we can understand each other. I am Laro, Erica's mate."

"Mate? As in husband?" Isabella asked. "Tanoth showed me some images on his pad, but I found it hard to believe it was actually a wedding."

Erica smiled. "Yes. I'm married. But let's go inside, and you can tell us everything."

CHAPTER FIVE

Isabella could finally understand the man . . . or lion? His deep, sexy voice was husky as he introduced himself again.

"My name is Tanoth. I am a lion shifter. I am sorry I scared you in the forest."

"A lion shifter? I thought that kind of stuff was all fictional, stuff you read in books or see on TV."

"Not on this planet. It's very real, Izzy," Erica said.

Though she was still deeply upset at the news of Hannah's death, Isabella couldn't help but be awed by the house and its surroundings. It was almost too much to take in. She had never seen anything like it on Earth.

"Are you hungry?" Erica asked. "Cook has prepared a late dinner for us. Tanoth contacted us and told us he'd found you. I had no idea that he was talking about Hannah's sister. His pronunciation of your name wasn't quite correct, and I had no clue who you could be. We thought we had all the survivors from the seven ships and the area was cleansed of all the debris from the Initiation Two. Your unit must have fallen far away from where the crash site was."

"I was surprised to find the unit. Yes, it was quite far from where the ship crashed." Tanoth helped himself to bread and cheese.

"Everyone from the relocation program is here?" Isabella asked.

"Almost. We suffered some losses, but many survived," Erica told her.

Sadness overwhelmed Isabella's heart. Her sister wasn't that lucky. Hannah was gone. She'd never see her again—the sister she was so close to, who had bent ass over backward to get her on that ship. Never would they sit together on her bed, giggling over stupid stuff, or play with each other's hair, concocting new hairdos. Hannah painting her nails, putting makeup on her face. It swished through her mind in flashes and pain pierced her heart.

Tanoth sat next to her at the dinner table. When she didn't touch the food, he took her plate and filled it for her. The last thing she wanted was to eat right now. Her grief was almost too heavy to bear. She'd had second thoughts about it all, then had agreed anyway, and now . . . here she was. By herself. No Hannah, who had been the main force behind the stowaway plan and had been so happy when Isabella had drawn the short straw.

"We can talk more tomorrow if you like," Erica said in a soft tone. "We'll understand if you want to be alone with your grief. And not to worry. I'll take care of you. Hannah was one of my best friends, as you know."

"No, I don't want to be by myself. I've been alone for God knows how long, so I'd rather talk. It has been months. I survived through the winter. I've become a master thief. I lived in a hollow tree. And somehow, I never got caught when I stole. Some guardian angel was watching over me. And the strangest part of it all, every night as I drifted off to sleep, a voice told me to be patient. He would come. And then he did, and he's sitting next to me right now. And even weirder, he was a lion first and freaked the living daylights out of me. I thought I'd met my end."

Erica cleared her throat. "Okay, first, you're on a planet called Ierilia. It's in a different universe. Our ships met with an asteroid belt and were badly damaged. We were hurled into this system, and all the ships and the cargo ships crashed here. We've found them all."

"The forest I woke up in was magical. It was fairytale beautiful. When I began to explore, I found a small village."

"That would be Xandero," Tanoth said.

"Whatever the name . . . the first time I snuck into the village at night I stole some clothing from the market. I had to blend in."

"Secondly, what's more important to me, how did you end up as a stowaway and how was this all possible?" Erica questioned.

"Hannah . . ." Her voice broke, and she stopped for a moment. "Hannah didn't want to leave me behind. Of course my cousins wanted to go, too. They're not much older than me. Their parents both died of the virus, so they had lived with us for a long time. It caused a lot of argument, and they had almost abandoned the plan. They all decided that we draw straws. Between my parents, who mortgaged their house and emptied their bank accounts to pay for almost everything that was needed, and my two cousins and their savings, they came up with a plan. Travis and Hannah chipped in whatever they had. But then it was still a toss-up who was to go out of the three of us. We drew the straws. I was the lucky one. Lucas and Jeff work at NASA. There were extra stasis units in storage. My cousins stole one of them. Jeff was in charge of the computer technology on the ships. He was able to wire one of the computers into the cargo bay of the Initiation Two. They built a crate to disguise the stasis unit. The night before take-off, they placed me in it, and closed the crate, then loaded me onto the ship."

"Wow. That's all I can say, Little Miss Stowaway."

"If you talk to Travis . . . you said he is still alive?"

"Yes, he is."

"Travis can tell you about the whole plan. Like I told you, he was heavily involved, as was Hannah."

"And you woke up in the forest near Xandero. It's beyond fantasy. Gorgeous. We were there not long ago," Erica said. "Tanoth, what did you think when you came upon this young woman?"

Tanoth grinned. Taking Isabella's hand, he squeezed it. "She was a mirage, the woman who stepped out of my visions. I've seen her so often in my dreams but dared not think she could ever be real. I thought I had conjured her up—a fantasy of how I would picture the woman who is to be my mate. I so regret having scared her. The forest was so beautiful, and my lion ached to roam, so I shifted, and my lion scouted the forest for a while. And then suddenly, this lovely blonde young woman stood before me. She was so afraid, she climbed up a tree and then tried to bribe me with some food."

"And I thought I'd be *his* next meal," Isabella added.

Laro chuckled. "Another match decided by the gods and goddesses?"

"Wait a minute." Isabella looked at Laro. What the hell did he mean? Their gods matched people? Like soulmates? Her gaze turned to Tanoth. When he smiled at her, her heart skipped a beat. She shook the feeling away. "That's just crazy. I'm only seventeen. Oops, no, I guess I'm eighteen now, going on nineteen. And how long was I in stasis? Does anyone know? I could be hundreds of years old."

"Old enough to fall in love." Erica gave her a pointed stare.

Isabella ignored that statement. "Erica, your house is beautiful. Will I be staying here?"

"Not sure yet. Nearly all the people from Earth have moved to Initiation Genesis. The king gave us our own realm. Province or state, but they call them realms here. We've almost finished building the first town. You're going to need some guidance, so maybe it would be best if you stay here. I owe it to Hannah to look after her baby sister. It's getting late. Tanoth, you're welcome to stay the night."

"Thank you, Erica. It is so late I would have hated to wake my brother to beg a room."

Erica chuckled. "Ivran is lucky I have sympathy for him." She stood and motioned to Isabella. "Izzy, let me show you to your room."

Isabella scrunched up her nose. "All my things are in the hollow tree I made my home after I woke up. What I am wearing is all I have with me."

"We can send someone to retrieve them. Don't worry. Are they important?"

"I don't know. I didn't have a lot. Some jeans, shirts, and the stuff I stole of course. The most important thing I have is Hannah's note, which I keep close to my heart. Oh, and I need my iPad. It has all the photos on it of my parents, Hannah, and family." She dug beneath her blouse and took the note out of her bra. "They had added a small bag with rations and water to my unit. That's where I found the note."

Erica read it, then handed it back to Isabella. "A memory to treasure. But now you must move on. Treasure your old memories and begin to make new ones."

Isabella had not slept so soundly and comfortably since she'd left Earth. She yawned and looked at the sun streaming through the windows, a soft breeze causing the sheer white curtains to billow into the room.

She got up and went to the bathroom Erica had shown her the previous evening. Gazing at the shower and the bath, she wasn't sure which to pick. A hot bath would feel heavenly. She turned the taps on, then went back to the bedroom to take off the nightgown Erica had lent her. To her surprise, she found new clothing in the closet. And in the drawers, new underwear but no bras. Didn't matter. She didn't have much to fill a bra anyway.

After inspecting the closet and chest of drawers, she hurried back to the bathroom. The tub was full. The taps had shut off automatically. Shampoo . . . oh, she could finally wash her hair properly. The bars of soap she'd stolen from the market had kept her hair clean, but there was nothing like a good shampoo, and she hadn't found anything like it at the market.

She soaked for a while, then washed herself and her hair. As she stepped out of the tub, it emptied on its own. "Nothing medieval about this," she muttered as she dried herself using the soft towels that were ready for her.

The dress was beautiful. Simple, but elegant. She felt like a princess as she inspected her reflection. The blue material really suited her coloring and matched her blue eyes. The dress was trimmed with lighter blue lace. Fine, pale blue embroidery decorated the bodice and just above the hem. She attached the translator to the bodice and scrunched her nose at her image in the mirror. She had lost weight since she had been on Ierilia. She was thin, her cheekbones were more defined, and her blue eyes looked too big for her face. *A princess?* She looked like a lost waif. She shrugged. Wasn't that exactly what she was?

Wondering about the time, she ventured out of the room and down the stairs. Food! Delicious-smelling food! Skipping down the last few treads, she followed the scent and found the kitchen. Erica, Laro, a teenager, and Tanoth were seated at a large table.

"There you are. You slept a long time. Morning, Izzy." Erica gestured to the teenage boy. "Izzy, this is Tomas, Laro's and my son."

Isabella raised her eyebrows. "Okay. You've been here just as long as me, not enough time to produce a grown teenager."

Erica smiled. "Laro was a widower. Tomas is his son, but now he is ours."

"Oh. That makes sense. Morning, everyone. This is breakfast?" she asked, looking at the many dishes on the table.

Laro grinned. "Lunch."

"Isabella, you look breathtakingly beautiful. Your hair is like spun gold," Tanoth complimented.

Isabella felt blood rise to her cheeks. "Thank you." She felt like telling him to continue talking that way . . . she'd probably swoon in his arms.

"I'm glad the dress fits you, Izzy. I'll get you more clothes, but I had to be sure of the size. It really does bring out the color of your hair and eyes," Erica told her.

Tanoth stood and pulled a chair out for her to be seated. She smiled and sat down. "Thank you." *And he's a gentleman, too!*

Her stomach growled. Loudly. Last night was the first hot food she'd had in a very long time. The scraps from the inn were always cold, and often meager, but it was better than nothing.

Tanoth had filled a plate of food and pushed it in front of her. "You need to eat, Isabella. You barely touched your food last night."

She took a bite of roasted vegetables and almost moaned. It was so good. "So, Erica, what do we do now? You said everyone else lives in another realm? Is that where I am going to go?"

Erica tapped her fingers on the table. "I have set up an audience with the king for you and Tanoth later this afternoon. But I think, for now, you will continue to stay here. It will give you time to adjust and learn the culture. We'll see what the king says."

Isabella gave her a confused look. "An audience with the king? Why?"

"He wishes to hear about how you got here and survived

all this time on your own. The king keeps well informed of everything that happens on Ierilia. He rules the whole planet."

She dropped her fork on her plate as fear pooled in her belly. Images of medieval torture filled her mind. Being thrown into a dungeon and left there. "Erica, I had to steal to survive. I can't tell a king that! I'll get locked up or worse. Don't they cut hands off for stealing? Like in the Middle Ages on Earth?"

Erica started giggling and shaking her head. "Izzy, calm down. It will be nothing like that. You'll see. King Biryn is a kind man. Now finish eating."

Isabella sighed. That was easy for her to say. Erica wasn't the thief. Maybe she should have stayed in her forest. At least there she understood how to survive. She took a bite of her food but had lost her appetite.

Isabella was glad Tanoth had to go with them to the palace. For some reason he made her feel safe, and right then, she was scared to death. To her surprise, she had found out that both Erica and her husband were a part of some elite team for the king.

They were leading the way to the king's private chambers. From what Isabella understood, the queen had just given birth to a set of twins earlier, and the ruler had no wish to leave his wife's side to hold meetings in the throne room. *Yay me . . . At least the story won't be heard by too many people.* She could already hear the chants to chop off her head.

They came to a stop in front of a gorgeous carved wooden door. Erica knocked lightly, and the door was opened by a tall man wearing a uniform much like Erica and Laro's.

"Captains." He motioned for them to enter. "His Majesty is expecting you."

"Thank you, Dunmore." Erica led them inside and gestured for Isabella and Tanoth to sit.

Tanoth sat beside her on one of the sofas and took her hand in his. "There is nothing to fear, Isabella. The king will understand."

Before she could answer, a door opened across the room. A tall man with dark brown hair and a kind face entered the sitting area.

"So this is the little girl found near Xandero. I am King Biryn." He walked to stand before her.

Little girl? Isabella didn't know what to do. Awkwardly, she stood, then curtsied. "Your Royal Highness," she mumbled.

"Sit, child. No need to be afraid. I have not eaten any of the Earth people yet."

Isabella sank back to the sofa and groped for Tanoth's hand. He took hers and squeezed it reassuringly.

Isabella scrutinized the king. She'd had no idea what she really expected. A royal figure wearing a red robe and a crown on his head? This man looked as normal as Laro and Tanoth and wore the same kind of clothing as the villagers.

Dunmore served them all with a glass of wine but handed Isabella a glass of fruit juice. It smelled heavenly, like freshly squeezed oranges. She stared into the tall cup. *Orange Juice? The real stuff?*

"Your name is Isabella, Erica told me, and you were a secret passenger on the Initiation Two. I would like to hear your story," the king said, his eyes focused on her face.

Isabella was completely honest, even branding herself a thief. When she finally finished talking, she watched his reaction. When he burst into bellowing laughter, she cringed and sat closer to Tanoth. What was so funny? Confused, she looked at Erica, who merely smiled.

"How old are you, Isabella?" the king asked.

"Eighteen, I guess. Almost nineteen now."

"That is in Earth years. You are not such a little girl. You are a young woman and a beautiful one. I apologize for laughing. I find it amazing that you managed to steal from the villagers and fool them, a little slip of a girl like you." Biryn laughed again.

Isabella felt some of her anxiety waning. Maybe her punishment wouldn't be that bad. "I didn't fool everyone. The waitress at the pub or tavern knew. She allowed me to eat leftover food and quite often left coins on the table for me. One day I would like to repay her for her kindness."

"Tell me, young lady, what is your education?" the king asked.

"I finished high school early. Then I studied child care for a year. I wanted to become a pediatric nurse. I love children."

Biryn rubbed his chin. "That is interesting. Especially since the queen and I have been looking for a suitable young woman to assist Cylena with Eliya and Aylie, our twins. Your punishment will be as follows. You will come and live at the palace and be a nursemaid to my son and daughter. During their sleeping hours, or when the queen and I wish to be alone with our children, and your evenings, you will study Ierilian culture and our language. What do you think of this plan, Erica? You told me you know Isabella well."

Erica answered him. "Yes, Biryn. She is the little sister of Hannah, who perished when the Initiation Two crashed. I can vouch for Isabella. She's a good kid."

"I wish you'd all stop calling me a kid!" The words slipped from her lips before she realized. She covered her mouth with her hand. How could she have blurted that out in front of the king?

"Sorry, child," Biryn said, smiling at her kindly. "You are a young woman, but you are so petite and look very young. Tanoth, I put you in charge of recovering Isabella's belongings, and reward the young waitress who was so kind to her."

"Your Royal Highness, I don't know how to thank you." Isabella almost stumbled over the words. "Helping to look after two babies will be no punishment at all. I love little ones."

"It is decided. Erica, take Isabella to meet Cylena and the twins, please? She will move to the palace tomorrow."

CHAPTER SIX

Isabella twirled before the tall mirror in her room. The new dress Cylena had given her was absolutely gorgeous. It was the palest pink, embroidered with small red roses and white lace cascading from a deep collar and at the hem. It was a dress fit for a princess. After surviving months on whatever she could steal, she felt so spoiled. She and the queen had connected instantly and become very good friends. Cylena kind of reminded her of Hannah. She loved spending time with her.

Though her heart ached at the loss of her sister, in a way, she was glad she'd woken up on Ierilia. The people here were kind, and in many ways so simple—even the king and the queen. They had embraced her like family and treated her as if she were their little sister.

She adored taking care of the babies. They had wriggled their way straight to her heart. They were starting to smile now and gurgle. Eliya had even started to roll over and Aylie, though much smaller than her brother, wasn't too far behind. She and Cylena had so much fun with them. Of course they still slept a lot, so during that time she studied the language and Ierilian culture religiously and was close to mastering the language.

The king and queen allowed her a lot of free time to visit Laro and Erica. She also spent a lot of time with Tanoth. It amused her that Erica always managed to invite Tanoth the evenings she visited. Isabella didn't mind at all. She looked forward to being with her handsome rescuer. She was becoming more attached to him each time they were together. A strange pull from deep within drew her to him like a moth to a flame. It was so odd. She'd never felt that way in her life, with any boy. Then again, they had been boys. Tanoth was all man. She peeked one more time at her reflection and grinned. She had never looked so happy, even back on Earth. Her cheeks were flushed pink, and she had a healthy glow. Her hair bounced around her shoulders in golden waves, and her eyes flashed with excitement. Laro was on his way to pick her up with his flyer after the babies had gone down for the night. She would see Tanoth again that evening. Sometimes she felt guilty when she thought about Hannah. But she had to move on with her life. Hannah was gone, her parents she'd never see again. This life on this planet was her destiny now.

Hand in hand they strolled through Laro and Erica's gardens. The moons and the big star that she had learned was called Polarium shone down on them. It was apparently a magical star that could be seen from all planets.

Tanoth stopped and twirled her to stand before him, then caressed her cheek. "Isabella, I have to tell you something."

She sighed. Every touch was like a shock sending tingles racing across her skin. She looked up at his deep blue eyes. "Yes?"

Her breath caught when he twisted a lock of her hair around his finger. "You are the woman the gods and goddesses showed me in my dreams. The woman destined to be my lifemate."

Isabella stood rooted to the ground for a few moments. Yes, he was her dream man come to life, but was she ready for such a commitment? "Tanoth, I've got feelings for you, but I'm still young. I have no life experience at all. I'm not sure I can commit to you at this time." She was so confused.

Her heart and soul told her he was the one, but her mind just couldn't wrap around it. What the heck was a lifemate? "I am so unfamiliar with your gods and goddesses and their plans. I am just a girl from Earth. How can I be your lifemate or whatever that is?"

Tanoth's sigh sounded like it came from deep within. "I understand your confusion. Maybe I should have waited to tell you."

"Hell, baby, there is a lot of chemistry between us. I feel it, too. My hormones are raging off the charts."

He shook his head. "Your language is confusing. Can we continue on as before? Just forget I said anything."

Standing on her tippy-toes, she nodded. "Yes, of course." She placed a butterfly kiss on his lips. They were so soft, she kissed him again. His hold on her tightened. Then his lips parted hers, and the kiss deepened, drawing the life from the depths of her soul. Feelings she had never experienced rushed through her body. It was exquisite and sexy, and oh, so hot. Her blood felt as if it were on fire. Her heart pounded almost out of her chest. Sure, she'd kissed boys, had dated, but it had never gone beyond that. This was different. This was very real. Too real.

He broke the kiss, but his lips still hovered over hers when he whispered, "I have fallen in love with you, my beautiful princess from Earth."

She took a breath to still the racing of her heart. "Hardly a princess. I'm just an ordinary girl."

He cupped her chin and placed a featherlight kiss on her lips. "*My* princess. And I will wait for you patiently."

Isabella almost hated to go back to the palace. She loved being with Tanoth. He told her such interesting stories about Ierilia, its magic, sorcerers, shapeshifters, and about his work and the excursions he had to go on to test soil samples. He'd been on just such an excursion when he'd found her — to make sure the soil where their ship had crashed was okay.

She loved the fact they could speak now without using the translator. Relaxing on her pillows, she couldn't help thinking of their kiss. The heat of his body against hers. The feel of his arms wound tightly around her. Her pulse rate kicked up a notch. Could he truly be in love with her? That pull she felt deep inside was so much stronger now. She knew she was falling in love with him, too. She smiled, looking forward to their next *date*, and slowly drifted off to sleep, but then something woke her. A strange sensation infused her body . . . her mind. Shifting uncomfortably on the bed, she tried to shake the feeling, but it wouldn't go away.

Her mind tried to blank out. It was almost as if another mind was trying to overpower her thoughts. A sharp pain pierced her skull, and a man's voice rumbled inside her head.

Let it go, little one. My name is Zohmes. Accept what is happening. I will release you when my mission is done.

An inky black cloud engulfed her. Flames and smoke burst through it like the smoke was on fire. God, she couldn't breathe. She was gasping for air, but the thick fog filled her lungs. Grabbing her throat, she coughed and coughed, but she couldn't expel the smoke. Black spots danced before her eyes and a wave of dizziness hit her. *Oxygen* She needed fresh air. She stumbled from the bed and threw open a window. Leaning out, she tried to take a big gulp of the crisp night air. It didn't help. She was choking. She was going to die. She fell to the floor, still clutching her throat. Darkness, then blessed peace.

Isabella sucked in a deep breath and opened her eyes. Everything was blurry, so she tried to rub her eyes. Her hands were stuck. They wouldn't move. Slowly her vision cleared. She lay on the floor near the windows. Like an automaton, she stood and dressed, then made her way to the royal quarters.

She was in the nursery bending over little Aylie's crib. Her hand stroked the baby's cheek, but she couldn't feel it. She could feel nothing. It was as if her body had been taken over by another being.

Willing her body with all her might, she tried to take a step. Her feet wouldn't budge. The nightmare. It couldn't have been real, could it? The man's voice, the smoke. Had she died? Was she in hell? The man's rumbling laughter echoed through her mind. His essence brushed hers. Anger. Pure unadulterated hatred. It poured off him in waves. It permeated her skin and every breath she took.

Then she realized. No, she wasn't trapped in hell. It was much worse. She was caged within her own mind. A mere spectator to what happened around her. And the worst evil she had ever felt was in control. *His* mind was in control of everything her body said or did.

Cylena and Biryn entered the nursery. When Isabella turned to greet them, malice filled her veins. Whatever had taken control of her body and mind despised the king and queen.

There was nothing she could do. She attempted to muster all the power within her to talk, to warn the royals, but it didn't work. It was like watching herself in a movie and not being able to change the script.

Who in the hell was Zohmes? Had she really heard all that in her mind? She'd been in the palace for weeks now, more than a month, well, what she figured was approximately a month, had long conversations with Cylena, but never had she heard mention of that name, though Cylena had told her many stories about all the magic on the planet.

Biryn picked up Aylie, and Cylena took Eliya out of his bassinet. The royal couple looked so happy and proud.

"Eliya feels very hot," Cylena said suddenly while feeling the baby's forehead.

"Your Majesty, I thought so, too. I was about to contact you. Maybe he has a fever?" Isabella shook her head. It was her voice, but it wasn't her talking.

"For goodness sake, Isabella, you always call me by my name," Cylena chastised her. "What do you think is wrong?"

"I don't know, Cylena."

"What about Aylie?" Cylena asked.

"She felt warm to the touch, too. They don't appear sick, but maybe the doctor should examine them both," Isabella answered.

She cringed. Whatever was using her to talk and act sure as hell didn't speak as she would. She hoped the king and queen would pick up on it and know something was wrong. *Very wrong.*

Isabella watched the royals fuss over the babies.

Before long, Catrice rushed into the room.

"Doctor Catrice, I don't understand. They haven't been fussing," Isabella heard herself say.

The doctor gave her a curious glance, then hurried to examine the infants. After she thoroughly inspected both infants, she turned her attention to Biryn and Cylena.

"I can't find anything wrong with them. Their temperature appears normal, and their vital signs are perfect. Why did you call me in?"

"My son was burning hot," Biryn told her.

"And our girl was beginning to feel very warm," Cylena added.

"My diagnosis is that they're fine. They don't have a fever but do keep an eye on them. Call me if you need me or if there is a change in their temperature." Catrice packed her stethoscope and thermometer back into her bag and smiled at the king and queen before leaving the room.

Isabella watched the little spectacle. So this whole charade was just to frighten the royals. To what purpose? Who in God's name was this serpent who had invaded her mind and was controlling her every move? How could she contact anyone to let them know what was happening to her? Tanoth and Cylena had told her so much about all the magic on Ierilia, the shapeshifter lions, the jewel dragons. Was this some kind of magic? But why her?

Maniacal laughter sounded in her head. She tried to bring her hands up to her ears, wanted to drown out that crazy guffawing, but couldn't.

"Isabella, what is wrong? You look pale." Cylena rocked Eliya back and forth. "Biryn and I will stay with the twins for a while. I will put them to bed after their next feeding. Go and rest for a few hours."

"Cylena, I'm fine. Thanks for worrying."

"Then you can go and study for a while."

They wanted to be alone with the twins. That was obvious. The entity inside her brain didn't want her to go, but with the queen urging her to, he had no choice and made her walk to the door and leave the nursery.

When she was in her own room, she fell on the bed and cried. Well, she did . . . sort of. The girl on the bed didn't shed a tear and just lay staring at the ceiling. Damn, she was seeing everything, hearing, and able to think. But she couldn't move freely. It really was an invasion of a body snatcher.

What do you want? Get the hell out of my head and body.

Again, that maniacal laughter.

Girl, I will let you go when I have what I came for.

And what is that?

That is of no concern to you at this time.

Silence.

She tried to sit up, but her body wouldn't cooperate.

Quite a while later, someone knocked on her door. She sat

up. "Come in."

Cylena came into the room and sat on the bed next to her. She laid a cool hand on her forehead. Isabella felt it, tried desperately to say something, but her lips wouldn't move.

"How are you feeling, Isabella?" Concern laced her voice.

"I'm fine. Really."

"Come and sit on the balcony with me. We will have a cup of tea."

"That sounds good. The babies —"

"They are sleeping. It is not time to feed them yet. Biryn is with them, so do not worry."

Cylena walked to the door and told Dunmore, who had escorted her, to bring them tea. "Now come and sit on the balcony with me and we will talk a bit. I have a feeling something is troubling you."

Ah, good. Cylena at least felt that something was awry. She got up off the bed and followed the queen out onto the balcony. It was a glorious day. She should be out in the gardens, taking the twins for a stroll.

Dunmore appeared with a tea tray. He set it on the little table between their chairs. "Will there be anything else, Your Highness?"

"Thank you, Dunmore. No, you can go." Cylena stood to pour tea, but Isabella stopped her.

"I'll do that." Cylena sat again, and Isabella lifted the teapot to fill their cups. A vial appeared in her hand. Where the hell had that come from? It was very small and fit in the palm of her hand. As she poured tea into Cylena's cup, the vial magically opened, and some liquid dripped into the tea. She poured tea into her own cup, but the vial had disappeared. How weird was all that?

"Thank you, Isabella." Cylena took her cup off the tray and brought it to her lips. With all her might, Isabella concentrated to try to knock the cup out of the queen's hand, but it was of no use. Her limbs wouldn't cooperate.

What the fuck did you put in the queen's tea? Poison?

The potion will not harm her.

Like she believed him. Isabella felt sick to the stomach. Had he poisoned the queen? Words came from her mouth, words she did not speak, yet she did.

"Cylena, what is a grimoire?"

"Where did you hear that word, Isabella?"

"Tanoth mentioned something and told me about a black gem. Discovered on his last excursion, he said."

"Tanoth should not have told you about it."

"Oh. Is he in trouble now? But what is it?"

"The grimoire is a very old book containing many spells that can be used for good or evil. The grimoire can be very dangerous in the wrong hands." Cylena drank her tea, then continued. "But I will tell you all about it. Please pour me another cup of tea?"

Whatever was in the vial had done no apparent harm to the queen, except she was very talkative. More so than normal.

"Will you be seeing Tanoth this evening?" Cylena asked.

"Yes. He is coming to the palace."

"I have a feeling you are very fond of that young man."

"More than fond, but it scares me."

Okay, so the idiot inside her head and body knew exactly how she felt about Tanoth? How damn invasive was that?

"Has he kissed you?"

"Eh . . . yes. But tell me more about the grimoire. I heard of such things in stories and movies on Earth. Can I see it?"

"No, Isabella. The king has hidden it in the royal treasury to which only he has a key. The grimoire is safely tucked away in a small, secret room."

"Wow. Sounds intriguing. Where is the secret room? Do you need a key to it, too? Does he keep the black gem in it as well?"

"Yes. It is a pity. The little box it rests in is so beautiful. I would love to display it. The secret room is behind a very large portrait hanging on the wall. If you remove the portrait, a panel slides open." Cylena finished her tea. "I should go back to the twins. It is almost feeding time."

"Where does the king keep the key for the treasury?"

Isabella could hardly believe the questions she heard coming out of her own mouth. She was astonished when Cylena freely told her.

"In the drawer of his bedside table. It is safe there." Cylena stood. "Goodness, look at the time. We had a lovely talk about you and your young man, Isabella."

After the queen left her room, Isabella sat on the side of the bed. Or . . . he sat. She just watched where he led her, forced her to sit, walk, or stand.

So what was all that about?

An old book that you are going to steal for me. And the black gem.

Like hell I will.

You might have noticed, you have little choice what your body does or what you say.

The queen will realize she told me too much and she'll hide the key.

The queen will not remember anything. The potion has worn off and with it her memory of her conversation with you, except your romance.

You're an evil bastard.

And you are a little spitfire. It is strange. I have possessed many, but never have any been able to talk back to me or know what I was doing while in their body. But not to worry. You will not remember any of this after I leave you.

And when will that be?

After you get me the book and the gem.

CHAPTER SEVEN

The asshole in her head and body had no patience with the babies at all. He let them cry. Isabella ached to pick up Aylie and comfort her, but instead, he forced her to walk to the balcony, close the door, and stand there gazing at the gardens.

You will get the key this evening when you bring the twins to the royal bedroom.

She'd fight tooth and nail before she'd let him get the key. Isabella shuddered. For that bastard to have full control over her was beyond horror. She felt so helpless.

At night, the twins slept in their cradles in the king and queen's bedroom. After that, she was free until the next morning.

He finally allowed her to go back into the nursery. Aylie had cried herself to sleep. Isabella gazed down at the baby. She was still red from crying, and her hair was damp. She felt mortified. *You bastard. Look what you did!* Again, that crazy laughter. She sat beside the cradle and thought about Tanoth. She was looking forward to seeing him that evening. But was the bastard in her mind and body going to allow it? If only she could tell Tanoth what was going on with her.

You will not tell your young man anything.

You can't stop me.

Oh, yes, I can. After he leaves, you will go to the treasury to get the book and the gem.

Just like that. I don't have the key.

You will have it.

116

Time crept by slowly. The bastard barely allowed her to tend to the babies. After dinner, Cylena came to feed them, and together they dressed the babies for the night. Isabella loved this evening ritual, but now all she could do was watch as her hands moved mechanically and listen to his griping about dirty infants. It horrified her.

Each carrying a baby, they went to the royal quarters and laid the infants in their cribs. Isabella was about to leave the bedroom when a commotion sounded in the dining room.

Cylena hurried to see what it was all about. Isabella found her feet flying to the bedside table. She opened the drawer, and there was the key.

With all her might, she tried to stop her fingers from grabbing it. To no avail. With the key tucked in her pocket, her feet carried her back to stand beside Eliya's cradle.

Cylena returned. "One of the servants broke a precious vase and was beside herself," she told Isabella.

"Poor thing."

"Accidents happen. Now be off with you. Your young man is waiting for you in the gardens."

Isabella felt the reluctance as she left the palace to meet with Tanoth. Normally, she would have gone to her room, put on a fresh dress, and brushed her hair to make herself look as pretty as possible. The bastard who possessed her had no interest in doing that. His reluctance to meet with Tanoth was evident. She felt it so strongly.

He stood leaning against a lamppost. When she approached, he eagerly stepped toward her. "Isabella. You're late. I was afraid —"

"Don't be stupid, Tanoth. Stop acting like a lovesick puppy."

Good God. Had those words really left her lips? She saw his hurt expression, and there was nothing she could do to soften what she'd said. "Well, let's find a quiet spot and get on with it." She took his hand and pulled him to the gazebo in the rose garden.

"You are acting very strange. Get on with what?"

"Sex, stupid. Isn't that what you want?"

Oh my God. Did she just fucking say that?

Shut the fuck up, snake. He's going to think I've gone crazy.

Tanoth gazed down at her, a concerned expression crossing his features. "Isabella, what is wrong with you? You're not acting like yourself tonight. Maybe I should leave and come back another time. Or wait until we see each other at Laro and Erica's home."

"Sorry. I've had a bad day."

You are spoiling my fun. You want him to take you. So, now is a good time.

Fucktard! Leave me alone. Leave Tanoth alone.

You need to stall Tanoth until the royals go to bed. Then you can go to the treasury to fetch what I need.

Tanoth placed his arm around her shoulders. "I'm sorry you had a bad day. What happened?"

"The babies were fussy."

Isabella saw Tanoth studying her face, her eyes. Then he bent down and kissed her.

Her body betrayed her. No, the bastard betrayed her. God, she was confused. Tanoth had awoken feelings within her, a desire she didn't know could burn so fiercely. Oh yes, she wanted Tanoth. It was a sweet, enticing ache that built within her each moment she spent with him. Not this time. That monster corrupted it. Now, her body moved against Tanoth seductively against her will. Her hands untied the string at the top of her blouse, then yanked the material down, exposing her breasts. Her nipples hardened. She pushed herself against Tanoth.

When he didn't move, seemed to stand there like a statue, her hands pushed the bodice down all the way. Isabella tried like mad to stop, to will her hands to behave, but it was no use. Her fingers had a mind of their own. They undid the clasp at her waist. Before she realized, she stood stark naked.

Throaty laughter in her head.

You do have a beautiful body. How can he resist?

Shut the fuck up! Dickhead! Stop this!

I am having a good time. Enjoy your mating.

Her lips smiled. Seductive words escaped. "Tanoth, baby, love me? Let me feel you . . ." Her hands found their way to his crotch, undid the string at his waist. She yanked his pants down. His cock sprang free.

Tanoth groaned. "Isabella . . . stop . . . I cannot—"

"Shut up." Isabella was mortified, embarrassed, as her body sank to the stone floor and she lay down. *Stop this . . . Please!* She tried desperately to stand back up. To shove the demon that possessed her out of her mind . . . her body. She couldn't. He had entrenched himself so deeply within her being, she had no hope of fighting him. Spreading her legs, she bucked her hips. Her arms lifted to invite him to take her.

She wanted to crawl into a corner of her mind and just disappear. What the snake was forcing her to do went totally against her grain. Naked, out in the open. Anyone could walk past the gazebo and see them.

He stood above her for a moment, his cock still free, pulsing. His jaw was clenched, and a troubled expression clouded his eyes. Suddenly, he yanked his pants up. Then he took her hand and pulled her to stand up. "Isabella! What has gotten into you? Get dressed."

When she didn't move, Tanoth retrieved her clothing and handed them to her. "Isabella, please."

"You are no fun." Isabella could feel anger boiling from her possessor. She jerked the clothing from his hand, yanked her dress on, slipped her blouse over her shoulders and tied the opening. "I will find someone else to fulfill my needs since you obviously don't want to."

Tanoth studied her face, an unreadable expression in his eyes. He shook his head. "I should not have stayed." He turned, strode away without looking back, and left her alone in the gazebo.

Isabella tried to call him to return to her, but her lips would not move. Her possessor's laughter filled her mind as he forced her to watch Tanoth walk away.

She sat down on one of the benches and smiled . . . or at least the demon did. Isabella was screaming. Her heart had been wrenched in two, her soul ripped asunder. How in the hell was she going to fix this mess? Tanoth would never want to see her again.

Why are you doing this to me?

Enough of your whining. Once I have what I want, you will be free.

The demon turned her gaze to the king's bedroom window. The lights were still on. The monster's rage was a steady burn in her mind as she stared at the window. She shivered. What could the king and queen have done to anger this beast?

He made her wait on the bench until the lights had gone out in the king's chambers. It was late. Well past the time she normally went to bed. Everyone in the castle would be sleeping, except for the guards that were on duty.

It is time.

No! I'm not going to steal for you.

She fought against him but to no avail. He forced her to stand and slip into the palace through the rear of the garden. Her heart beat faster with each step, and dread filled her. She knew this was not going to end well. How could it? Guards were posted throughout the palace. When this was over, what would happen to her?

She knew where to find the treasury. Cylena had pointed it out to her during one of their strolls through the palace.

Too soon, she stood in front of the dreaded door. She palmed the key and opened it, then stepped inside. The portrait. She instantly spotted it and removed the picture from the wall. Behind it was the secret room. She felt the bastard's elation when the door automatically disappeared into the wall. Right in front of her on a shelf was an old book. A gold filigree box stood on top of it. She seized them both and stepped out of the secret room.

She tried to grab her throat. Oh God, she was choking again. Black smoke poured out of her mouth and nostrils. A wave of nausea rolled through her. She coughed and gasped until the thick fog of fire and ash expelled itself. Laughter echoed around the treasury. Then suddenly the black cloud of smoke swirled and faded into nothing. The grimoire and gem got sucked into the vortex with it. The gold box lay open at her feet. Next to it, the key. She bent to pick them up and without thinking stuck both in the deep pocket of her skirt.

Dazed, she took a deep breath of fresh, clean air. Was he gone? Was her mind truly free? She didn't feel him anymore. She wanted to laugh and cry at the same time.

"What are you doing in here?" One of the guards entered the treasury.

Another guard joined him. "How did she get in here? She must have stolen the key. Off to the dungeons with you. The king will deal with you in the morning. He does not tolerate thievery. Where is the key?"

"In . . . in . . . my . . . p-pocket." She was about to burst into tears, but she managed to restrain the urge.

One guard held her while the other felt her pocket. He withdrew the box and the key and held them up triumphantly. "I must return these to the king immediately. Can you handle her on your own?"

"This little girl? Go. But do not wake the royals now. Give

it to the guard on duty."

"No. The king must have it. It cannot be in anyone else's hands. Take her to the dungeons."

"Let me speak to the king and queen? Please?" Isabella begged. "I can explain everything."

"Hold your tongue. You can save your explanations until morning," the guard snarled. Then after binding her wrists, he dragged her along.

CHAPTER EIGHT

Isabella lay curled up on a bed of straw in the corner of her cell. She cried now until she had no tears left and dry sobs wracked her body. She felt drained, exhausted. But sleep would not come. Her anxiety at what would become of her now overpowered all else. Except her thoughts about Tanoth. He was going to think her a slut. The thought of losing him for good, devastated her. Worse, what would happen to him? The king and queen would assume it was Tanoth who had told her about the grimoire, gem, and the gold box.

Eventually, she did drift off, only to have nightmares about the tormentor who had possessed her. His demonic laughter woke her up. Her face was soaked with perspiration. Desperately, she tried to shove it all in the back of her mind.

A guard pushed a bowl of food and a goblet of water through the bars. "Eat, wench. The king will be here soon."

There was no frigging way in hell she could eat. At least she managed to drink the water. Her throat was parched. She waited, but the king didn't come. Finally, Dunmore, the king's personal aide, came.

"Isabella, the king sent me to fetch you and bring you to the throne room."

She stood. He didn't shackle her or tie her wrists, but he did hold her arm in a vice grip. "A trial? Already?"

"The king wastes no time if a crime occurs on Ierilia, especially one in his own palace."

She expected to see a crowd of spectators, but the throne room was virtually empty. The only people present, were the king, queen, Laro, Erica, Brenn, Ciara, and Ivran, Tanoth's brother. Isabella was so glad to see Erica standing near the royals. The king dismissed Dunmore, but just as he left, two guards brought someone else into the throne room. She looked behind her and to her consternation saw Tanoth. He didn't meet her eyes. His face was stern and forbidding. The king dismissed his guards, too.

Once the doors closed, the king addressed Isabella. "Young lady, what do you have to say for yourself? You admitted to being a thief when you were found. You swore it was only for survival. Yet here, you have everything you need and want, and you choose to steal from us?"

"Your Majesty, I am so sorry. It wasn't me. Honestly, I love the twins and Cylena is my dear friend."

The king stood, his face thunderous. "How can you say it was not you when you were caught in the treasury with my key and the gold box. Where is the gem that was in it? Where is the grimoire? Is Tanoth your accomplice?"

"Your Majesty, I am not. I know nothing of this," Tanoth interrupted.

"Silence. You will answer when spoken to. Isabella, what possessed you to steal from us and the people who helped you?" Biryn stood before her now.

"H-his . . . name . . . w-was . . . Zohmes. He possessed me."

"Who told you where to find the gem and the grimoire?"

Isabella's tears began to flow. She couldn't stop them. "T-the . . . queen."

Cylena stood and joined Biryn. "Isabella, that is a lie. I never told you."

"Your . . . H-highness . . . A vial magically appeared when

I poured your tea on the balcony. It made you talk. The demon inside my head asked the questions. I was helpless. I heard and felt everything, but I couldn't stop him. He was an evil bast—"

"You have heard stories about Zohmes and Odoxon and his possession of people. You are lying, Isabella." The king angrily strode back to his throne.

Cylena said, "Isabella, I feel so betrayed. You have hurt me deeply."

"Cylena, it . . . it . . . wasn't . . . me . . ." Isabella sobbed.

Biryn looked at Tanoth. "And you, young man, what is your story?"

"Your Majesty, I never told Isabella anything about the grimoire or the gem. I swear on all I hold dear. All I can say is that when I met Isabella in the gardens last night, she did not seem or behave like herself."

The king was silent for a few minutes. He rubbed his chin, then stood again. "Tomorrow morning we will hold the trial by fire for both of you."

Erica jumped toward the king. "Biryn, for God's sake! No!"

Ivran grabbed Erica by the shoulder and pulled her back. "Erica, this will not help them."

Biryn pinned Erica with a hard stare. "Captain Martinez, I have spoken. If the girl and the young man are telling the truth, as you know, they will not be harmed. The girl's tale does not ring true. Anyone that has been possessed does not remember or know what happened to them. How is it that she claims to have been possessed by Zohmes and remembers everything?"

Erica turned to Ciara. "Can you do something? Can you talk to Rania? Can the goddess help?"

Ciara shook her head. "I am sorry. Rania is silent on this matter."

"Call the guards and have them both escorted to the dungeons," Biryn ordered.

Isabella felt like she was going to faint. They almost had to drag her from the throne room. Trial by fire? Were they going to burn her at the stake? Like the Salem witch trials?

They locked her in her cell and Tanoth in the one next to her. She knew her story was unbelievable. Yet the king had admitted to others being possessed. But she remembered everything, each detail. After she calmed a bit, she thought about what she had told the king. She'd left a lot out. In her distress, her mind was scrambled. Like the smoke and stuff that had come out of her mouth and nostrils. Why didn't she mention that, among other details? She'd left out the part of her attempted seduction of Tanoth. It was too shameful.

"Isabella?" Tanoth called out to her.

"Yes."

"I do believe you were not yourself last night."

She scrambled up and hurried to the bars. Grasping them, she sobbed, "Oh God, Tanoth, I'm so sorry. I wasn't myself. It was some satanic demon inside of me. I could hear him. He talked to me and made me do everything. Honestly. I swear it on all I hold dear. My body wasn't my own. He controlled me. And then after I had the grimoire and the gem, all this smoke and fire came out of my mouth and nose, and suddenly I was back. But then the guard caught me with the gold box and the key in my pocket."

"Did the queen truly tell you about the grimoire and the gem?"

"Yes, she did. The bastard made me put the potion in her tea, and it made her talk. He was the one making my mouth and lips ask the queen questions."

"You are telling me more than you told the king. Tomorrow morning, before the trial, the king will ask you again to

126

repeat your story. Tell him everything. Even the part that involves me, you trying to seduce me."

"Noooo . . . I can't. I am so ashamed of what he made me do . . . of the things he made me say." She choked back a sob. "Tanoth . . . I've never . . . I'm a virgin. I've never been with a man." She wished she could see him. Even though she reached through the bars, the wall between them was too thick "What is the trial by fire? Are they going to burn us at the stake?"

"I believe you, Isabella. Do not fear the trial. The fire will not harm those that speak the truth. You and I both know in our hearts what the truth is. But more important, I love you, and I believe you. Zohmes is an evil god. He will stop at nothing to gain what he wants. So now he has his hands on the grimoire and the gem. The spells written in the grimoire in the wrong hands can wreak much havoc. I cannot tell you more. After the trial, if the king and queen allow it, I will tell you everything."

"Tanoth, thank you for believing me. I was so afraid I'd lost you forever after what happened."

"My princess, I was angry and deeply hurt at first. I thought the gods and goddesses had deceived me about my lifemate. But the more I thought about it during the night, it became clear to me that your behavior was not that of the young woman with whom I fell in love. Then at sunup, the king's guards came and took me to the palace."

"I'm so sorry. It's all because of me. If you hadn't found me, you wouldn't be in this predicament. And now tomorrow you are facing the same punishment as me, and you didn't do a damn thing!"

"Isabella, I understand why the king suspects me. He thinks I told you about the grimoire and the gem. Right now I do not think he is thinking clearly. How could I have known where he keeps the key to the treasury? How could you have known? Only the king and queen know what they keep in their private bedroom."

"Yes. But the queen doesn't remember she told me. That demon said after the potion wore off she would forget everything. Tanoth, has anyone ever survived this trial by fire? Have you witnessed such a trial?"

"No, princess. No one has ever survived it. And it is a trial created by the gods. It is always held in private."

"That sounds ominous," she said in a small voice. "Aren't you scared?"

"Yes and no. I know I speak the truth, and so do you. The only solace is you and I will perish together."

CHAPTER NINE

They spent the day and a good part of the night talking until sleep overtook them. Isabella had no idea what time it was when the guards came and took them to the waiting hovercraft.

Isabella saw the arena below. It reminded her of a Roman arena. Was there going to be a big crowd cheering the trial on? No, Tanoth had said it was always held in private. She had no idea what to expect. She'd so hoped that Erica or Cylena would come talk to her, but neither did. The king probably forbade it.

Six guards marched them into the arena. They had to wait behind a barred door. Her heart thudded, resounding in her head and ears. She was terrified.

A guard opened the gate and motioned them to enter the arena. Her feet sank into warm sand. She looked for stakes with piles of wood and straw at the bottom but saw none.

The six guards who had escorted them to the arena marched them to stand before a raised platform. The king and queen, decked out in royal finery and their crowns, sat in the center. It appeared the whole team was present. But Isabella saw no spectators. The bleachers were empty, much to her relief.

Her mind felt so numb. Next to her, Tanoth whispered loud enough for her to hear, "Tell them everything you told me last night. Do not leave anything out."

The guards stepped away and stood behind them. Isabella heard a soft hissing sound. When she glanced around, she saw large metal circles appear from the ground.

Biryn stood, a gold scepter in his hands. "How do you plead, Isabella?"

"Not guilty, Your Majesty."

"Tanoth, how do you plead?"

"Not guilty, Your Majesty."

Clouds appeared above them, blocking the suns. "The gods have made their presence known. You may now speak in your defense, Isabella. When Isabella is finished, Tanoth, you may speak."

Tremors of fear shook her body. She trembled from head to toe, but somehow, she felt Tanoth's calming presence. Suddenly, through the clouds, a ray of light enveloped them both. She dared to glance up for a split second. Polarium? In broad daylight? Its calming golden ray sent a delicious warmth through her body, and her fear disappeared. She began to talk, this time not leaving out the slightest detail. She even dared to talk about her wanton seduction of Tanoth. When she was finished, Tanoth told his tale. When he stopped, the king stood again and held his scepter up.

"Let the gods judge if you both spoke truthfully. If you did, the fire will not harm you, and we will have judged you wrongfully. You will step through each circle. After each circle, you have a chance to speak the truth. The last largest circle will be your final judgement. Isabella, you are first."

She turned and saw the circles burst into flame, the flames reaching the center. How did one get through that without getting burned? Strangely enough, the intense fear had settled, and she felt completely calm. It was as if Polarium had infused her with strength. She walked toward the circle and heard Erica scream as she stepped through the flames. "Okay, if I'm to burn to a potato crisp, so be it." As she lifted her foot, the flames turned a blue color, and she felt nothing but a cool breeze.

She ran to the next circle, and it was the same. More confident now, she continued on, until the last, biggest circle. The circle of truth. So far, not a hair on her body or her head had been scorched. Knowing she had spoken truthfully, she bravely stepped into the last circle. The flames instantly extinguished, and she stepped unharmed onto the sand beyond.

She turned and watched Tanoth do the same. After he stepped through the last circle, he rushed to her and took her into his arms.

He held her tight, and she felt so safe. "See, I told you not to be afraid. The gods say the trial by fire will not harm those that speak the truth."

"You telling me last night that no one had ever survived it didn't help, but Polarium infused me with strength. Did you see the star shine down on us?"

"Yes. For Polarium to appear in daylight is magickal."

Erica came running toward them. She clasped Isabella in her arms. "Izzy, I'm so sorry this happened to you. I had nothing to say in any of this. Are you okay?"

Isabella suffered Erica's inspection from head to toe. "I'm fine, except all this stuff is messing with my head."

Ivran wasn't too far behind Erica. He had pulled Tanoth into a hug. "Mother would have had my head if you had perished, little brother. But I knew you spoke true."

Cylena joined them, too. She stood before Isabella. "I must apologize from the depths of my heart for doubting you. Your story was so unbelievable. Will you forgive me?"

Isabella saw the sincerity in the queen's eyes. "Frankly, I wouldn't have believed my story either."

Erica squeezed her hand. "I witnessed one of these trials, and I was scared shitless for you. Thing is, the others that were possessed didn't remember anything. The king will want to talk to you. And the team."

Ciara sauntered up. "Rania just informed me that Isabella has been infused by Polarium. That is why we saw its rays envelop her and Tanoth. It's miraculous. The gods and goddesses favor you both."

"When I felt Polarium's rays all my fear melted away." Isabella stood closer to Tanoth.

From the platform, the king announced, "We shall return to the palace. Lunch awaits us."

"Tanoth, I don't want to go back to the palace. I just want to be alone. Well, not alone, with you, but not with them."

"We must, sweet. The king commanded it."

She sighed. "So be it, but stay close, okay?"

When they arrived at the palace and went to the royal quarters, lunch was ready for them. Isabella wasn't hungry. After her ordeal of the last two days, she couldn't eat a bite if she tried. She looked at the team sitting around the table. Laura and Julia gave her curious glances. Of course they would. They didn't know anything about what had happened.

Biryn raised his glass. "To a very brave young woman. To Isabella. And to her mate, Tanoth."

Mate? Really now.

All sipped from their wine. Then the king began talking. "Some here do not know what has happened in the last few days. First, Zohmes has the grimoire and the black diamond. We must get it back."

A murmur among the team members. Biryn continued. "I apologize to Isabella for putting her through a grueling ordeal — the trial by fire. But I had no choice. I needed to know the absolute truth. Now that I know she has spoken truthfully, I will let her tell you what happened and how Zohmes was able to obtain the grimoire and the black diamond."

Isabella repeated the whole tale again, except she left the

seduction part out.

"We cannot leave the grimoire or the gem in Zohmes' hands. There is too much damage he can do to our world using the spells within," Astiana stated.

"Whoever Zohmes is, he is an evil, hateful man," Isabella said vehemently.

"He is not a man. He is a fallen god who wants the throne, similar to what we know as Satan," Erica told her.

Tanoth caressed her arm. "Ciara, you said Polarium had infused Isabella. What does that mean?"

Isabella looked at the dragon princess. She and her cousin Taylith were often in meetings with the king, along with the rest of his elite team. "I'd like to know, too. My first night on Ierilia, Polarium shone so brightly. I felt very safe beneath its glow. I know the star helped me to survive all those months I was in the forest."

"In your case, Polarium has protected you from harm." Ciara smiled at Isabella. "We do not know what Polarium's origins are. All we have are legends passed down through the generations. Some believe that the goddess of the moons, Asla, created the star to guide and protect travelers on their journeys, but the star is so much more. Many of us believe that Polarium infuses Ierilia with magick. I doubt we will ever know the truth of when and how it was created and what its powers are."

"Polarium kept me safe, even when the Initiation Two crashed." Isabella toyed with the food on her plate, then set her fork down and glanced at the king and queen. "It has been a very rough couple of days. I am still trying to process everything that has happened. Do you mind if I get some air?"

Biryn rubbed his chin, then gave her a broad grin. "I think, young lady, both you and Tanoth have been through quite an ordeal today. I am giving you both a week away from your duties." His gaze turned to Tanoth. "You have been traveling throughout many of the realms for your work. Take the girl sightseeing. Introduce her to Ierilia. I command it."

CHAPTER TEN

The next morning, Tanoth picked her up at the crack of dawn. The first place he took her was the town Bernie had been building, and the excavation site of the temple. Bernie was all too happy to meet her and show them around. Isabella was awed when she saw the grocery store. "Real tomatoes! And lettuce, and strawberries. Tanoth, can we buy some?"

Bernie grinned. "Laura has been very busy having the gardeners plant all our Earth seeds."

Tanoth stocked up on some of the fruit Isabella pointed out and lettuce and tomatoes. She could hardly wait. She'd not had any of it on Earth. Again . . . it was only for the rich.

After Bernie had shown her his house, Tanoth decided they should continue their vacation. "I'd love to look inside that temple," Isabella said. "Is that really where you found those . . . eh . . . items?"

Tanoth laughed. "Bernie was with us. And no, not inside the temple, but beyond it. But he does not know what has happened."

"Like what items and what has happened?" Bernie questioned.

"It is a long story and I am not at liberty to say. You will need to speak to the king," Tanoth said. "But let us continue on to the beach."

When they arrived at the beach, Isabella drank in the sight. A blue ocean, a beautiful white beach, sand that looked like it had never been walked on.

After Tanoth pitched a tent, she took her sandals off, and they walked through the warm sand to where the waves rolled onto the beach.

Isabella had never seen anything like it. She had grown up near the sand and surf of Florida's beaches, but they looked nothing like this. The beaches on Earth were littered with garbage and tents and makeshift shelters of the homeless. The water was contaminated, and sea life was dying off in droves. Quite often she would see all manner of fish and fowl floating dead on the surface. Cleanup crews went out daily to remove carcasses from the water. She'd seen people swimming in the ocean in old movies, but she'd never set foot on a beach, let alone even dipped her toes in ocean water.

But this beach was pristine, and the water was crystal clear. Below the surface, she could see an array of colored plant life, small fish, and crustaceans. The sand was pearly white and silky fine. It reminded her of snow.

Tanoth held her hand as they walked along the edge, ankle deep in the water. She'd knotted her skirt above her knees. The sand squished between her toes. She relished the feel of the fine sand. Now and then she bent to pick up a beautiful colored shell and tucked them into her pocket.

"This is incredible!" Isabella took a deep breath of the fresh salty air. It was exhilarating.

Tanoth stopped and pulled her into his arms, then kissed the tip of her nose. "Not quite as incredible as you."

He held her as they gazed out over the ocean. It was late afternoon, and the suns made the water sparkle like diamonds.

She looked up at Tanoth and sighed. "Damn, I wish I had a bathing suit."

"Why would you need a suit to bathe?"

Isabella giggled and shook her head. "They aren't to bathe in, silly. They are worn when one goes swimming. If I had known you'd be bringing me to such a beautiful beach, I would have asked Erica about one."

He gave her a lopsided grin and winked. "Who needs a suit to swim?"

"I am not going skinny dipping! What if someone sees us? So, what *do* Ierilians wear when they swim?"

"Your Earth language is mystifying. What is skinny? I know what dipping means."

"Eh . . . naked. The word can also be used for someone that is undernourished."

"Ah, I see. First of all, most of our towns and villages are not close to the sea. Many of them have rivers nearby. Some of those have very strong currents, so it is too dangerous to venture into deeper waters. When we do go into the water to bathe or play, the men wear their undergarment, and the women wear a short tunic. Also, there are oceans where one could encounter dangerous water species, like the Glahm Ocean. It is the home of dangerous serpents. People naturally stay away from those waters, unless they are in a boat."

Isabella wrinkled her nose. "Is this ocean safe?"

"I believe so. I have not heard of dangerous sea life here."

Oh, she longed to go swimming. But all she wore under her dress was underwear. She sighed. "Oh, look at those big fish. They resemble dolphins. They're extinct on Earth now, but again, I have seen them in old movies."

"They are orkallions. A friendly fish and very playful. It is said they are highly intelligent. We can be sure there are no dangerous species here because of their presence."

"See, just like dolphins. Are there sharks here?"

"Sharks?"

"A huge fish that can bite you in half or take off your arm or leg."

"That sounds like a sciskes. Yes, we have something like that in our oceans, but not here. I am hungry. How about we go back to our tent and roast the fish I caught?"

Earlier, he'd amazed Isabella as he'd fashioned a spear from a branch and speared a few fish for their dinner. She watched him build a fire, rubbing two sticks together to ignite the wood. He really had to teach her how to do that. Not that she ever thought to be alone and lost again, but it would be nice to know how.

Tanoth had come well prepared. He handed her a metal plate with a chunk of bread, some fruit, a tomato, a leaf of lettuce, and cheese. The aroma of roasting fish teased her nostrils. Just as the suns were beginning to dip below the horizon, turning the sky into a myriad of color, reflecting onto the now smooth sea, he handed her a fish on a stick. "Fingers?"

"Yes, love. We are camping." He grinned and sat next to her.

Isabella thought she'd gone from hell to paradise. And maybe that's what all this was. She'd died in the crash, got tested for months, then by a hellish god inhabiting her body, and now she was in Heaven. Whatever it was, it was all too real, and she planned to relish every second of it. And the man meant for her had already lived there. He had been waiting for her. Maybe she was still young, but no way in hell was she going to waste her time with him either.

"You are deep in thought, Isabella. You do not like the fish?"

"Yes, sorry. It was delicious. I was thinking about everything that has happened to me since the ship crashed. I think I died, and now I'm in Heaven."

Tanoth burst into laughter. "You mean the realm of dreams? I am afraid this is all very real. This is not the afterlife."

"Are you sure? None of it feels real to me."

"I am very sure. You have been here such a short time and experienced much. From now, we will lead a normal, safe life." He took their plates, brushed them clean using some sand, then turned to her and pulled her against him.

A warm breeze caressed her, sending the fragrance of perfumed flowers through the air. It was so quiet around them. The beach had been deserted all day, and still was. She snuggled against him. "Where do we go tomorrow?"

"If it were up to me, we would stay here the whole week. Alas, the king ordered me to show you some of Ierilia. We will fly to the next realm, and I will show you its main city, Tardala."

"Did I ever thank you for getting my belongings from the hollow tree? Not that most of that clothing from Earth is any good here, except for underwear. Did you reward that young waitress for helping me?" she asked.

"Yes. The young woman, her name is Dranina, was happy to learn you were safe. I told her your story. She was well rewarded and hopes to see you again."

"I'm glad. Without her sharing her tips, I would have become a worse thief."

He lowered her to the warm sand and tenderly kissed her lips. Her heart sped up until it was a staccato rhythm pounding against her ribs, echoing in her ears. She pushed up against him, pulled at his body until he lay on top of her. "Tanoth, this feels so right," she murmured against his lips.

And it did. Unlike the fiasco in the garden, she was no longer confused. She was in control of her body and her mind, not the monster that had possessed her, and she wanted Tanoth. Each taste of his lips . . . each caress built a sweet ache of need within her, yearning to be fulfilled.

The kiss deepened. His tongue explored the crevices of her mouth. His tongue teased hers until she felt like she'd explode. Her whole body was on fire. A slow, steady burn pulsed between her thighs. Spreading her legs, she pushed up against him.

"Are you sure, love?"

"Yes, as sure as I'll ever be. I've fallen in love with you, too, my gorgeous alien."

He yanked his head back and gave her a mischievous grin. "Alien? You are the alien here."

Isabella giggled and pulled his head back down to her lips. She felt his fingers fumble with the laces of her bodice. He slipped it down. Then he loosened the belt of the dress and slid it down to her ankles. All she wore beneath was a pair of panties. He fumbled with it until she lay naked before him.

He stood and removed his tunic and pants, then gazed down at her. His eyes blazed with passion as he admired her naked form. There was no embarrassment, not this time. He made her feel beautiful and alluring. Like she was the air he breathed.

"The moonlight makes you look like a goddess, love. You are exquisite. Your hair is like spun moonlight rays, your eyes the blue of the ocean, and—"

And he looked as if he could have been a Greek god. All muscles and tawny skin, his long, wavy hair blowing in the breeze. Polarium's light shone brightly, casting him in an ethereal golden glow. She ached to touch every inch of him.

"Keep telling me stuff like that, and I may just attack you. Come here," she ordered and held her arms out.

She felt his cock throb against her belly as he lay on top of her, his chest pressing against her breasts. His lips caressed her forehead while his fingers combed through her long hair. He kissed her nose, her temples, her chin, then claimed her lips again, drawing the love from her heart and soul.

He broke free for a moment and murmured, "Never could

I have imagined the gods and goddesses would send you to me."

"Did you really see me in your dreams?" she whispered.

"Yes, I did. You are the one. My lifemate. Will you join with me, my princess?"

"I'm not sure what that means. Are you asking me to marry you?" Isabella asked uncertainly, not at all sure if she was ready for marriage. All she knew was that she wanted him. That her body was on fire for him, and those flames needed to be doused.

"Marry? Yes, if this means betrothal, yes again."

Isabella had to think for a moment, but not for long. "If this means we're engaged, yes. But I don't want to get married right away. Allow me to come to terms with everything that has happened first? But enough talking. For God's sake, continue what you started."

"I love you, sweet princess. I want you to be sure before we—"

"I'm sure, now shut up." She grabbed him by the hair and pulled his head close to hers. His lips crashed down on hers and revealed all the built-in passion within him. She moaned under his caresses. When his hand kneaded her breast, she pushed his head down and arched her back. He took her nipple into his mouth and sucked hard while his other hand massaged the free breast.

Her belly felt like it would burst into flames any minute. Her clit pulsed. His lips rained kisses across her breasts, and his fingers tweaked both nipples while he kissed his way down her chest, to her belly, to finally stop just above her pubes. He sat on his knees between her legs, gazing down at her. She spread her legs wide for him, drew her knees up. The breeze caressed her opened folds.

He bent low and licked her juices, then gently nibbled on her clit while his fingers found her throbbing and waiting vagina. When he entered a finger and began to rotate it within her, she squirmed. "Take me, Tanoth, please," she moaned throatily.

She watched him sit on his knees again, take his cock in his hand, and guide it to her waiting opening. She drew in a sharp breath when she felt the tip enter. Oh, it felt good, so good. Like nothing she'd ever imagined. He was so big, he had to enter her slowly. When he was halfway in, he lay on top of her and took her into his arms, his lips claiming her in a neverending kiss that took her to the brink of insanity.

She pushed up against him, wrapped her legs around his body, then felt him push in all the way in one thrust. It didn't hurt like hell, as so many of her friends had claimed. Sure, she felt a ping of pain as he broke through, but then he filled her, completely. He lay still for a few moments, caressing her, kissing her and fondling her hair. Then he began to move, and she thought the exhilarating rollercoaster ride would send her over the edge.

"Yes, baby, oh yes. More, please . . ." she called out.

"I love you," he said in a husky voice.

"And I love you," she managed to get out. Her libido was in overdrive. She was so ready for him to fulfill that desperate need, to come. His body began to tremble. He gasped, and she matched him thrust for thrust as they rode the final wave of passion.

He collapsed on top of her and just held her, panting. They lay quietly for a little while until they got their breath back. Isabella leaned away from him. "Now I'd like to go for a swim."

"Now?"

"Yes, why not? You know all of me now. I'm no longer ashamed to be naked in front of you." She scrunched up her face. "Besides . . . this sand gets everywhere."

Pushing him away, she stood and raced toward the gentle

tide running onto the beach. The water was so calm now. She turned to see him just standing there, watching her. "Come on! The water feels balmy!"

"You look like a moon nymph. I can't help just watching you."

"But I want to play. Join me," she shouted and waded deeper into the water. When she was waist deep, she dove in and swam a distance.

Something grabbed her from below and dragged her beneath the surface. She choked, spluttered, fought . . . then surfaced to look into his grinning face. "I'm going to get you for this!"

They played and frolicked in the water until finally he scooped her into his arms and carried her back to their campsite. "Time to bed down for the night, princess."

She pulled his head down, seeking his lips. "Sounds like the perfect plan to me."

The week had flown by. Before she realized, it was time to head back to Cront. Tanoth had to resume his duties at the mine in Xynnar, and she had to go back to the palace and help Cylena with the twins. It would not be a permanent job. She knew that, and so did the king and queen, and she was especially glad of that now. She and Tanoth had discussed getting married — or joined, as it was called on Ierilia. She wanted to wait a little while, and he understood.

Isabella sighed and looked at the rising suns just peeking above the horizon, sending their beautiful colors across the sky. They were spending their last day together at the same beach where they had first made love. She decided it would be her favorite vacation place in the future. Their future. Leaning against him, she heaved a heavy sigh.

"What's wrong, sweet?"

"Nothing. I almost hate to go back."

"Yes, as do I. But I'm afraid work calls for both of us."

"I feel so happy, so content. I love you so much," she said softly.

"And I you." He kissed the top of her head.

"Now if only all strife on Ierilia would stop—if that ugly sorcerer and Zohmes would just go away, life could be perfect."

This time he sighed. "Life can never be perfect. How dull would that be? I wonder if the king and his team were able to recover the grimoire and the gem."

She turned and kissed him. "I suppose we'll find out when we get back home. Now let's enjoy this last quiet day together. It's unfortunate there are some people on the beach this time, or I'd be stripping off my clothes and running into the water."

He laughed. "You are a little vixen."

She wrapped her arms around his neck and grinned. "No, just an illegal stowaway who has finally found a home."

This story is connected to the Crimson Realm Chronicles. Many of the characters appear in the following books.

1 In Search of Pride—e-Book and Print (includes Carnal Twilight)
2 The Dragon's Lion—e-Book and Print
3 Sword of Betrayal—e-Book and Print
4 Sword of Judgement—e-Book and Print
5 Testing the Crown—e-Book and Print
6 Shard in the Mirror—e-Book and Print
7 Initiation Genesis—e-Book and Print

The e-Books are available at extasybooks.com, amazon.com, and many other 3rd party sellers.

About Taryn Jameson and Gabriella Bradley

Taryn Jameson is a mother, artist, and avid reader who lives in an enchanted forest that sparks her imagination to create. Her latest outlet is the written word. She is the alter ego of cover artist Angela Waters.

Gabriella Bradley is a mother, a grandmother, and runs a busy business. She has been a writer and artist all her life. Her hobbies include hiking, gardening, swimming, sewing, embroidery. Favorite movies are old timers like Gone with the Wind, Spartacus etc. Favorite TV series are Fringe and Lost, Favorite music is Abba.

WHITE STAR
BY
BELINDA MCBRIDE

CHAPTER ONE

Attigua — The Blue Planet

He woke with the lingering memory of green fields and skies of the deepest cerulean blue.

Brock Uhern lay sprawled in what was probably the largest bed in the city, red silk entwining his bare limbs, wicking the cold sweat from his skin. He stared at the decorative mural on the ceiling, at the sumptuous carving surrounding the shuttered windows, and breathed the softly scented air. The sun didn't shine past the shutters; the sky outside would be grey and ominous, the clouds heavy and low and a perfect match for his mood. The Blue Planet was nowhere near its romantic name. It was wet and cold and grey.

He could count on his hand the times he'd seen a blue sky over the past seven years.

He rose, visited the toilet, and stepped into the shower, frowning at the return of the scaly growths on the slate walls of the chamber. They flourished in this climate. Lately, they were returning more quickly after cleaning. The canisters full of tuffa rock weren't absorbing the moisture from the air as they should.

Ignoring the lichen, he ducked under the water, shivering slightly as it sluiced over his head, down his shoulders, and then his body. It was tepid, but he didn't mind. It was clean and abundant.

Stepping out, he wound sheeting around his body. It was bleached white, the fabric course and absorbent. At home, he'd have lounged naked in the bathing yard, allowing the cleansing bright light of his planet's sun to dry and warm his skin. He was still darker than most of the locals on this soggy planet, but his skin had paled from russet to bronze in the seven annums he'd spent away from home. He barely recognized his own reflection when he saw it.

One by one, he lightened the tall windows, praying for some view other than the cold grey sky, but was disappointed. He then saw a fleeting break in the sky. The blue shining through was pristine and pale. His heart leapt in hope, but the clouds quickly reclaimed their dominance. To his horror, his eyes filled with tears. He hadn't cried in — he didn't know how long. Forever, perhaps.

He sighed and didn't turn as the door to his chamber opened. He couldn't afford to allow anyone to see his weakness. It would be reported to the trainers, and he'd have that to deal with as well.

The soft shuffling step told him it was the cripple, the slave who was curiously independent. She rarely did housework. He mostly saw her attending King Jamis, or slipping innocuously along the hallways, face averted, arms laden with books and data wands. She must have slipped up and angered someone, to be assigned to cleaning.

He opened his mouth to remind her to tend the shower but stopped.

He'd be gone soon. Six weeks. Six more engagements. He'd then walk out of these rooms and never look back. He'd go home and pray for forgiveness. His parents would be stiff and hurt but wouldn't withhold their love. He'd repent his sins and bring them the riches he'd earned. He'd work his hard muscles in the fields, or up in the sky farms. Anywhere they wanted him, as long as he never had to fight again.

He'd build them a new farmstead if they wanted. Buy

new equipment. But he wanted to go home. The need ached in his chest and tightened his throat. He stared out the window, out at the congested city down below, and further out, to the rough, grey ocean.

The door opened again, and a pale young man delivered a tray laden with his morning meal and the scarlet tea that never failed to wake him. Once the table was arranged, he sat, staring down at the plate, trying to extend the illusion that he was alone. He ignored the paperwork set to the side of his plates.

The young man helped the crippled girl with the bedding. It would be changed out with another color, but was always the filmy silk produced so abundantly on this planet. The damp conditions encouraged the growth of a slug-like invertebrate that wove intricate webs that laborers harvested on a daily basis. The farms sprawled up into the hills and mountains and were the backbone of the planet's economy. It even grew wild, and a cottage industry had risen based on the silk . . . more crude and rough than his luxurious clothing and bedding. They grew some grain, but it was prone to spoil, so wasn't stored. His meals consisted mostly of fish and fowl, and the few greens that flourished with the moisture and limited sun.

It seemed fitting that this planet was wealthy from the silk of a slug. The whole place was wet and slimy on the best of days.

He sighed again and sipped the tea, wondering if he'd have withdrawing pains when he left Attigua and no longer had access to the stuff. The food was well-prepared, though heavily spiced. The bitter clarity of the tea cut through the rich flavors. He ate methodically, efficiently — fully aware that his survival hinged on his physical well-being. He must remain healthy and robust, his mind sharp as a blade and his reactions quicker than those of his competition. He primarily fought bipedal humanoids like himself, but the competition had grown more challenging the past few matches. He was coming home with injuries, and far more fatigued than he'd ever been in his life.

He looked at the empty plate before him. If someone wanted him to lose . . . He pushed the plate away, staring down at the surface of the table. It was a rich, dark inlaid wood. The wealth they squandered on one lone fighter was breathtaking. He was so famous, he couldn't leave the palace complex without being recognized and sometimes mobbed.

His image was everywhere. If he were to walk into the travel-port and purchase a flight off the planet, that news would spread planet-wide in a matter of minutes, and he'd be apprehended. He knew that because he'd tried.

Losing him would be a huge financial blow to the planet. With that grim thought in mind, he touched the papers and scanned the newest version of the contract, wishing they'd provided a translation in Common as well as in his own Braccin language. That way he could compare both translations to the original.

Not that he didn't trust the Royal Gladiatorial Foundation and the king who headed it.

Actually, he didn't trust them with his life.

Literally.

He read again, wincing at the terms. The first contract they'd offered last week reflected the exact duplication of his original terms, but for an abbreviated term of five annum rather than seven. He'd been offered better housing. A few nicer advantages and a higher lump sum wage. A bed slave. The original wage had sat in an off-planet bank for seven annum, quietly collecting interest. He'd diverted most of his prize earnings as well and had converted it all into Coalition credits. He'd lose on the fees, as he'd have to travel outside his system to recover it, but the stability was its own reward.

This second contract left him in his current housing. It wasn't a significant downgrade from the original contract. Just enough to let him know he wouldn't do better. Next week, they'd withdraw something else. The wages would drop. They'd withdraw some of his trainings.

And his fights would grow increasingly dangerous. It seemed the RGF didn't wish to lose their top fighter, nor did they want anyone else to take him. They were willing to kill him to prevent that. As he was their star, his fall would be spectacular, and the victor would quickly take his place.

He shoved the papers away and carried his tea to the window, gazing out at the unchanging view. Wet rooftops. Wet streets. Vehicles splashed through potholes that were never adequately repaired. Out on the ocean, the water was choppy.

There was a white glow behind the clouds on the horizon. It wasn't this planet's sun, but a distant star called Polarium. When he'd first arrived, the clouds had broken, and for a few moments, he'd witnessed the star's brilliant, white light. He'd thought it was beautiful. Now, it just seemed weak and drab.

As though responding to his mood, a minor tremor ran through the thick stone of the floor. They happened daily, as they always had. Even the planet itself was miserable with its lot.

Behind him, dishes rattled, and he turned, watching the crippled slave stack them on a tray. She picked up the sheaf of papers, neatened them and centered them on the table.

"Take them away."

She turned, surprise quickly suppressed by her normal submissive behavior. She quickly ducked her head, hiding her face, but he'd seen enough to hold him still, shock running through his body.

She was beautiful. She was damaged, as many of the

slaves were, a dark bruise staining her left cheekbone. She was shockingly pale, as most of the people on this planet were. They lacked exposure to their sun's light, and it showed. But she wasn't pasty white like the others. Her skin held a tawny hue, with time under the sun, she'd be golden, like the royals, who had the leisure to take journeys to other places, or even to spend time in artificial light.

Her eyes . . . green. Green as the greenest fields reflecting the gold of the summer sun. Green as the most precious gemstone in a dragon's hoard. Her eyes made him want to weep. Her hair was tightly bound, but the same tawny bronze that her skin should be.

Before she turned away, he saw sharp intelligence in her expression, curiosity, and cunning. She boldly met his gaze, and then lowered her head, unable to hide her true nature beneath the mask of a slave. After she left, his gaze lingered on the door. His heart pounded, and for once the arousal of his body was spontaneous, rather than manipulated by a bold hand or a cunning mouth.

He didn't like the fact that slavery was an institution on Attigua, but no culture was perfect—his included. This planet didn't have prisons—violators became property, often for their entire lives. They were marked according to their crime. Given her limp, she might have been a runaway servant or a thief . . . one who'd stolen shoes. He grimaced at the thought. Cruel as it seemed, he'd seen worse. She was an anomaly, as she appeared to spend time with the king, who was infamous for his disgust at physical imperfection. When Brock had been presented, King Jamis had glanced at him and turned away, repelled by the dark marks and armridges that had still been visible back then.

Alone again, he paced the room, bored and lonely. He had a party later that night, but today stretched before him, empty. He had one day a week away from training and the gym. He could visit the city, where someone was bound to recognize him. He could visit an entertainment house, or dine at a kiosk, or even take a boat out onto the choppy ocean and search for an elusive bit of sky.

He could hike into the mountains in search of a dry spot. He could visit the library in the palace and catch up on events in the system. Or he could sleep. Because when he slept, he flew home, seeing the green fields, the gentle sun, and the rich, dark soil of his family farm.

He lay on the freshly made bed, noting the silk was now vibrant green. *Like her eyes.*

Minutes passed, and he lay quietly, willing the faces of his loved ones to come to mind, but they remained stubbornly elusive. He clasped himself through the rough toweling he still wore, but his body refused to be lured to response. He let his mind wander, touching lightly on the last match he'd fought, feeling the ghostly pain of a bruise to his ribs, the fire of a slash to his upper arm. Fontet was his friend in training, but in the arena, he'd become a formidable foe. Brock was afraid he'd soon be forced to eliminate the other man completely. More and more fights were ending that way, with Brock bleeding and his opponents unresponsive. They woke badly damaged and unable to fight.

Another cost to the royal budget.

With a sigh, he rose and dressed quickly, without care. In a few hours, dressers would come and prepare him for the event that night. Afterward, he'd be praying for alone time again.

He left his rooms and strode to the library, determined to pass the long morning in a constructive fashion, one that didn't involve blood, sweat or pain.

Or rainwater, either. He was sick of the rain.

Outside of the giant's rooms, Verda stepped aside, letting Val walk past her. Though burdened with laundry, he'd move faster than she. Stooping, she picked up the buckets full of brushes and rags and hobbled down the corridor to the supply closets.

Housework wasn't her job. Her body wasn't suited to labor. Oddly, the royals hated a cripple clattering around their private spaces, tending to their private needs. She supposed it was strangely uncomfortable for them to view imperfection. She wished it was guilt they felt, but that would be overly optimistic. They knew no guilt.

She leaned against the wall for a brief, forbidden moment, her hand resting over the center of her chest. Her heart raced, and her breath came fast. She'd seen him! Right there, just yards away, and he was as big, beautiful, and vibrant as she'd been told. He moved like a beast . . . not like a great, lumbering animal, but smoothly, so swiftly that it was hard to track the tiny movements that telegraphed his intent. And she relied heavily on such cues to manage her survival. He was dangerous in his stealth, and in his beauty.

She pushed off the wall and hobbled down the corridor, automatically smoothing her expression, careful not to betray the agony that accompanied every step. She folded her hands, cast her eyes to the floor and did her best to blend into her surroundings. The residences weren't her normal territory. She usually stayed to the web of corridors leading from the archives to the research library, and up to the royal residence. When she was lucky, one of the small, personal shuttles was at her disposal. Today, she was denied such assistance. She was being punished. She wasn't sure why. Maybe she hadn't bowed low enough or effaced herself to some royal's satisfaction. She didn't care. It would soon end.

She averted her mind from the pain by imagining the powerful warrior she'd encountered. She'd never seen him fight . . . not in person. Such entertainments were forbidden to her. But in the city, his image was displayed in shop windows, and moving vid captured some of his more notorious moves. Great leaps through the air, twisting rolls, and near-suicidal attacks. Training manuals bristled with statistics and drawings, all promising to unlock the mystery of his fighting style. Gossip sheets speculated about his lovers, his fortune, and rather breathlessly speculated about the fate of his upcoming contract. Would he sign again? Would he travel off into space, to his mysterious home on a distant planet?

Brock Uhern was a fantasy, a hero. He was nearly a legend, and as she'd seen, he was very, vividly real. And there was no mystery to his fighting style. He was simply a slightly different species of humanoid — he'd been raised in higher gravity than existed here. His body was large, his bones and tendons and sinews functioned to support his mass. She saw nodes on the outside of his forearms, indicating some sort of boney growth. He didn't feast on raw flesh. He ate fish and porridge, and he drank red tea. He was a good fighter, not really brilliant. His training was limited, and his advantages were those of birth. If he faced off with another of his own species, his wins wouldn't come so easily.

Rather than being arrogant and cocky, the fighter seemed wistful and sad. He was a creature of the light, and out of place here on a rainy planet. Verda didn't think he'd renew his contract. The man was aching for something he hadn't found here. He'd be leaving soon. If he was allowed to leave.

She paused, catching her balance as a mild tectonic shift rolled through the ground below. No one seemed to notice the gentle quakes these days, but they were growing more frequent. She had no way to measure the intensity of the quakes — the king refused to invest in technology to monitor the seismic activity of the planet. But lately, dishes toppled from shelves, and it wasn't unusual for an object too close to the edge of a table to fall. She could time them, though, and they were lasting longer.

She hurried down the hall, hoping to avoid Ser Lanham, who'd taken a caning from Princess Maghe. She was angry now, and eager to pass her humiliation on to an easy target like Verda. Winding through corridors, she passed from the spacious guest quarters where Brock Uhern resided, to the less elaborate rooms reserved for visiting dignitaries. From there, she took a downward curving passage that was far narrower than those above. The walls grew closer, the ceiling lower, and the air was dank and moist.

Just yards from the room she shared with Yala, the laundress, she came to an abrupt halt. Ser Lanham paced the corridor, her stride jerky and abrupt. She was still angry but managed to contain her emotions.

"*He* wishes to see you." Her thin lips twisted. "Now."

Verda's heart dropped. All she wanted was to sit for a minute, to ease her leg. The journey to the audience room was not only long, she'd face a curving ramp that rose to the royal heights. She wasn't allowed to use the lifts to climb to the higher levels. She fought back a sigh and nodded meekly.

"I'll be there as quickly as possible." She turned, ignoring Ser Lanham's stifled snort.

"I'll take you. He's in a hurry."

Damnation. She spent so much of her time in and out of his favor—they should just assign her a dungeon cell with a direct lift to his apartments.

She hated riding double on the trolley with the slave mistress but was grateful for the ride up. It was little more than a wide board with a steering handle, elevated by a magnetic reaction to the iron in the stone beneath them. It hummed along quietly, almost silent, which is why Ser Lanham left a few unsuspecting servants sprawling as they passed. Verda grasped the brace behind her, straining to avoid contact with the thin, rigid woman in front of her. Ser Lanham wouldn't wish to be actually touched by one of her charges.

In less time than it took for her to walk from Brock Uhern's lodging to her own, they negotiated the guest wing of the palace, then crossed out through the gardens until they arrived at the royal wings.

They bypassed the library and archives, and she released a small sigh at being denied her normal workplace. That was the real punishment. Not the labor.

He knew her too well.

Another minute took them up the various curving ramps to the receiving rooms. To her surprise, they continued to the private level where the royals actually lived and moved. They turned down a corridor, bypassing one hall that Verda recalled all too well. Rigidly, she avoided gazing that direction. There was no point in looking. That life was now dead and gone.

Ser Lanham slowed, allowing Verda to step off, leading with her good right leg. Well . . . her *better* leg.

"I'll be nearby, just return here when you're finished." She sounded like she was talking through stinging, sour spite. The Ser didn't particularly like any of her slaves, and perhaps disliked Verda more than the others. It made no sense to keep a lame slave alive, but the Ser didn't question orders from above. She followed directions to the letter and found her pleasures in punishment when she could.

CHAPTER TWO

As always, Verda counted every step to the door, using that time to mentally compose herself, to shove away emotion and cloak herself with an extra layer of humility. She straightened her shoulders, lengthened her spine, and bowed her head appropriately. Before she could touch the door of the king's private apartments, they swung open.

She entered, sizing up the room, looking for hidden dangers. There were no clerks or courtiers; no other members of the family. The door closed behind her, and she felt the absence of the bodyguards.

Her skin prickled in warning, but nothing happened.

She was tired. The continual flow of adrenaline into her system suddenly failed her and Verda struggled to maintain the posture and the quiet dignity she wore like armor. Belatedly, she lowered her gaze. King Jamis hated her eyes. Thankfully, the king was preoccupied with a large ledger. Which was odd, given his revulsion of the written word.

She arrived and stopped precisely six feet away, sinking awkwardly to the floor, braced on her fists, her head dropped forward.

He left her there until the pain in her leg was unbearable. But she bore it. Her vision grew hazy as she waited. She counted down the seconds, forcing control over her pain.

"Ah. You're here. Get up, Verda. That's just embarrassing." His mouth twisted as she rose awkwardly to her feet. He drew some pleasure from her discomfort. He always did.

He was a large man, a head taller than she, wider through

the shoulders than the middle, though that part was catching up. His short chestnut hair was greying in an artful fashion. His narrowed eyes were an odd shade somewhere between brown, green, and blue. Strange eyes, she'd always thought. Suitable for a strange man. He was only partially dressed, still in only pants and his fine silk shirt, though a more suitable outfit was probably waiting him in his dressing room.

No need to dress presentably for a slave.

He continued to study the ledger, and she stood quietly, not letting her guard slip for a moment. She studied him, though her gaze was directed downward. Abruptly, he slammed the book closed and stood. She clenched her teeth and stood her ground.

He opened the book again, turned it in her direction and rose, arms behind his back, turning away from her.

Bold move. Or just stupid. Or totally confident that this particular slave lacked any ability to harm him.

"Tell me what you see in there."

He strolled to the window, gazing out at the grey-green vista, out toward the mountains in the distance. Verda walked to the desk and careful to touch nothing, looked at the open page. Numbers were neatly inscribed in rows . . . handwritten. Archaic.

"Profits and losses. I'm sorry, I can't venture more than that." There were dozens, hundreds of notations. It meant little to her without time to study. Many statisticians had their own secret methods of recording numbers.

"Profits and losses." His voice carried contempt. "I'd think one as brilliant as you could see more clearly."

Her cheeks went warm. She was grateful he wasn't looking at her face. She continued to study the page.

"These appear to be numbers from the Games."

"Aha," he murmured.

"Profits are on the rise." She then saw the pattern. Every Seven Day, the numbers spiked. That was the main night when the most popular fighters appeared. She went back through the weeks, noting a steady rise in attendance. The previous two weeks, that number rose on Third Day as well.

"Brock Ahern is fighting twice a week now," she said. "The numbers are rising in conjunction with his appearances." And Brock was unhappy. And tired. And his contract would soon end. Again, her skin prickled. Perhaps her labor that morning hadn't been punishment. Perhaps it was surveillance.

"Yes. And you know what will happen when he leaves."

He didn't say it, and she didn't need to. The kingdom had a fierce hunger for money. Every week, seawalls crumbled, and rather than build new walls and relocate citizens, structures were repaired, patched and cobbled together while the family and their courtiers adorned themselves in exotic goods from off-planet. The loss of the planet's most popular fighter would cost millions. Perhaps more.

"You tended his room. Was he there?"

"Yes, my King." She stepped back from the ledger, turning to fully face him.

"His mood?" The king examined his immaculately polished fingernails. The nail on his smallest finger was chiseled to a sharp point, as was the current fashion. A fashion he'd set and would soon abandon.

"He appeared . . . melancholy."

The king didn't reply. She glanced at him, gauging his mood. He appeared to be in tolerable control of his temper. But there was that shirt, not fully fastened. His hair wasn't quite styled. He'd not tolerated his servants that morning. This was a dangerous moment.

She tried again. "He paid little notice to me, but I believe he realized I wasn't his normal attendant. He gazed out the window all morning. He ate because he had to, not because he relished his food, or even hungered. The only trace of enjoyment I noted was when he sipped his red tea." And there was that moment he saw her. Looked into her eyes and for a second, seemed diverted. "A stack of papers was placed beside his food. He ignored them."

The king growled slightly. She fought the urge to step away. If she did so, he'd follow, and fate only knew what punishment he'd lay on her damaged body this time. She remained perfectly still, reining in her urge to flee.

Or to fight. She'd rather fight. She'd like to sweep his feet from under him, twist his arm and —

"What of the rains?"

She swallowed, smothering her impotent fury. "This spell is projected to last approximately ten days. The readings show enough sun after that to encourage the grain to germinate at the proper time. Ser Felden tells me the fields aren't draining as well as he'd wish, but the modified grain he integrated into the seed stocks should improve the yield."

He was losing interest. His gaze skittered about the room, and Verda knew she should cease. But still . . .

"The seismic events — "

"What of them," he said snappishly. "They're nothing new."

"I've recorded their frequency and the duration — "

He waved her off, and she promptly backed away, knowing she was risking a flare of his temper. But still —

"They grow stronger. Yesterday's tremor brought down a section of seawall — I was told — "

"Enough. Out."

Backing up, she did her best to hide her limp but knew the effort was to no avail. He didn't want to hear her theories. Didn't care to know of the hours she'd studied, the maps and measurements she'd consulted. He didn't care to know the source of the rain and the flares that took down their energy grid. He did not care. He'd focus on the limp. It fascinated him. She turned to leave.

"Verda."

She stopped, not looking back.

"Brock Uhern must sign the contract."

She turned slowly. "I have no influence on him."

"Then figure out how to influence him. If he doesn't sign . . ." he trailed off ominously. "Befriend him if he's lonely. Fuck him if you must. Your failure is your life."

The words echoed in her ears. "But unc—Highness—" Oh fate. That error would cost her. She rushed to continue before he comprehended what she'd almost said. "I have no beauty. I'm lame. Ungainly. Without appeal." She'd been told that so many times before. She didn't even own a scrap of a mirror and ignored the one hanging on the other side of the room she shared. Her appearance was irrelevant. It did nothing to ensure her survival.

Or it hadn't in the past. How was she to charm the fighter into friendship?

"Out." He turned away, already forgetting her, and for the briefest moment, she saw him as vulnerable. His guard was down. He'd never expect an attack from her. She clenched her hands and narrowed her eyes.

She'd never survive the attempt. And survival was very much on Verda's mind these days. Somewhere off this planet, somewhere in another world, there were people she needed to find. There were people she'd kill to find. But not today.

She walked to the door, ignoring the biting pain in her leg, ignoring the massive bodyguard waiting for her.

She stepped on the trolley behind Ser Lanham and leaned back, again avoiding brushing against the grumbling Ser. She dropped Verda in a service corridor a painful distance from her quarters. Verda walked slowly from the soft carpets to hard stone floors, entered her room and noticed the dampness at the edges of the room and shivered. She sat on her narrow bed and studied the grey walls, and made a plan.

CHAPTER THREE

He'd nearly lost the last fight.

A long, shallow wound burned across his ribs. The healing flesh pulled as he slowly, steadily, lifted a heavy cylindrical weight.

His opponent was new. An off-worlder who'd undoubtedly been recruited much as Brock had been, lured away with promises of wealth and fame. He lacked Brock's arm span and height but compensated with his speed. And his skills were superior. That wasn't comforting knowledge.

Brock had damaged him badly, catching him on the short spur of his lance and shattering his ribs with devastating blows. He'd be sidelined, but Brock had spotted several new faces down in the holding cells, where the fighters were segregated from one another for their own safety. Next week, Brock would enter the ring with a disadvantage. His wound was healing well, but he'd be tender, and that scar would be a target. The trainers had denied him healing beyond what it took to keep him alive.

He returned the bulky weight to its rack and began a series of cardiac and agility drills, sprinting up ramps, clambering ladders and dodging between poles. When he finished, he mopped the sweat from his face, using a length of woven sheeting. He paced, allowing his heart to gradually slow, then leapt to a hanging bar, using his own weight to stretch his engorged muscles. His entire routine was familiar. He'd modeled it off the games of his youth when he and his cousins had prepared for the fields and sky farms. It relaxed him, took him back to better times.

He dropped to the floor, landing easily. He'd trained alone again; his coach was probably diverted to the new fighters.

It was a message. Maybe a threat.

He should give it another hour, but strength wasn't his issue. He needed training. Skills. He had four more weeks. And they'd doubled his matches.

Brock stripped, showered under water as hot as he could bear, then pulled on his trousers. Barefoot and shirtless, he left the small gym and hurried down the back corridors to his quarters. Though he was the darling of the royals, they didn't particularly want to see him outside of parties and the arena. He lived a very strange existence.

When he reached the stone-flagged outer corridors, the cool, damp wind chilled him, so he pulled on his shirt and shoes. Movement in the garden below caught his attention, and he peered out the open, arched window, down into the dull green foliage.

He curled his lip in disgust.

One of the courtiers was battering a slave. He watched, his stomach churning. Then the hair on his neck stood on end: it was the crippled slave. The one with green eyes. He debated dropping down into the gardens, to put an end to the atrocity, because the woman had a rod of some sort and was ruthless.

But he paused.

The blows weren't landing. Granted, a few slid off the slave's arm or shoulder, but she was deftly turning the attack, and the courtier was too enraged to notice that she was inflicting no harm. In spite of her awkwardness, the slave moved nimbly and with control. She appeared to cower but was blocking. She was directing the energy of the woman's rage elsewhere.

His heart began to race. The slave was trained to fight. And she did it well. Far better than he did.

He watched until the woman with the rod exhausted herself. She kicked at the girl's bad leg, and the slave collapsed to the ground, seeming injured. But again, she'd avoided the full force of the blow. She remained on the ground until the woman left, and then rose awkwardly to her feet. The damage to her leg was real, and it was profound. If she'd been whole, she wouldn't be a slave. A fighter like her would never allow it.

She looked about the garden and used the abandoned rod to support herself as she hobbled away. So that kick had landed and done damage.

Not certain what he intended, Brock broke into a run, heading back toward his quarters. He needed that woman. He needed her knowledge. He ran easily, weaving through the crowded corridors, ignoring the gasps and laughter as he dodged servants and guests and other staff. He needed her banked fire and her brilliant green eyes. He knew nothing about the girl, other than the fact that she could very well be his salvation. She was a warrior hiding beneath a mantle of humility.

And no one else saw it.

He reached his room, slapped his hand on the lock and entered, breathing hard, his gaze scanning the apartment till he spotted the contracts. Three new incarnations of the document were neatly stacked on the table. He pulled out a chair and read the newest one, his anger bubbling as he read the terms. They'd withdrawn his trainer. He was now to report to communal eating areas, rather than dining in private. It was a clear violation of his original contract, but he didn't care. He wasn't going to debate the issue.

He found a stylus and penned notes in the margin. He proposed two amendments. He then tossed it back on the table and started for the door. He paused. Ser Comptyn oversaw the business dealings of the Gladii. If he was going to haggle, he'd far rather do it privately. He opened the rarely-used desk array and laboriously composed a note to the Ser, requesting his presence. He then closed the unit. He didn't need a translator for verbal dealings, but the written language of the Attig was complicated. He'd need someone to review all documentation. And he recalled that the scribe he'd used in the past was now visiting a settlement on the other side of the planet.

Convenient. And possibly serendipitous.

Brock chose his clothes carefully and dressed. He combed and bound his unruly hair, then rolled up the sleeves on his closely cut tunic, allowing the spurs on his forearms to emerge, just slightly. He had spurs elsewhere but opted to continue concealing those. He inhaled deeply, standing tall and erect, using his full height to build on his physical presence. Even at home, he was larger and taller than most of his peers. But he hadn't felt much different than others. Here, he was acutely aware of his size. He'd met the king on several occasions and found it amusing that the leader was insecure enough that he always greeted Brock from an elevated dais.

There was much to communicate with the body. Pride. Superiority. Danger.

Right now, Brock summoned all three. He knew that though the dignitaries feted and flattered him, they really thought he was a dolt. All muscle, no brain. And while he wasn't a scholar, he was smart enough. One didn't design and build multi-level sky farms without some knowledge of higher education. One didn't settle on a strange planet and quickly master the language without some sort of skill. One didn't defeat numerous enemies without killing them by default. Brock's challengers lived, though they left the arena on litters.

He walked to the window wishing desperately for sunlight. He generally appeared at his most intimidating in brighter lights. There was no light, and out of nowhere, he was struck by unhappiness. He wasn't certain he could bear another month here. If they'd just let him leave, he'd gladly return half his pay. With interest.

He laughed ironically. His fights brought in more on a nightly basis then they'd initially paid him. Now that they'd doubled his schedule, he'd be even more valuable. They'd use him until there was nothing left.

Brock might wind up leaving the planet early after all. In a coffin.

He heard the soft knock on the door and turned, giving the command for the guest to enter. Ser Comptyn came in, his color high, his mood bristly. His hair was iron-grey, the facial hair he wore was streaked with black. His pale eyes were cold and blue. He was past his prime, but still dangerous.

Comptyn slapped a contract on the desk, next to the one Brock had made notations on. "You finally ready to sign? Because this stubbornness isn't working out to your benefit."

"I want to go home," Brock said. "I've served out my contract. I'm weary. In time, another fighter will catch the public's interest. You don't need me."

Ser Comptyn shrugged. "True. And that's been put before the king. But he doesn't agree. He'd like you to stay on." He ran his tongue over his teeth. "I have some leeway with you. Will you talk?"

"Only with a translator." He studied the fight master's gruff face. "I can read your language, but not fluently. I'd like a written translation."

"That will take time." Ser Comptyn frowned. "The official scribe is journeying east. However, I can bring in Verda."

"Verda?" Brock asked. His skin prickled. "Can this person

translate in Common as well? Written and verbal?"

"Definitely in Common. Not sure about your tongue." He palmed the communications patch on the table. "Find Verda. Send her to Brock Ahern's rooms. Immediately."

Brock walked back to the window, thinking fast. What other conditions could he put on the contract? They wouldn't be surprised if he made foolish requests. It was expected that the idol of so many would be spoiled and arrogant.

The slave. He needed the slave. She had green eyes — the word for green —

The door chimed, and he released the locks. He heard the sound of soft footfalls — uneven. The sound of someone moving with a limp.

Verda.

His heart raced. He turned, scanned her, looking for signs of injury. There was an abrasion on her cheek. She was garbed in long sleeves and full, loose trousers, so he couldn't tell if she was hurt elsewhere. She looked calm on the surface, but there was apprehension in her eyes. Fear of every unknown situation and he was certainly part of the unknown. She met his gaze and ducked her head, looking down to the floor.

The other times he'd seen her, she was always laden with books or papers or some other sort of data. She dwelled largely in the archives and library. She was a slave, but not the usual sort.

"Verda, we need translations." Ser Comptyn waved at the table where the contract fanned out in an unsteady stack. "Common, and," he waved his hand toward Brock. "His language."

She picked up a page, not looking at either of the men. "This is already translated."

"I don't trust it," Brock said. "And I don't read your language well enough to compare."

She started to gather the papers.

"You can stay here. I need all three contracts translated. For comparison." He cast an angry glance at Ser Comptyn."

"It will take some time."

The Ser huffed impatiently. "Do you have tasks of a more pressing nature?"

Her cheeks darkened, and she gazed down at the floor. "No, Ser Comptyn."

"Then get to it. I'll notify Ser Langham." He looked from Brock to the girl. "Do you think this will take time?"

"Several hours, I'm afraid. Perhaps into tomorrow. I'll need a scribe."

"I'll send a unit up." The Ser looked at Brock, his thick arms folded over his chest. "Do you have demands?" He put up a good front, but he was anxious. His position as Ser was probably riding on Brock signing those papers.

Brock glanced at the slave. Verda. He then looked back at Ser Comptyn. "Perhaps. Yes. I may have a request." She glanced at him sharply, then back down at the paper. She saw the notes he'd made and glared at the page. Another slip in her servile façade.

The Ser gave a contemptuous smile. "We'll speak again tomorrow after I review your changes. You're with staff tomorrow for coaching. Be prepared."

Brock nodded, feeling an odd relief. He shouldn't. Being grateful for access to coaching was infuriating. Humiliating. It was frightening. But now he had hope. Once the Ser exited the room, he turned to the slave, looking at her from head to toe. She picked up the first contract and started reading.

"Put that down."

She looked at him in surprise.

"Put that down," he repeated. "And remove your tunic." He didn't miss the disappointment on her face as he left the room, returning quickly with a small jar. She'd slipped off the tunic, revealing fabric bound over small breasts. He didn't linger over her anatomy, that way led to potential exposure. Embarrassment. Because just looking at her triggered a slow burn, a dangerous arousal he'd never before experienced.

He was no virgin, and he'd certainly taken lovers but avoided passionate entanglements within the court. He'd been offered his choice of slaves, courtiers, and even the royals, but turned them away. His liaisons had been brief, hurried, and furtive, generally among the other off-planet fighters. They all knew better than to get emotional, to fall in love. Any could die in the arena at any time. A quick fuck in the dark corners of the stadium went a long way to maintaining the need to touch and be touched. The occasional royal or aristocrat still called for his services, but the novelty had largely worn off. Celibacy wasn't so great a challenge.

Until now.

He studied her lean arms, impressed at how firm they were. There was a bruise on her right shoulder, where he'd seen the rod land. He opened the lid and begin applying the balm to her bruise. She looked over her shoulder.

"What is that?"

He handed her the jar, watching as she sniffed.

"Bruise balm. I make it from herbs I brought from my home."

She handed it back.

"Where else were you struck?" His voice sounded too deep, too rough.

"How did you know I was hurt?" Her voice had a pleasing pitch, slightly lower than the affected accents of other palace dwellers.

"I was in the corridor above the garden." He applied the balm to her forearm, over another rough looking bruise.

"And I saw what you were doing."

She looked straight ahead. "What was I doing?"

"Trousers, please."

"No."

Her refusal took him by surprise.

"Yes," he countered.

She stood utterly still. "There are no injuries to my legs." She was lying, but he stepped back, returning the lid to the balm and handing it to her.

"Go to the changing room and put this on your bruises." Interesting. She had no issues with disrobing on top but resisted baring her lower body. She didn't appear misshapen, but her limp suggested deformity.

She left the room and returned within minutes, the scent of the balm drifting in with her. As always, the herbal fragrance caused a sharp pang to resonate through him. It reminded him of warm days and sunny fields. His mother made the balm every year, filling jar after jar, sending them out with the field workers.

That was his last jar.

She turned again to the contract. "Do you want me to read these aloud?" She flinched when he took the paper from her hand. Another spark of anger burned. She'd been struck enough that her reactions were automatic.

"No. I want to talk about the fight I just saw."

"We weren't fighting." Her voice was firm. "Ser Langham felt it appropriate to discipline me."

"And you blocked every blow. Otherwise, you'd be laying senseless in the garden. Most likely bleeding."

He paced the room, and finally stopped, gazing at nothing but the wall. "What you did down there . . . it was brilliant. And I need you to teach me."

"What?" Her face was incredulous. "I have nothing to teach you!"

Again, she reached for the contract.

He held it out of her reach. "I need to learn what you did. The blocking, the deflection. I'm too large to have your speed, but—"

"You're amazingly fast for a man your size." The words erupted, and she looked like she'd choke on them. "I mean . . . uh . . ."

"I have raw strength, good speed, and balance. But this past month, my opponents are better trained. Closer to my size. Soon, I will fall."

"All fighters sometimes lose."

"They mean me to lose. And if I don't sign that—" he nodded to the contract, "—they don't mean for me to leave alive. I have no intention of staying here, and I don't mean to die in the process of escaping this sodden, moldy planet."

"You're bluffing about the translation." Her green eyes were keen and intelligent. She was sizing him up, not as a fighter, but as a person.

He nodded. "I can read it just fine. Common would be easier, the translation is poor, but I read enough of your language to decipher most of the terms. Every week, I lose another privilege. I don't mind. But I no longer have daily training with a coach."

"Not that he was serving you well. Argus is a lazy coach." The humble trappings of the slave had fallen away. She let the papers slip to the table and studied him. "You are a tolerable fighter. You have more talent than most, which is how you've adapted and been able to survive, but you are correct. Your opponents are being imported and are far better trained than you are."

"Damn." He was right. He didn't want to be right. He just wanted to finish his time and go home.

"Will you help me?" he asked.

"Will you help me?" she countered.

"What can I do for you?" Brock looked at her in question.

She stared down at the floor. Over the past few minutes, her entire demeanor had changed. She looked taller. Stronger. She hadn't been born a slave. More likely, she'd been a war captive. An enemy of some sort.

"I had a task. It was a repellent job, but I swore to do it. By any means." She looked at him, and he felt he knew her. She was a comrade. Someone who shared his dilemma. "You are a prisoner here." She said it as if the realization was new. "Just as much as I am."

"Well." He smiled. "Not the same, I have free access to the city. And I'm quite popular at certain parties."

"You can't leave, though. I suppose you're watched constantly."

"I suppose I am." His smile faded. "Leaving won't be as simple as completing my contract and taking a shuttle to a station."

"When you go, I wish to go with you."

"*What?*" Had she heard his words?

"When you leave . . ." she spoke slowly, "I want to go with you."

"I can't just take a slave and leave. I don't even know if I'll live long enough to get out of here."

The true peril of his situation finally settled on Brock's shoulders. Having someone to talk to, made his plight very real and very frightening.

"If I leave," he said, "I'll have to escape. And when that time comes, I may not be here at the palace."

Aside from that, he had no plans. Not even a vague idea of how to flee.

"I know where there's a planet-side spaceport. It's small, and it houses mostly smaller craft for atmospheric travel. But there's a ship."

"A ship?" His disbelief echoed in his voice. "A *ship*?" He

laughed shortly. "I have no idea how to pilot a ship in space!"

"I do." Her reply was quiet. "And once we're away, I can teach you."

He looked at her again. "Who are you? Because no slave would know how to pilot a ship. Or even know the location of a secret port."

She shrugged and crossed to the large window that looked out over the city below. She was quiet for a long time, and he left her to her silence. It had taken more courage than he realized to verbalize his plight to her . . . a stranger. She stood far more risk of betrayal than he did.

He watched her, though she showed him only her back. Though the sun wasn't shining, the light from the window brightened her. She was tall for her race, slim and elegant in her movement, even with the awkward limp. Her hair would spark gold in the sun, or by candlelight. It was braided back, exposing stark, regal beauty. With her usual submissive attitude, she could be mistaken for plain and humble. Standing there silently, she was showing him her true self.

She turned, looked at him steadily, as though she saw deep into his soul. Her cheeks flushed when she caught him staring.

"This world hasn't always been this way. Once, the sky was blue, white clouds sailed overhead, and we were always brown from the sun." She walked toward him, the limp more noticeable. "I wasn't always a slave."

"I suspected that."

She smiled absently. "I grew up beloved. Spoiled. Passionate. The change in my circumstances was . . . abrupt."

"What happened?" he asked.

She shook her head. "It doesn't matter. Not now. But we both need to flee, and we need each other to do so."

"I can finish out my contract."

"No. I was tasked to encourage you to stay. I was to do anything to prevent your leaving, up to and including seduction." She flushed again and gave a depreciating smile. "There are undoubtedly others better suited for that purpose."

"No."

She looked at him sharply.

"No, there aren't others better suited for that." If his amber skin could show it, he'd be the one blushing now. And he knew it was time to change the subject.

"I need a covert route from the planet. You know where there's a ship. What do you need from me?" He studied her, learning everything he could just from the way she moved, her slow consideration of the problem at hand. Sizing up his opponent was his best skill. And she wasn't really an opponent. She was his ally. He hoped.

"The port isn't far, but I can't—" She paused, and looked down at the floor, her humility again on display. "—I can't get there by myself. I'm . . ." She trailed off. It wasn't humility. It was shame. "I must be carried."

"And I'm the only person strong enough to carry a woman as large as yourself?" It was meant to be teasing. She was slender. Almost thin. She smiled slightly.

"I did consider Peri Stroop."

He snorted in amusement. His friend Peri . . . clever, sneaky, and not a model of benevolence.

"We have to approach the port with stealth. Thus, we have to stay off the roadways."

At one time, she must have been an elevated person. Priceful. Now she'd fallen, and he believed she was stronger for it. Something in his chest grew warm. His throat grew tight. She suddenly seemed far more than beautiful.

"I will teach you to fight and survive if you promise to

come to me when the time arrives." She turned away from the window, walking back into the dimly lit room, and leaned on the table.

"When will that be, Verda?"

She sat at the desk, and he sat facing her, shocked when her green eyes caught his. She was crying. For the first time, fear prickled his skin. This was real.

"When the planet dies, we will run."

CHAPTER FOUR

"We need more time together."

The door hadn't closed behind her when Brock made his demand. For it was a demand. All these years of being petted and indulged had insulated him from the impossibility of her dropping all her duties to attend him.

"We haven't had a chance for you to teach me."

"They may be humble," she said waspishly, "but I do have duties to others in the palace." She brushed past him and set the completed translations on his desk. "Besides, it's only been a day." Her leg ached, so she sat, shedding the skin of the slave before this great, massive man. He looked slightly wild today. He'd been stressing. No doubt he was facing a fight without the support of a trainer.

"Who's your next fight with?"

He shook his head. He was so . . . lovely with his amber skin. His hair was silken, falling to his shoulders in waves several shades darker than his skin. His eyes were the same color, but dark, rimmed with jet black lashes that looked as though they'd been painted on.

She stifled a sigh. It was no wonder he graced the covers of so many publications. He was delicious to look at.

"They won't let me see the schedules. I don't know if I go in tonight or the next night."

"Tell me who worries you most," she said. They'd have to do this the hard way. But he needed to be prepared. They could always change opponents at the last minute, even if he did know who he was fighting.

179

"Lareth. I've never fought her, but she's better than most of the men."

He was right to rank her as a threat. Lareth was mostly Landaun, a massive, war-like species with tough skin, savage natures, and very few vulnerabilities. The females equaled the males in size, even possessing a phallic appendage. There were few this far from the Coalition in which they resided, so she'd never seen one before. But when Lareth arrived two weeks ago, she'd done some research, mostly out of fascination for the huge, savage woman.

"I'm glad you see her as a worthy opponent. Just because she's female doesn't mean she's not lethal. And the Landaun females have a tradition of raping their defeated opponents."

"Oh. I suppose I'd better not lose," he said dryly.

"That's not a joke, Brock. The king knows that citizens are suffering, so he's staging larger spectacles to divert them." She got up and rotated her right foot, trying to loosen permanently stiffened tendons and muscles. "The Landaun strive for death rather than defeat. When they fight in the arena, they prefer to dishonor their opponents than kill them. So, the good news is that if she beats you, you'll survive."

"The bad news?"

"You'll wish you were dead."

He looked slightly sick. 'Then how do I fight her?"

"First, forget she's female. It makes absolutely no difference. Then prepare for her to be swifter than you are. Her skin is tough. If you chose a weapon, chose one to puncture rather than slash."

He nodded. "How do I fight her hand to hand?"

She took his arm and tapped his wrist, elbow, and shoulder. His skin was smooth, his muscles hard. He was warm. She struggled to focus on her task.

"Landaun use brute force. Thus, you will do well to learn to block and deflect and then attack vulnerabilities. We don't have enough time for you to learn nerve locks tonight, so we'll focus on redirecting attacks and breaking the joints."

"Breaking joints," he murmured. He sounded disturbed. "The joints are vulnerable. But I prefer to focus on the torso and head."

"You'll continue with that, but you need to learn finesse and subterfuge. Let your opponent take your arm . . ." she extended an arm to him, so he clasped it. Verda twisted his arm, rotating his elbow and gently exerting pressure. "That would break the elbow. Now do it to me."

They traded, and he repeated the move again, and again. When he had it down, she made him repeat it. She then moved on to the shoulders. And then the knees.

After an hour, they were sweating, and Verda's leg felt like it was on fire. She held up a hand and stood still, gathering the courage to take a step. Before she moved, she was swept up in a pair of strong arms. Brock carried her to a massive sofa and gently set her down.

"What can I do to help?" He dropped to his knees and massaged her calf through the thin fabric of her loose breeches. She gasped as pain rocketed up her leg. Abruptly, he let go. When he looked at her, his dark eyes were almost black, with a reddish gleam behind the pupil. It was fearsome. He lowered his brows, and she found it hard to breathe. She couldn't imagine how it felt, coming face to face with this man in the arena. He was angry, but not at her.

"Heat? Ice?"

She blinked, looking down at her leg. He still supported it, gently holding her foot.

"Heat," she murmured.

He set her foot down and hurried out of the room, returning with bandages and a small heat pack. He wrapped it in place, and the slow, mellow warmth of the pack radiated into her leg. She wanted to melt. She had no access to such luxury. She spent many nights awake, shuddering as pain seared her leg.

"How'd it happen?"

He didn't ask what the injury was. Or even if she'd been born with it. He assumed it was an injury.

"It was a long time ago. I barely remember," she said, not willing to share the horror of that day.

"It always gives you pain?"

She clenched her jaw and then relaxed. She nodded.

"Is this why you want to leave?" He rose gracefully to his feet. "This and the coming . . . whatever's going to happen?"

Verda looked at her leg. She closed her eyes and nodded again. It was all too much. He was too much . . . too big, too alive. Too gentle. "I've heard there is a species in Coalition space. Healers. It's rumored they can fix almost any injury."

Brock knelt in front of her, cradling her foot in his hand. His head was bowed so she couldn't see his face.

"You're willing to risk your life escaping, then travel galaxies in order to chase down a rumor?"

"Yes," she said. "This life . . . I was not meant for it. If I stay here, I'll die, one way or another." Every day, Jamis came closer to striking the fatal blow. Every night, she gave thanks that she'd survive to see the sun again. One day, though, he'd strike. "The same is true for you, Brock. You aren't meant to be here."

Outside, it was growing dark. The wind was high, and rain slashed the windows. The lights around the room were slowly rising, but still dim. Brock cradled her foot in his massive hand and ran his thumb down the sole, massaging her tight, sore muscles. It was a luxury she'd never experienced. Her eyes slipped closed, and she leaned back, relaxing into the moment. One big hand circled her ankle, rotating it gently, and she stifled a gasp. He ceased the movement.

He gripped her calf. She went still, her eyes closed, her breath catching in her chest. The heat from his skin ran up her leg, triggering arousal she hadn't expected. She looked at him, her heart racing, torn between the need to flee and the desire to explore him, to touch him in return.

His eyes were large, startled. Only when he started to push up her pant leg did she move, curling up in a ball on the couch.

He let her go and continued to look at her.

"What did they do to you, Verda?"

Verda shook her head. She remembered what happened, hour after hour, every day of her life. She wasn't meant to forget. They'd made sure she wouldn't. With the memories, her mood shifted from lazy arousal to painful tension.

She didn't relax, and when Brock smoothly settled on the sofa next to her, she was too frozen to escape his presence. His body was warm and solid. He was right next to her, large and unmoving. He gently pulled her into his arms, not holding her tightly, just remaining as a presence.

She counted the seconds in her head. Then minutes. He didn't move. She relaxed slightly, her muscles loosening, her body shifting over to his, as though he was a magnet. Another minute and her head rested against his chest, his arm looped over her shoulder. She listened to his heart, felt the steady breath and synched hers to his. She shifted, allowing him to gather her up, to hold her securely.

"You can tell me, Verda. It goes no further than this spot."

"I tried to escape," she said, almost before he was finished. Her voice sounded harsh. "I tried to escape and injured three guards. Each man was allowed to retaliate."

She heard his breath pause and waited for an explosion. But he remained quiet. "I was made to stand before the king, my hands bound to a beam over my head. Each guard was allowed to strike, but only my legs, so I'd never try to escape again."

"Oh, Verda." His lips were pressed against her temple, not in a kiss, but a gesture of empathy. "How old were you?"

"I was old enough to damage three grown men." She felt her mouth pull up in a smile. "Perhaps twelve . . . thirteen Common years."

He pulled her tighter. "I knew you were born to it. When did you learn to fight?"

"Right from birth, practically. My father and mother had different styles. My brother and I learned right along with walking and talking. What I'm teaching you is my mother's techniques. They depend more on small moves and speed. I can no longer do my father's art justice."

She pulled away from him and gathered her dignity. "In a week, we should see the sky again." There was something to her voice, a throb of pain. Of longing. She swallowed it away. "Out there behind the clouds, there's a star. It's called Polarium."

"The White Star. I've seen it just a few times since I've been here. It's very beautiful."

"It's killing us." Never before had she spoken those words out loud. "Solar flares, perhaps. Or some sort of gravitational force. I don't know what exactly. But scientists have pinpointed the instability in our planet to forces coming from that star. The rains never end, and the seismic instability is increasing."

He frowned. "Then the king must know, correct? Why hasn't the public been alerted? They could at least have the option of evacuating."

She turned and looked at him sadly. "The researcher who brought it to his attention was assassinated. The others needed no other warning."

"Verda, why would a king deny such a thing? Why would he keep them in ignorance?"

"Because he's not fully sane." He was mad. She should simply have said the ugly truth. The king was dangerously unstable and was growing worse. She knew it. Others knew it but still protected him with their lives.

Brock took a deep breath and exhaled slowly. Fear flashed in his eyes and was gone. "How much longer?"

"The remaining men and women who know of this have quietly continued their research. Several left the planet and haven't returned."

"That close, then?" The fear was gone from his face. Now, his sensual mouth was grim. He'd faced death before. He was preparing to fight again. A different battle, and perhaps a hopeless one.

She nodded. "It can happen anytime. I thought we had longer, but the breaks in the rains are less frequent, and the number of tremors doubled. They are occurring deeper in the planet." She stood and walked to the window again. And finally, she put her greatest fear into words.

"I can barely navigate the palace, Brock. How will I escape the city and climb to the port?" The fear she lived with daily threatened to break loose . . . to overtake her and crush her spirit.

He rose and went to stand behind her, looking outside. His window looked out over a sheer drop. It had taken over a year, but he'd eventually learned that his room was an effective cell. A very luxurious, comfortable cell. There was only one way out. If the door was locked, there was no escape.

"I will find you, Verda."

"My lodgings are several levels down from here. You may not be able to reach me. Or you may be elsewhere when it happens. Or I might be with the king, and he'll—" She stopped, pressing her lips tightly closed. She'd said too much, yet couldn't stop.

"He'll kill you." He said it simply. Sadly. Because he knew there was a reason the cruel, unstable king had ordered to damage her and then kept her close. "Who is he to you?"

Verda's hands tightened on the sill of the window. Her breath fogged the glass. She stared at the condensation as she spoke. "I am his history." She turned to face him, leaning back to take the weight off her leg. "I'm the daughter of the woman he couldn't have, and the brother he could never defeat."

"Oh, fate. He's your uncle." There were multiple levels of shock in his voice. "Your uncle maimed you."

Without speaking, she nodded once.

"He was your guardian?"

"He was my regent."

Silence hung in the room. She saw horror on his face. Pity. Fury. And Verda knew she was no longer alone. She had an ally.

He shut his eyes tightly. "He was the younger brother?" She nodded again. "You were to be the queen."

"Do not ever speak of it. To do so would mean your death. Instantly. Those who remember were sent away years ago. My name was removed from the record. I am no one now, except a crippled slave." Her voice was soft. Intense. Angry. She let the emotions run through her, and after years of denial, she embraced them.

"You are a warrior," he said, cupping her face. "Powerful. Strong."

"Broken and afraid." She met his eyes frankly. "I'm property. I have no family. No friends."

"I'm a friend." It could have been a trite, easy declaration.

Yet it wasn't. It was the truth and froze the air in her chest. She wanted this man to take the burden from her, just for a moment. She wanted him to tell her he'd fix it. He'd fight for her and win. She wanted to be rescued yet was all too aware that she might be the one rescuing him.

"What can I do," he asked. "To help you when the time comes?"

She couldn't unburden herself completely, but they could share. Her eyes burned with unshed tears, and she glanced away.

"We need to stay close. I know I can't be at your side all the time, but—" She lifted a single brow. "The king gave me an order. To pressure you to sign the contracts. We can work with that."

As though it had been timed, a chime alerted him that someone was at the door. Ser Comptyn. Verda took up a stylus and sat at the desk. Brock released the door and then paced, his agitation rising as the fight master entered, wearing his anger like a cloak.

"You've not signed yet."

Brock glared at the man. The Ser paled slightly and focused his ire on Verda. "Haven't you finished the translations?"

She fought not to grit her teeth. "Yes, Ser Comptyn, I just need to check the three copies against each other." She turned in her seat, extending all three packets to Brock. "Please take your time to read them over."

Brock took them and remained standing, scanning each sheet with care. He joined her at the desk, taking her stylus and making notations in the margins. He felt tense as stretched wire, and her tension rose. Across the room, the Ser sighed impatiently. He paced the room, casually picking up and examining the few personal items Brock displayed on shelves and in cases. Trophies, mostly. A figurine of a girl. A broken blade. A lump of green and gold glass.

"I requested changes. Please include them in the final copies." His voice was cold and arrogant. The fight master took the pages and scanned them, glancing at Verda, and then back to the contract. He finished reading and set the pages on the desktop.

He folded his thick arms, tilted back his head and looked down his nose at Brock. That was a feat, considering Brock was a handspan taller. "That's all?"

"That's what I want," Brock replied.

The Ser smiled, and Verda's skin went chill.

"No need to make another copy. Set your name to the page."

Brock looked at Verda. She knew what he'd requested. She nodded slightly.

He signed the page. And then the second, and the third.

And Verda cursed herself for praying that she was right because if she was, this dying planet would take millions of lives.

But if she was wrong, Brock might never escape to go home. And she would die at her uncle's hands.

CHAPTER FIVE

Sitting on the hard, narrow bed she'd slept in for over a decade, Verda looked around the tiny room. She'd known no other home for most of her life.

The crumbling plaster walls were rough and painted dingy white. Once the room had been bright and almost cheerful. Years of neglect and encroaching moisture were breaking plaster from the rock walls. Water stained the wall under the high window. Some of the stains were fresh, and there was moisture creeping along the floor and into the room in shallow pools.

There'd once been rough wooden shelves on the walls, set to hold their necessities and their few personal items, but those shelves were now on the floor, propped against the drier inside wall. Lichen grew up the rock. It was ugly but harmless. The slaves scoured it from the walls of the upper rooms, but down here on the slave level, it grew at will.

She drew a deep breath, deliberately calming herself. Her heart beat too fast. Her skin was too warm. She thought of Brock, and the warmth inside matched the heat on the outside.

His looks attracted her. That wasn't unusual. She'd seen many compelling men as they visited the palace. She'd carefully chosen her first lover, determined to control that single aspect of her life. He'd been a visiting scholar, one who'd given silent support to his mentor in the arguments about the White Star. He'd treated her like a human and had been a gentle lover. And as she'd expected, his time in the city had been shortened by the displeasure of the king.

Hopefully, he'd escaped the capital city. Hopefully, he'd escaped the planet. She'd liked him.

What she felt for Brock was different. She liked him, too, but felt edgy in his presence. He was a big, gigantic contradiction. He was a fighter, a deadly warrior. But his skills were rough, and he relied on strength and instinct.

He was gentle. And he was lonely.

He learned quickly. He was smart and adapted easily. He'd need to, he was fighting Peri Stroop in just days, and Peri was wickedly dangerous. All of her reading on him suggested that he learned with every fight, and though he'd had some losses, they were few. Whatever mistakes he made were never repeated. Peri was hungry. And Brock called him 'friend.'

She stood and took a few moments to adjust to the pain that flared with movement. Her sessions with Brock had taken a toll on her. She'd adapt to the pain. She was good at adapting.

"Verda!"

She jerked in surprise, gasping as the old wounds on her legs pulled. She fought not to pant with the pain, slowly building up the stoic face that hid her from the world.

"Yes, Ser Lanham." Her voice was steady, betraying neither her pain nor her fear.

The slave master glared at her, disdain and anger showing on her hard, pale face. Perhaps there was a hint of fear there as well.

"You're to report to Brock Ahern's quarters. Indefinitely. Gather your—" She looked around the room, her lip curled in contempt. "Gather your possessions and leave now. I'm moving the new ash girl into this room."

Verda felt as though her throat had closed. It was time.

"I'm not sure if being a fighter's slut will be a step up

from being the king's whipping girl. At least you'll have better clothes. For now."

She was walking away, obviously not expecting Verda to follow. Once she was out of sight, Verda gingerly lowered herself to the bed again. She looked around the room. What did she have to take? Her comb and the strings she looped through her hair to secure it? The chipped mug next to the water basin? Her spare shift, with the darned holes?

Quickly, she hobbled around the room, gathering anything she had any use for, leaving the rest for the new resident of the miserable room. She made a bundle of her robe and pushed the flimsy rolling door closed behind her. She walked up the ramp to the ground level, looking at a tiny rivulet of water as it trickled downward.

How had the Ser not seen that? How could anyone miss what was happening? Before she took another step, the ground rolled ominously beneath her feet, and she struggled to keep her balance. Around her, slaves and servants hurried along, showing no concern. No fear. She walked close to the wall, head down and eyes on the floor. A uniform-clad child dashed past her, delivering a message of some great urgency. Most likely some noble wanted something of paramount importance . . . a meal served on dishes that would color coordinate with their clothing. Perhaps Princess Janine coveted a caged fowl whose feathers reflected the blue of her eyes. Up there, no one worried about water seeping through the walls or chunks of plaster falling on their coiffed heads.

But those grand towers stood on feet of rapidly crumbling clay.

Her legs hurt, but she set one foot in front of the other and dreamed of the day when the tendons and muscles would be healed. When she could run as swiftly as the page, and spin and feint and train with Brock, once again nimble and whole. Stupid fantasy, but it occupied her mind for a moment.

She rested, leaning against the wall, gazing out a high window. The gray clouds roiled and raced through the sky, and bemused, she watched as they broke, revealing glimpses of greenish blue sky before tumbling into place again.

Greenish blue. The sky should be *blue*. She hurried along, ignoring muscles that pulled and caught. When she reached the tall red door of Brock's quarters, she lay her palm on the lock and heard the chime sound. The door slid open, and she entered, heading through the foyer, past the dining space, and into the spacious living room, her attention divided between Brock, who lounged on the massive sofa, and the window.

"Brock. You should see this." She gestured to him, and as silently as a mountain panther, he was up and moving across the room. He joined her at the window. It filled most of the wall and had controls to adjust the visibility. "Open it all the way," she instructed.

"Window, full open," he murmured, standing close behind her. His light accent burred in her ear. "What are we looking at, other than clouds and rain?"

"The sky," she said. "Watch the clouds. Something's happening."

He stood behind her, towering over her, and she felt as though there was a wall at her back. A warm wall, with just the right amount of give. He wasn't embracing her, but there was contact, and she fought the urge to sink back and close her eyes. To let him be strong for her, just for a moment.

As though reading her mind, Brock moved closer and slipped an arm around her waist, taking enough weight to ease her legs. She ignored the flutter of her heart.

"There. Right there." She pointed, but it wasn't necessary. Behind her, she felt his breath catch. She felt his heart speed up. Tension corded his arms, and she glanced down, seeing the ridges at the outside of his arms begin to protrude.

He was alarmed. Perhaps frightened. Those bumps were a defensive response. They lengthened into alarming, jagged points. But in his arms, she was safe. Verda leaned back, and he looped one arm around her waist, the ridges pointing downward, toward her belly. She wondered how they were used. Were they a vestigial trait of his people? They looked like battle gauntlets, wicked and dangerous. She wondered . . . were they bone? Cartilage? Some organic material she'd never encountered?

"What's happening?" His deep voice was almost a whisper in her ear. She didn't answer until the wound in the sky closed over, hidden behind the storm clouds.

"I don't know. I remember years ago the sky was very blue. But once when our family was traveling inland, a fierce storm arose. It was windy, and the clouds were high. The light falling through the sky was green. Like a bruise." She continued scanning the sky. "The winds were fierce. We sheltered in a series of stone caves. They tunneled far back into the mountain, and I remember the sound of the storm. It sounded like the screams of the dying. It felt as though the wind was reaching into the mountain, struggling to drag us out."

"Has there ever been a storm like that here, near the ocean?"

"Not that I know of." She leaned forward, breaking his hold on her. "I can't imagine . . . if winds like that are near water . . ." She took a deep, shaky breath, and then turned. Brock wasn't looking at her. He was looking out toward the ocean.

"Oh, Geaha . . . protect them." He fished a medallion from the front of his shirt, drawing a pendant to his lips and kissing it. She turned back, straining to see what he was looking at. His eyesight must be incredible.

She squinted, seeing nothing but roiling skies and white-capped waters. Finally, she saw a boat. A large, deepwater boat, pitching and bucking, vanishing down into troughs, and bursting up through the waves. She pressed her fingers to her lips. "That's a ferry. There are likely hundreds of people onboard. Those waves . . . oh, mercy." She pressed a hand to her belly, sick with dread. So many lives . . . all on the edge of death.

He didn't reply. Instead, Brock pointed to the south of the boat. Water twisted up into the sky, funnels, and spouts, bursting up like bizarre, sinuous creatures from the depths of the sea. They raged onward, just a mile . . . perhaps less, but bearing down on the ferry. When Verda was sure the craft would vanish from this world, the water spouts collapsed, folding in on themselves, dropping into the still choppy water.

The clouds looked tattered and frayed. Polarium was in view, its lights slashing and bright, like broken glass in a pool of water. Pushed by the wind, the clouds parted, and light poured down from the sky, illuminating the grey, wet city below them. Colors dazzled her. She squinted her eyes, blinking tears away. How long had it been since she'd seen the sun? She held out her hands, feeling radiant warmth soak into her skin. Her breath caught in her chest. She hadn't seen the sun for longer than brief moments since she was a girl.

"Verda, your hair—" She turned to look at Brock and froze. His skin was always a warm, amber hue, but as she watched, it changed. His black hair was now a shade of red . . . dark and rich and vibrant.

"My hair?" She was still staring at him as his skin darkened. Swirls and patterns emerged along his arms, up his throat, and onto his face. "Your hair! It's changing color! And your skin—you're photo reactive?"

"You're golden." He looked at her with the same wonder on his face that must be on hers. "Your eyes are the color of *eppha* grain." He must have seen a look of confusion on her face. "New green. Bright. Almost pale. And your hair—" He touched it, examining it closely. "I knew it was gold, but now it's the color of freshly polished gold. You're a blonde." He smiled awkwardly, his full lips pulling upward. He then looked toward the sky, his smile fading. "How long will that last?"

She turned back to the window, fear creeping back into her gut. "Not much longer. I'm afraid . . . I'm very worried there will be more storms. More like the one from when I was little." But these storms would not be on dry land. These storms were over water. The idea of their destructive power terrified her. But the sun exhilarated her. Her hands trembled.

They stood at the window, gazing out at the sunlit world, occasionally glancing at each other in wonder. From behind, he wrapped his arms around Verda, and she leaned back into him. She was warm. She'd forgotten how that felt. She looked down at his arms, seeing the sun etched patterns on his skin. The ridges running down his forearms were darker than the rest of his skin. She lay her head back against his chest, hearing his heart, feeling the heat of millennia radiating from his skin. Braccis was an agricultural planet. Solar light would be everything in a place such as that.

"What are those patterns on your skin?" she asked.

He lifted one arm so she could see the elaborate, filigree-like patterns. "*Gresha Geaha*," he said in his own language. "The touch of the Goddess. It's what sets sky farmers apart from others. We can bear the solar exposure at higher altitudes." He lowered his arm and tentatively, she stroked the smooth skin of his forearm, running her fingers over the ridges on his outer arm. "What are these for?"

He flexed his arm, and the ridges suddenly grew, curving back like serrated teeth. She gasped.

"They're called *tengs*. We move rapidly through the framework of the sky farms. The tengs enable me to catch a lattice or a branch if my hands are full. Or if I slip."

Verda touched the *tengs*, shivering as he retracted them.

"They seem more like weapons."

He twisted his arm, extending, then retracting the wicked-looking protrusions. "I have them on my feet, too. And elsewhere." He was silent after that. But his hands were not still. He touched her lightly, smoothing his hands over her arms, stroking the soft skin at her throat.

"Why did you leave your home, Brock?"

His arms tightened slightly, one around her waist, the other crossed over her chest, his palm on her shoulder. He sighed.

"Why does a young person ever wander? I sought adventure. I went looking for fame and fortune. And I found it. I had that drive, you know. It told me I was meant for bigger things than toiling in the heat or scrambling through the sky farms."

"But at what cost?"

He gave a small laugh. "My honor. Sometimes my dignity." He was quiet for a long moment. "My family. My freedom."

"But you can go home," she said, knowing that his freedom to return hinged on their escape. She'd projected clearing skies, but not for several days. She'd been wrong about that, what if she was wrong about the catastrophe she'd been preparing for? What if the planet continued to survive the solar flares? Perhaps this brilliant day signaled the passing of the crisis.

Then they'd both be trapped.

He didn't answer. Instead, he touched her hair, unfastening the firmly threaded coils, so they cascaded down past her shoulders. He stroked her temples, his fingers unexpectedly gentle. She knew where this was going. She wanted it as well. She imagined their limbs entangled, their bodies joined, and she shuddered, feeling the taut pull of desire. She couldn't bear to close her eyes against the brilliance of the sky, marveling at the light until her eyes watered.

He moved then, one hand tracing the curve of her waist. His lips were warm as he whispered kisses down her throat, down to her shoulder. She took his hand from her shoulder and laced her fingers into his, then carried it down till his warm palm covered her breast. He groaned softly, his breath tickling her cheek. Smoothly, he turned her to face him, angling them, so they were both fully in the light, and she studied his features. His skin was gleaming, dark copper, and his eyes were the vivid dark, with sparks of fire within. The grim lines that bracketed his mouth faded and instead, he smiled.

She couldn't stop looking; he was bright and brilliant in the full, unfiltered light. Even under the vivid lights of the arena, he'd never looked this bold and electric. He was powered by sunlight. She wondered if it made him stronger. Faster. More dangerous than she knew him to be.

He bent to her, and the kiss was both bold and gentle, awkward and painfully familiar. Unexpectedly, Verda felt tears in her eyes, and she moved closer, hungering for the touch of his skin, for the warmth and comfort of being held by another person. How long had it been? He seemed to sense — or even share her need. He wrapped her up in his arms, holding her tightly.

She let her legs go soft, and he lowered her to the floor, where a thick carpet softened the exotic quarried tiles. He lay beside her, gazing at her. The sun dazzled her eyes, but she still saw the softness on his face. The desire. Briefly, she thought of the ridges on his arms and wondered where else he might have them. His feet. Maybe his legs. But where else? Tengs, he'd called them. He considered them tools. Knives were also tools. And some tools were weapons.

She caught the edge of his shirt and pulled it over his head, then studied the whorls and delicate lines on his skin as the sun drew them forth. How had he survived here in the rain and gloom? She glanced up at the window. Dark, riotous clouds studded the sky, but there were still vivid patches of blue. The sickly greenish shade was gone. She looked at Brock, and he was also staring at the sky. He was less sensitive to the light than she. Had they both adapted to their environments? Would she always wince at the light?

He met her gaze then and leaned in for another kiss. This time, it was passionate and intense. His tongue came to her lips, and she let him in. The kiss became carnal. Sensation swept her body, warm and welcome. She rarely felt sexual, and when she did, there was no privacy. She never touched herself. She'd taken few lovers, and her relationship with the king must have afforded her some protection, as she'd never been forced. Years of celibacy crashed into her in that one moment and need gripped her like a vise.

He hadn't been celibate, she knew that. She'd seen lovers enter and then leave. One fine lady had boasted of her conquest of the aloof gladiator. She'd only wanted him for the novelty of taking, and then discarded him. Had he been as lonely as she, these past seven years?

Except for the marks and ridges, he was like most men she'd seen. He had flat, oval nipples and a navel. His muscles were hard. His hands calloused and rough.

They felt like heaven on her skin.

The name Verda suggested lush, green and verdant growth.

The woman in his arms was not lush. Her golden skin was pale, shimmering slightly in the sun. But her eyes were vivid green, her hair shimmered like the autumn eppha that flourished on the surface of his planet. Up high in the Ariel frames of the sky farms, he used to look down, marveling at the miles and miles of grain that morphed from pale green to the hard, dark green of emeralds, finally mellowing down to gold. As summer's heat waned, the grain was harvested . . . an entire planet's worth, and then it was shipped to other worlds, and the entire cycle began again.

All the while, Brock, and his family, scrambled in the structures high in the sky, tending to delicate fruits that would eventually provide wine for the people of Frashee, or to be served as a delicacy for some distant feast. His feet had rarely touched the solid soil, and when he did go down, it was to sleep in his family's home, to laugh with his parents and toil in the fields when the grain was ready to harvest.

His life had been ordinary.

His life had been splendid.

And his seven years of misery on this soggy cesspit of a planet just might be worth it if Verda's plan for escape proved sound. He'd take her home. He'd wed her. Take her to the sky — but she could never live in the sky. Her skin was too fragile, and her legs —

He ran his hands down her arms, easily brushing coarse garments from her skin. She was strong, her hands were capable, though not roughened from work. Her shoulders were slender, and her breasts were small but beautiful. Her body tapered . . . from shoulder to narrow waist, and out to gently rounded hips. He pushed the loose trousers from her hips, sliding them down her legs. Unexpectedly, she went stiff and rigid, and he looked at her and remembered. Her eyes were tightly closed, and her full lips were suddenly tight. As though feeling his gaze on her face, she opened her eyes and met his gaze.

She nodded.

He sat up and gently bared her legs.

Her poor, ravaged legs. The fronts were almost unmarked, only a few shimmery scars marred the skin. The back though—he ran a hand down her calves, feeling ridges and indents of old wounds. Deep scars. Damage that undoubtedly ran down into tendons and ligaments. Damage designed to maim and cripple and cause endless pain.

Rage overtook lust, and Brock drew deep breaths, gathering the courage to turn her to her belly and fully view her legs. One foot drew up oddly, the result of poor healing. They'd cut her with knives, or some other blade. Some wounds had been shallow. Others had sliced to the bone. They'd been deliberately allowed to heal badly. Every one of those wounds could have been treated and could have healed without leaving marks.

Exhaling, he leaned down, placing gentle kisses on the worst of the marks. He blinked against tears. In the arena, he'd seen worse injuries . . . wounds that could easily kill. He'd seen fighters dragged back to the staging areas, their innards spilling, bones crushed. Sometimes they died. Often, they survived and fought again.

"This is why you are desperate to leave," he said softly. "Even if the planet lives on, you must escape." He lay on the floor beside her, and she rolled over to face him. She kissed him softly.

"There is a species of humanoid called the Vash. They live within the Summer Coalition. It's said they can heal. I believe they can repair the damage."

"I've heard of them," he said. "They are a myth, Verda." Her eyes lost their shine. Her gaze dropped, and he felt he'd been cut off from her soul. "And if they are real, how will you travel there? How will you pay for their services?"

She closed her eyes briefly and then looked at him steadily. "I don't know. But I refuse to surrender to this, Brock. I will work any job. I will bear the pain. And I will prevail."

As he looked at her, the light began to fade. It wasn't cloud cover, though. It was dusk. But even in the waning light, her eyes were vivid, and her hair glowed. The marks on his skin began to vanish, and his skin was fading down to night levels. He'd almost forgotten how he looked in the brilliance of daylight. He'd almost forgotten who he was.

Yes, he was a fighter and an adventurer. But he was also a farmer. A son and a brother. His hands weren't hard from the sword he fought with. They'd been toughened by hours using a hoe and a cutter. His muscles were iron-hard from hours in the Ariel frames. He'd built speed and agility from countless hours swinging and leaping from frame to frame. His steady nerves resulted from hours spent a mile above the ground, with no solid footing.

He leaned in and kissed her again, feeling at once exultant and ashamed. He'd do his best to free her, but in the end, he couldn't take her home. There was no place for a woman like her on a planet like his. She couldn't live with him in the sky.

The idea of letting her go . . . of her fading from his life—it was intolerable. Desperation swept over him, the knowledge that their time was finite. In the end, he'd lose her, either to death in the arena or to this failing planet. If they survived, she'd begin her quest, and he'd go home.

Home. The word unleashed an ache in his soul. Loneliness so profound he wanted to weep.

She was undressing him, slipping off his low boots, tugging his trousers down his legs. She was slender and pale, her breasts tipped by golden nipples, the hair at the juncture of her thighs was sparse and gilt. He ran a hand down her arm, it was smooth and slender, lacking the distinctive ridges a woman of his own species would bear.

She wrapped a hand around his member, stroking and fondling, drawing a gasp from him. She bent, her hair cascading over his thighs, and took him in her mouth, sucking and licking while she cupped his testicles. She serviced him, and he ached to touch her, to place his mouth on her, to taste and feel and invade every inch of her body.

As though sensing that he could bear no more, Verda rose, crawling up his body to cover him, to press her mouth to his as he guided his shaft into her body. She was warm and slick, she smiled against his mouth, then caught her breath as he pushed in. She rose, straddling him to ride, but Brock pulled her down, needing the feel of her body on his, her skin and his skin touching. He cupped her ass, guiding her, holding her tight. Their movement quickened, and seconds before he lost control, she moved faster, harder, grinding against this groin. He felt the flare of her body-heat and the clutch of her body as she came. She panted, her face inches from his. Her groan was guttural, and the sound alone was enough to make him lose control.

"Come, Brock. Let go." Her voice was a harsh whisper. She was indistinct now, a silhouette in the darkness. She surrounded him. Commanded him. She drew the climax from him, leaving Brock in ecstatic bliss. He came then, his body bowing up into her, feet digging into the expensive rug, and he crushed their bodies close, his teeth bared, his cry on the cusp of a snarl. He fell back, still shuddering, his body spent, his mind hazy and soft.

With his seed slipping from her body, she drew away from him, rolling to his side. He drew her close, wrapping her tightly in his arms. Together, they lay like that, eyes wide open in the darkness.

"Look at that," he murmured in her ear. Outside, the clouds still filled the sky, but they were illuminated from behind, as though a spotlight shone behind a curtain. The effect was hauntingly beautiful.

"The White Star." The source of all the deadly forces shattering this planet. "So beautiful," he said. "So damned."

"It brings life to some. Takes it from others." She lay her cheek against his chest. "That's the nature of existence, is it not?"

It was indeed the nature of existence. Life and death. Chaos and order. It was beautiful, and it was dreadful.

CHAPTER SIX

Three more fights. One more week.

The mercurial king hadn't been happy with the changes to Brock's contract. He wasn't willing to permanently surrender his favorite whipping girl to a gladiator, so he'd torn up the contract. He'd sent another, which Brock refused to sign. In retaliation, Brock had been pulled from his apartments in the palace and sent to the barracks, with little more than the clothes he'd worn and a few items he'd hastily shoved into a bag. He didn't know where Verda was, or if she'd been punished. Asking for ownership of her had been a risk. They'd both known it.

So, he was back into crisis mode. No coaching. Fights were added to his schedule, so he was sore and weary. Now he stood on the hard sands of the arena, facing a friend. Peri Stroop taught Brock much of what he now knew. He welded a set of double-edged blades, whereas Brock was unarmed.

Peri was his friend, but Brock had no illusions about their relationship. They'd trained together, partied together and fucked as a team, way back when Brock was full of youth and idiocy. Peri was older. Harder. Hungrier. Peri never hesitated to kill, where Brock had always spared lives when he could. He'd killed the Landaun female and found he lacked the stomach for death.

Peri knew damned well that Brock relied on strength and speed rather than technique. He'd been readying himself for this fight for years. Brock hadn't. He'd never truly believed the time would come when he'd face his friend in a death match. He hadn't prepared until Verda had forced him to do so.

They'd spent hours on a mat in his quarters, training in secret. In spite of her wounds, she moved with speed and cunning, able to deflect his attacks, using his weight and strength against him. She'd thrown him to the ground more than once. She'd used tiny movements to deliver flaring pain up and down his arms, paralyzing his hands. He rarely kicked at his opponents, but when he did so, she'd delivered blows to his inner thighs and behind his knees. He'd fallen like a tree. Now he knew what to do when faced with high kicks. She'd studied all the fighters and forced him to do the same, viewing hours of footage, graphing their strengths and weaknesses.

Together they trained, they made love, and they slept till he was called away to another fight. When he came home, he'd soothe the anxiety from her face, and she'd begin again. Drilling him. Sharing every skill she knew. And together, they made plans. And plans in case those ones failed.

And now, he stood yards from his friend, nervous. Regretful.

Frightened.

Peri smiled, idly swinging one of his blades, playing to the crowd, which roared in encouragement. For the first time ever, Brock knew the people massed in the stands were not on his side. He fisted his hands, grateful his sleeves covered his arms because adrenaline brought his *tengs* out in a primal display. He didn't need Peri to see his alarm.

They both lowered their stances, grounding themselves before one attacked. Their gazes locked. The crowd went silent.

Before they could move, there was a commotion in the crowd. Brock didn't look away from Peri, but from the edge of his vision, saw the royal colors flying in the plush boxed area kept reserved for King Jamis and his guests.

There was silence in the arena, taut and heavy with arrested violence. The crowd was falling to their knees for the king, some with reverence. Many more with anger and resentment on their faces. Across from him, Peri dropped to his knees in complete humility. The man was a consummate actor. He thought King Jamis to be an insane fool. But he lowered himself till his forehead touched the sand.

Slowly, Brock lowered himself to the hard floor, leaning on one fist, hoping his unruly hair covered the resentment on his face. There was another stirring in the arena, and Brock dared look up, shoving himself to his knees when he saw a figure tumble from the royal box to the floor of the arena.

Verda hit hard, and he saw blood running down her legs, bruises on her face. She lay still for a moment, then looked up, her face radiating fury and pain. King Jamis followed her down, landing lightly for a man his age. A pair of bodyguards bore down on Brock. He pushed up, ready to fight.

"You." The king strode over and stopped before him. His boots gleamed, and his breeches were pristine and white. "You cheated."

Brock didn't hide the surprise he felt. "I . . . cheated?" His voice echoed around the arena. They were being broadcast.

"I don't know how you knew about her, and her miserable history, but using a cripple as a fight trainer is probably not the brightest thing you've done." He gestured, and one of the behemoths behind Jamis dragged Verda closer. You were denied a trainer as discipline. You got one of your own. You cheated." He strutted, glancing up at the crowd. "Your hero is a cheat!" he shouted, and his voice echoed. Still, the crowd remained silent. All these years, Brock had been aware of the whispers of the king's cruelty. He was rumored to be insane. Perhaps he was, but Jamis was in full control at this moment. He was playing the crowd like a musician strummed a lute.

He turned back to Brock. "I'm not sure how she convinced you to join her pitiful rebellion. Did she tell you she was a princess in disguise? A poor soul who was damaged out of royal spite?"

Jamis shook his head. "No, sadly, little Verda is merely the unwanted child of a long dead bed slave. A whore. No one wanted her, so she grew up . . . undisciplined. Running wild in the alleys and low places of the city. She eventually developed a nasty habit of thievery. So, she was caught, taken in hand and punished. I then gave her a place. She's no one. Just a worthless slave."

He laughed harshly. "Do you know the betting is against you tonight? It's no secret that your *friend* has been studying your style, Brock. It's no secret that he's the better fighter. And that you're weary, what with fighting almost every night this week. And of course, training on the other days. Hours and hours of training. Verda did her job well."

Brock gritted his jaw and looked at Verda. She was pale as the parchment the contract had been written on. She didn't speak, and one glance told him she was terrified. But she didn't contradict the king. She let him speak uninterrupted. Just yards away, Peri stood, his hip cocked, his blades gathered in one hand. There was an expression of bemusement on his face as he watched the drama play out. Then a look of alarm. A swift tremor ran through the arena. It was subtle but sharp. Different. They all faltered for a moment, catching their balance.

Peri cleared his throat. "My king —" a lie since Peri was from a planet in a different galaxy. A democratic planet. Beyond his contract, he owed — and felt no allegiance to King Jamis. But Peri was good that way. He understood protocol. He understood money and fame. He pushed silky black hair from his face. "What do you wish of me?"

Jamis looked from Peri to Brock. He then looked at Verda, who'd awkwardly risen to her feet. The king's smile was slow and cruel.

"As Verda is such a gifted fighter . . . skilled enough to train the best among us, perhaps she should take Brock Ahern's place in the arena."

Brock felt his heart go still. His mouth went dry.

"No," he whispered hoarsely. The crowd was now silent, leaning in, listening. This life and death drama was being broadcast. "That is cruel. You must not taunt her that way."

He looked at Verda and knew . . . the king wasn't taunting. He was serious. He looked at Peri, saw the man's jaw flex. He'd gone slightly pale. But his grip tightened on his weapons. He would do it. His eyes were tortured, his face grim. He knew he was to be executioner this day. The rules of the game had changed. Peri was now in it for his life, not for money and fame.

"Please, Peri. You call me friend, you have a heart. You must not."

Peri looked at him, his grin looked like the rictus of a dead man. "I prefer to live."

"If you take her life, I will take yours." He said it simply. A promise. And almost before the words left his lips, the king's bodyguards had him bound with heavy ropes. He was helpless.

"Peri, she is his niece. The daughter of his brother. He did that to her. *He* did that." Brock pointed with his chin. He looked at the king, whose smile had faded.

"Brock, don't!" Verda said. Her face was so still, her lips barely moved.

"He was afraid of a child, so he had her maimed."

Peri faltered, glancing at Verda. The crowd was murmuring, a few voices raised in anger.

"She was the daughter of the king!" he shouted, making sure it echoed through the entire structure. "He was her regent, and he did this to her!"

Brock was struck from behind. He staggered but did not fall.

Liar.

Pretender!

Cheat!

The crowd's anger wasn't directed toward Brock.

"How *dare* you!" Jamis hissed. His face was red with fury. He stalked up to Brock and buried a fist in his gut. Brock doubled over, coughed and glared. He'd taken worse blows, but not while bound. His own fury spiked. He spat at the floor of the arena. Another blow, this time to the kidney. The bodyguards were far more efficient.

He struggled to stay upright, then leaned toward Jamis. "This will not go well for you."

The king glared at Brock. He gripped Brock's hair, spat in his face and turned away.

"At least show her the honor of arming her," he shouted at the king who had returned to the side of the arena, mounting a stair to his box. Seeing no response, he looked to Peri. "Please. If nothing else, arm her. Even just a staff!"

Peri turned away from Brock, facing Verda. "I am very sorry." He looked up at the stands, scanning the audience, who were now shouting, cat-calling and stomping their feet in fury.

Let her go!

Kill her!

Fights broke out. The entire place was on the verge of rioting. Brock struggled against the bonds, and one guard left him, striding out to the center of the ring. "Fight," he commanded. Peri swallowed. He looked sick. Verda stood tall and straight. All fear had left her face.

Peri bowed to her, rose and tossed one sword to her feet.

It was too long, too heavy, but she picked it up and gave it and experimental swing. How long had it been since she'd held a blade? A decade? More? She clasped the pommel in both hands and passed it to her right hand. Her movements were smooth and efficient.

Peri suddenly looked worried.

"I'll try not to kill you, Peri Stroop." That was all she said. She lifted one hand and gestured to the tall, dark-haired man. In a flash, Peri was on her, his deadly blade gleaming under the lights of the arena.

But Verda was no longer there.

CHAPTER SEVEN

Years and years of unrelenting pain hadn't prepared Verda to leap and roll, sword in one hand and an attacker at her side. But those years had trained her to move through the pain, so though her landing was awkward, she managed to roll, twist and slash out at Peri Stroop's unprotected legs.

The blade sliced clean, though shallow, and while he wasn't crippled, the fight was suddenly more even. She rolled, gaining enough space to rise to her knees, and then to her feet. She glanced at Brock. His guard was in place but hadn't noticed how Brock struggled with the heavy rope around his arms.

Stupid. Stupid. Stupid.

She nodded at him and returned to the fight, keeping an eye on the other guard. Now that Brock had announced her secret to the world, there'd be no escaping.

Peri was up, charging her with pain and fury masking his face. Pain usually prompted men to commit acts they'd wind up regretting. If he killed her, Peri might lose a few night's sleep. Or he might be haunted by her death forever. But if she could, Verda meant to spare him that inconvenience. He came at her, and she ducked his swing, coming up to slam the flat of her blade into the base of his skull. He went down again, face first. His sword had fallen inches from his outstretched fingers, and she kicked it away, then backed toward it, not willing to turn her back on him. Already, he was moving, groaning out a low curse.

She should kill him.

She looked over at Brock again and watched as he sawed at the bindings. Those nubs on his arms weren't actually blades, but they served their purpose. The rope snapped and in that very movement, Brock stepped back, swung an arm, and a gaping red wound appeared in the guard's throat. He attacked Brock, then abruptly fell to the ground, gouts of blood spattering the sand.

With both blades in hand, Verda backed away from Peri, who was on his hands and knees, slowly shaking his head back and forth. He was probably concussed. When he retched and vomited, she turned away, facing the second guard.

Brock stalked that guard. The sleeves of his tight shirt were shredded, his *tengs* flared out like long, serrated teeth. He bore down on the guard, blocked a flashing knife, and punched at the big man's belly with the heel of his hand. He jerked his hand back, blood shining red on a prong-like spike extending from his wrist.

She stared for a moment, horror and fascination warring in her mind. He was a lethal weapon. He hadn't needed swords or blades to defeat his enemy.

"Brock!" she shouted, gesturing to the wall of guards leaping into the arena from the king's box. She extended the extra sword and tossed it to him. He caught it in time to lop the hand off a royal guardsman. There'd be no fixing that injury.

In seconds, they were both surrounded. She was fading fast, the weakness in her leg, the wicked pain taking a toll on her stamina. But she kept on, never moving from her spot, always twisting, ducking and striking at those who kept coming. Those who kept making the same mistakes, over and over.

One guard moved on her, forcing her back, step by step until she felt the softness of a body beneath her heel. Glancing down, she saw Peri, still on the ground. His legs lay in a pool of blood. She swallowed and held her ground, blinking her eyes as they burned and watered. Just yards away, Brock was taking the bulk of the guardsmen, and now other fighters had been sent into the arena. Some came at Brock like hungry animals, while others stood their ground, guarding him. Several took up arms in his defense.

No—in her defense. An older fighter with a broken nose sketched a quick bow, saluting her with his sword. Another grinned.

"Knew your parents, miss . . . I mean . . . Highness. Fight on!"

And she did. She caught the occasional glimpse of Brock through the melee, his skin had darkened, the etched lines and patterns were in high relief. His hair was blazing that red-black shade so unique to him. She glanced up and saw that through the skylights, the sky was clear and blue, there wasn't a cloud in sight.

She wasn't the only one who'd noticed. All around, fighters were looking up, then turning back to their fights. The crowds were pointing up. There was cheering. And there was blood.

She took a blow so hard it knocked her off her feet, and Verda went down hard, the breath slamming from her chest. She struggled to rise but couldn't. She was dizzy and disoriented. She screamed, but she couldn't possibly be screaming so loud that she deafened herself. She rolled upright and went down again, seeing the other fighters struggling as the world upended. Cracks opened and sealed themselves in the arena floor. Massive sections of the walls came away, the sodden plaster heavy and wet. In the stands, spectators were stampeding out, but the floors were giving way.

King Jamis was surrounded by his nobles and his guards, but as she watched, the supports gave way, and the dais began to list. Brightly garbed men and women fell, some leapt. Screams mingled and got lost in the roar of the earthquake. Once again Verda struggled to her feet and was flung down.

"Verda!" It was Brock, struggling past the violent tremors, leaping over downed men and women, crawling when he could no longer keep his feet.

"Brock!" The quake eased. Dust and dirt filled the air. The abrupt silence revealed the groans, the piteous sounds of the dying. The screaming shriek of snapping timbers snapping filled the air and stone tumbled and collapsed, blocking the aisles. All around them, the building was shattered, dumping its burden onto the sands of the arena.

"Brock!"

Heeding her warning, he spun and pierced his attacker with the extended *teng* of his hand and slashed at another with his free arm. King Jamis stood supported at the end of Brock's arm, his fury fading to puzzlement. He looked at Verda.

"You did this . . ." he croaked, blood trickling from the corner of his mouth.

"No, Uncle. You ignored my warnings." She watched as Brock drew back his shoulder, and the body of Jamis slid to the ground.

He still lived.

"We must go." Verda could barely stand, much less walk, but it was time. She clasped Brock's arm, seeing the shock at what he'd done. A guard lay at his feet, bleeding from a grisly wound down his chest, and Jamis lay, blood trickling from a perfectly round hole in his torso. He might survive that, but she had the feeling there was more to come.

As though in agreement, another tremor shuddered through the ground.

"Where?" he asked, swinging Verda into his arms. He ran, leaping over bodies both alive and dead. He scrambled over piles of rocks and timber.

"North, to the mountain behind the palace!"

He ran, never seeming to grow weary. He ran with the burden of Verda in his arms, and when he could no longer run he walked, pausing only to brace them through another tremor. When the climb became too steep to carry her in his arms, she rode on his back, silently praying his strength wouldn't fade.

The clear blue of the sky turned red, as though the very world bled and died. Sunset was beautiful, and it was horrible. Verda hid her face in Brock's shoulder, imagining she could hear the dying screams of her people.

Her people.

If she'd ruled, would she have gotten them away in time? Would she have done better? She was weary and in pain. Riding on Brock's back was making her nauseous. She thirsted. She wanted nothing more than to lie down and sleep.

"Verda?" Brock's voice was breathless, and she felt a tremor in his muscles. "Is this it?"

He stopped, and she slid down his back to the ground, looking at the massive flat pad that jutted from the side of the mountain. Against all odds, it was still intact. And for the first time, she began to believe that this insane plan would actually work.

"Look." She pointed at a huge recess in the side of the mountain. "Those are the hangar doors." She walked, her left leg barely able to move. Brock steadied her, looping one massive arm around her waist. She found the thick iron door and stroked the panel hidden in the dark stone. It lit up with an eerie amber glow. Taking a deep breath, she lay her hand flat on the panel.

For a moment, nothing happened. She bit her lip. She'd gambled everything on this. She'd trusted in the chaos of the riot and the earthquake. No one should have suspected —

The door groaned, and when she depressed another spot on the pad, the hangar doors parted in near silence. Few people knew of the mechanic's entrance to the port. The seconds gave way to minutes, and when the doors fully opened, she knew their time was short.

Someone had activated the emergency systems. The planes and ships were all powering up. All save one.

"That one."

The darkened ship sat alone, dwarfing the other craft. It was older, but not archaic. She limped toward it, moving as fast as she could. "We can't get out till the other craft are moved."

Brock again scooped her up, hurrying toward the ship.

"It's the only one equipped for off-planet travel." She shouted over the noise of the readied craft around them. "They can fly elsewhere on the planet, but ultimately, they won't find safety."

"Looks like it hasn't been used in ages."

"It hasn't."

He set her down as they approached, and she found the access panel on the ship's belly. This time, she lay her hand on the plate with confidence. The ramp dropped smoothly, and Brock had them up and in before it fully deployed. Once in the dimly lit interior, she retracted the ramp and locked them in. Dim lights activated as they moved through to the bridge.

"Welcome to the *North Wind*. This was my parent's personal craft. It was keyed only to them. And to me." She looked around, remembering hours spent on this ship, her father laughing while her mother set Verda on a jump seat on the bridge, strapping her securely into a webbing of straps and restraints.

"Can anyone else board it?" Brock gently took her arm,

steadying her as they ascended up a ramp to the upper level.

She shook her head. "Not without some major equipment. And maybe a bomb or two." He smiled at her quip, and she smiled back. It was happening. They were escaping. Finally.

Within minutes they were in the cockpit. It had been a long time, but the pre-flight checks had been drilled into her brain as a child. Their familiarity brought comfort. She nearly felt her family onboard this ship, giving her guidance and strength. "Take that seat. Strap in." She pointed to the larger of the two seats. The one her father had used.

Brock followed her instructions. "You know how to fly this?"

She grinned at him weakly. "I did when I was a kid. Of course, my mother or father were always with me. But they let me pilot the ship once we were out there." She imagined the depths of space. The silence and solitude. "They taught me to use auto-pilot and to engage the DV Drive. I can also calculate navigations." She nodded to the bound sets of charts that were neatly secured to her left.

"You know where we're going, then?"

"Away." She switched the arrays onto low power and powered up the computers. They were dated, but still in working order. She'd update their data later. Now was the time for business. "There's a station about a day's journey out, but we'll bypass that one. I've heard its rough." Not to mention, they might be intercepted by her uncle's people as they rushed back to Attigua.

She shared a display to his station, using her finger to highlight their destination. "We'll go here first, to re-provision, check our energy levels and update my charts. After that—" She highlighted a larger, better-known station. "Here. And we can make plans." Plans, because Brock was dead-set on returning to his home. Verda would continue on her quest for a healer. They'd be in different systems, countless miles and hours apart.

Feeling slightly sick, she continued through the checklist while Brock sat in silence. She thought about provisions and water. It should still all be in place, albeit a bit stale. They'd survive. The power levels were up, the fuel crystal was in place, and finally, Verda drew a deep breath, held it, then let it out. She powered up slightly more, giving them a good view of the port. Others should be coming in just minutes. She desperately wanted to go. To get the hell away from here.

"I could blast through their ships," she said. "The North Wind is armed."

"You could." Brock grinned. "Whose craft are these?"

"They belong to the royals. That's Jamis's personal ship." She nodded toward a sleek winged craft. "They have no business evacuating. They're the leaders. They should be on the ground, helping with the recovery."

"We could do that. Just blast our way out of here. Then they couldn't leave."

Verda sighed. She sat back in her seat. "I shouldn't be leaving either."

Brock just looked at her without speaking.

"These are my people, Brock."

"Jamis was alive when we left the arena. Chances are, his political machine is intact. It was only because of the quake that we escaped with our lives."

She stared straight ahead, looking at the instrument array, then out at the view screen. She felt a tear trickle down her cheek. "My father didn't want to be the king. He wanted to leave . . . to see the universe. Jamis didn't need to kill him. My parents would have abdicated." Another tear. And now her nose was running. "Oh, Brock. He didn't need to kill them!"

He unfastened his restraints, gathered her in his arms and

held her, easing back into the wide seat she'd assigned him. He held her while she cried for grief and for pain. For fear. She gripped his shoulder, then pounded it lightly.

"I didn't know if you were alive! You were just gone, and he took me to his quarters. Locked me back in my old rooms. He questioned me repeatedly. He was sure I was planning a rebellion." She sniffed. "Some rebellion . . . just the two of us."

He squeezed her, and she lay her head on his shoulder. "I think you may have started a rebellion back there. Or maybe I did, exposing you like that. For which I'm so very sorry."

"It was time. I may not be here to lead it, or even to help my people flee, but Jamis's treachery has been exposed. If the city survives, he may not survive with it."

"What then?" He reached up and stroked her hair. "Who will step up as leader?"

"Perhaps there won't be only one leader. Maybe there will be many, as there were in the past. Or maybe there will be none. The leadership under Jamis was bad. If he didn't survive, whoever steps in may be worse. Though that's hard to imagine." She straightened, looking out the view screen. "Oh, look."

People were appearing, running from the rear of the hangar, stumbling over themselves in their hurry to reach the readied crafts.

Verda gave a rueful sniff. "The royal family's quarters connect directly to this hangar, so they can access their craft using the commercial ports."

"There are lifts? And you had me carry you up the side of the mountain to get here?"

"You're strong." She smiled. "And it was safer. I'll bet the palace has started crumbling."

She watched as people she knew pushed their way into crafts that were overloaded. She didn't see King Jamis anywhere. She did see Janine . . . her cousin. As Verda watched, the older princess ran toward a waiting craft and came to a sudden halt. She stood for a long moment. Verda toggled the viewfinder, zooming in on her cousin. And her heart nearly broke. Janine looked over her shoulder, her face white and tears streaming down her cheeks. She looked back at the craft, and her shoulders slumped. Someone leaned out, screaming at her, hands reaching, but Janine didn't move.

"She's staying," Verda murmured.

"If her father's dead, then she's the queen." Brock looked at her. "Well, officially."

Janine trembled so hard she nearly slipped to the ground. Turning away, she stumbled, her delicate dress in tatters, and sudden resolution on her face.

"If she survives, she's earned her seat on the throne." Verda closed her eyes, praying for her cousin. "There may be nothing left to salvage here, other than survivors." And the pull to remain behind hit her hard. She pushed up off Brock's lap and winced at the pain. She wobbled, her legs unsteady. And the truth was exquisitely painful.

"I'm no use here."

"Verda?"

She looked at Brock, barely able to see him through tears. "I can't do anything to help."

"Perhaps not on the ground. But we can help from a distance. We can send ships. I have money."

She shook her head. "This isn't your battle. Nor is it mine. Not now. Maybe in the future, if Janine will accept me." They'd never gotten on. Janine was one of the few who knew the entire truth about Verda and her parents. She wasn't amoral like her father, but she'd done nothing to intervene with him when she could have.

But then maybe she couldn't. Maybe she'd been just as much a prisoner as Verda. And Brock.

The ships were moving out of the hangar in slipshod fashion. The first to take to the air bobbled and dipped, and she wondered where they'd eventually land. There was no knowing the damage across the planet. Not yet. Another took off, and another. Within fifteen minutes, they were alone in the hangar.

"It's time." Verda began the sequence to power up the North Wind, using an old, brittle checklist to remind her of all the steps. To her surprise, she recalled the entire process.

"What do you need me to do?" Brock asked.

She looked at him and smiled, her vision misty with tears. "Just be here. Be safe." She turned back to her panel and gingerly levitated the massive ship. Unlike the others, it didn't roll or slide to the pad. They wouldn't launch out over the cliffs and climb to the sky. Instead, they hovered, inching forward till they were clear of the rock walls.

"Here we go," she whispered, and manually launched the ship into a vertical takeoff, straight up into the sky, piercing heavy, wet clouds, and out into the brilliance of a sky lit by the sun, and by a great White Star that shone with brilliant, colorful light. Polarium.

She didn't look back. There was nothing to see but clouds.

CHAPTER EIGHT

They lay together in a hired room, knowing their time together was almost at a close. Brock sipped a cup of red tea. The sweet-bitter liquid washed through him, and he knew this would be his last drink of the herb. It had kept him awake and stimulated for far too long. He hadn't had a chance to pack any, and that was just as well.

His heart was breaking.

Verda was healing. Her bruises were fading, and her wounds were closed. They'd visited a healer after landing at a small station several days from Attigua. They'd moved on quickly, getting lost in the rush of rescuers and refugees from the devastated planet.

It was as bad as Verda had feared. The cities were crushed, hundreds of thousands known dead, and as many more missing. Evacuations were being organized by the new ruler, Janine. She'd dropped her title and declared herself Chief Councilor rather than queen. At her side . . . Peri Stroop. Apparently, his injuries weren't as severe as they'd seemed. Brock suspected he'd faked his end of the fight. The Peri he'd known wouldn't have fought Verda.

Verda's hand rested on the table, and he settled his own over hers, marveling at the difference in sizes. They'd never had a courtship or a flirtation. They'd slept together a few times, fought for their lives together, feared for one another. Yet he loved her as deeply as if they were long-time spouses.

"Come with me, Verda," he said softly, knowing even as the words left his lips, they were futile. She'd never adapt.

Or perhaps she would, but she had her own quest.

"No. Take the *North Wind* and go to your home, Brock. Maybe when I'm healed—" She broke off, and they both knew the separation was coming. Forever. "We agreed, you'd buy the ship, and I'll purchase fare to the Coalition. From there, I'll find them."

The Vash. Who turned out to be very real, though very elusive.

Her plan was good, the *North Wind* and her DV Drive were out of date. In her parent's ship, the journey would take years. There were massive cruisers that moved through deep space, slipping into alternate dimensions to reach their destinations. Her journey would be long but wouldn't take a lifetime. Brock sat up, set his cup on a table and turned back to Verda, leaning down to kiss her. It was a sweet kiss, she licked at the tea lingering on his lips, and cupped his jaw. She looked up into his face and studied his features, as he did hers.

"I will never forget the way you look right now." Brock kissed her eyelids, her cheeks, her nose and finally dipped to her mouth. He heard her swallow and tasted her tears. She gripped his hair and kissed him harder, her teeth drew blood. She cleaned him up with her tongue.

Never once, had she asked him to travel with her.

She'd sat with him in the station's communications center and listened in as he spoke with his mother and father for the first time in seven years. She'd cried, though she tried to hide it. She'd kept out of sight of his parents, and they'd laughed, sobbed and berated him over the years he'd been gone. His brothers had found him on remote news channels and followed his career with increasing alarm.

They thought he'd died in the quakes.

They'd all cried at his story, hurt and angry and afraid, but ultimately forgiving of their wandering son. Brock had to go home. He could wait no longer. And Verda agreed. So, they'd written a contract, she'd sold her one item of value to Brock. She'd taught him to fly and pre-set the navigation for Brock to return home. Without his knowledge, she'd taken them off her course. The station they'd arrived at was just a short journey from his home. In two days, maybe three, Brock would be home, and Verda would be traveling to another planet. Another galaxy.

And Brock was dying inside.

"Perhaps there are healers closer . . . or surgeons. There are exceptional doctors — "

She smiled sadly and shook her head. They'd visited doctors on every station they'd visited on their flight from Attigua. They'd offered no hope.

"I'd marry you, Verda. Right here and now."

She quirked a single brow. "Here?"

He gave a little laugh, though it hurt to do so. "I'll drag you naked down to the Station Captain. This moment. Say yes."

She didn't answer. Instead, she sat up and pushed him down to the pillows. They'd paid extra for the largest bed on the station, and it still wasn't large enough. But it was a bed, and it was soft and clean. Brock lay back, grinning as Verda straddled his torso. She ran her nails softly over his chest, tracing the faint lines and swirls in his skin. She pinched his nipple, and he gasped, wrapping his hands around her slender waist.

"Take me, Verda." What he wanted to say was "Take me with you," but Brock was going home. There would be celebrations, friends and neighbors would come from all directions, abandoning the sky farms and fields to welcome Brock home.

She ran her hands up the ridges on his arms, they were almost flush to his skin now, the welts on his wrists nearly invisible. He cupped her breasts, thumbing her nipples, grinning as she gasped. Her hair cascaded down over her shoulders, brushing like a curtain around his face as she bent down to kiss him again and again.

He was hard, nearly weeping with desire, and when she clasped his cock, he cried out at the pressure of her hand, the slick moisture of her body. And then he was inside, clasped tightly, and she rode him, tears running down her face, dripping onto his cheeks.

"I love you, Brock. I love you . . ." and she came, her body dropping over his, her hips slamming down on him, nearly drawing him into this own searing climax. He rolled her to her back, mounted her and moved in her slowly . . . so slowly that she groaned again, clearly not finished.

"Greedy," he murmured. She was so small under him. He kept his weight on his arms, kept his *tengs* firmly sheathed so he didn't accidentally injure her. He moved with care, supporting her legs, drawing them up gently till he was wrapped in her body. When she clasped his ass, driving her nails into his skin, he knew she was there, so he let loose his control. And the leap of faith he took with Verda was just as frightening as leaping from the upper deck of the highest farm level, with only his *tengs* to control his fall.

He would let her go, but in his heart, he'd never lose her.

When it was done, he curved his body around her, holding her to his heart. He looked into the darkness of the small bedroom and waited for her to drift off to sleep.

When she woke that morning, he would be gone.

Her legs were more painful than usual. Of course, she'd been injured not so long ago, and the fight in the arena hadn't done her any good. Still, they hurt bad enough that she'd acquired walking braces and hated them more than she hated her legs. But as she journeyed down the sleek hall to the gateways, she was grudgingly grateful for their support. She could have taken a transport down, and was foolish not to, but the passage on the cruiser had been shockingly expensive. She hadn't told Brock how much, because he'd have tried to transfer more credits to her account. As it was, she'd discovered he'd paid far more for the *North Wind* than it was worth. And yet the cruiser was worth far more than any sum of money. It was the sole remaining artifact of her parents and her life with them. Painful as it had been to sell the ship, she was glad it had gone to Brock.

Now he could find his adventures when the time was right.

He hadn't offered to go with her. She hadn't asked. All she'd needed to see was the man he'd been with his family. With them, he'd laughed and cried. He looked young and really, he was young. It would be heartless to ask him to journey with her because he would not refuse. And she could no longer bear the pain of her injuries. In his world, everyone worked, and Brock would soon be back up in the sky farms. It wasn't a life for someone like her.

She glanced at the signs directing her way and groaned. She should have taken a transport. But, this was why she'd left an hour early. She'd packed the supplies she'd purchased into a rucksack that nestled in the small of her back. She wore clean, simple garments, loose trousers, a cinched tunic and a long, flowing vest. It was similar to the clothing she'd worn for years, but they were hers. Not the king's. And they were colorful, blue and green and gold.

She stopped to rest and saw the sign for her shuttle not far ahead. She leaned against the wall, tamping down panic. This was insane. It was futile. How would she negotiate a journey to another galaxy, when she couldn't even walk to the shuttle docks?

With a growl, she pushed herself upright and continued on. "I will throw these braces in the trash as soon as I find a can," she mumbled. But — she was moving faster and steadier than normal. She was just frustrated and tired. Heartsick. Lonely. The two weeks since Brock left had dragged on endlessly.

She'd always been alone and lonely, that was nothing new. But now she'd known friendship and love and the camaraderie of a kindred soul. Now she truly knew the ache of loneliness.

"It wouldn't have lasted anyway." She sighed at her own lie. "It could have lasted forever."

She reached the gate and hobbled forward, her brand new data unit gripped firmly in her hand. There was a crowd milling around, and she cursed under her breath. Boarding would be problematic at best, but there was a crowd of massive, huge . . . men. And women. All speaking in Braccin.

Her heart twisted, and Verda collapsed into a molded steel seat, dropping her head to her hands. She listened to the babble of their language. There was laughter, and there were tears. She didn't understand the spoken language that well, but they were bidding farewell to someone. Their voices were gruff and warm, and she felt a stab of homesickness for a place she'd never been. Verda struggled to her feet and pushed into the crowd around the attendant who was checking passengers. She'd take a shuttle from the station, out to the distant moorings where the huge cruiser awaited. That would be her new home for far too long. She had no idea how she'd pass the time.

Would she see the Braccin who was traveling? Would they know Brock? She laughed at the idea. It was a massive planet with millions of residents. Of course they wouldn't know Brock.

"Brock!" A woman's voice called out just yards from her,

and Verda looked up into the woman's beautiful face. Like Brock, she was dark, with whorls and swirls etched into her skin. She blinked at the similarity.

"Brother, is this her?"

She stood up, dumbfounded. The crowd grew tight around her and Verda felt dizzy and unstable. If someone were to bump into her . . .

The wall of people parted, and the wall of a man's body took their place. He wore white. She didn't remember him ever wearing white. The shirt was a light fabric, the trousers loose and flowing. She looked up into Brock's face, and he was smiling.

No, he was grinning.

Before she had the chance to leap into his arms, he'd caught her up and held her in the air above him. She steadied herself on his shoulders, and she laughed.

"Got her!" he shouted, and a cheer went up. "Didn't think I'd let you get away, did you?"

"Brock!" He lowered her till she was comfortably cradled in his arms. "What are you doing?"

They were surrounded now, by a wall of Braccin. A sea of Braccin! They were large, forbidding, and all grinning happily.

"Verda, my love. Meet my family. My father, Pyotr. My mother, Dorna." He swung her in the direction of a handsome older couple. Their coloring was the same as Brock's, and his face resembled his mother more than his father. "Sister Lettie and my brother Bram. My younger brother Evan." He went on to introduce wives and cousins and neighbors from down the road. She nodded, baffled at all the names and faces. There were other introductions . . . family and friends. A city leader. Perhaps a complete stranger, was in there as well. Her hands were clasped, her cheeks kissed. Several were crying.

"You understand, we just got him back, it's so hard to see him go again." His mother spoke softly, yet clearly over the chatter. "But nothing is forever, and we know now he's going for a good reason."

"This time," Brock's father growled.

"Leaving?" Verda glared at Brock. "Put me down."

"Nope. Not letting go till we're both on board that behemoth out there."

She blinked rapidly, not sure what she was hearing. Or that she was hearing it right.

"You're going?"

"I'm coming with you. I got the last available fare. Thankfully, I was able to upgrade to a double, for larger species."

"You're coming?"

"No dirty talk," he whispered in her ear. "My parents—"

She smacked his shoulder. "You're coming with me?"

"I couldn't let you go, Verda. What would my life be without you?"

She stared at him, framing his face with her hands. And then she kissed him.

There might have been laughter, and there might have been cheers. Brock set her down as he exchanged long, hard embraces with his parents and family. He then looked critically at the braces on her legs.

"We can do better than that, Verda."

She let out a heavy sigh of relief. "Thank goodness." He bent to pick her up again, and she stepped back. I'm doing this part myself."

He smiled. "I think that's a very good idea." He bent down and kissed her softly on the forehead. "I love your strength, my warrior," he whispered.

"Can you do this, Brock? Can you leave them again?"

"For you, Verda, I can. It's what people do when they love each other. Now I'm free . . . we're both free. And my family will be waiting for us."

"You love me?"

He touched a finger to her lips. "I love you."

She kissed the tip of his finger. "I love you, Brock." It was a quiet declaration of forever.

That was it, then. They were going together. And someday, they'd come back.

They turned, looked at his assembled family. He started to speak, but she put a hand on his arm.

"Thank you for the gift of your son." She looked up at Brock and slipped her hand into his. "We'll be back. I promise."

With a final, lingering look at the people who lived in Brock's heart, Verda walked down the gentle slope of the ramp, feeling his presence at her back.

EPILOGUE

The Vash were real. And they were magical. Miraculous.

Somehow, they'd heard the story of the banished princess who'd been crippled by her uncle, and they'd been waiting for Verda. Perhaps the gentle, nocturnal species had abilities other than their vaunted healing skills.

The procedure had been difficult, as so many years had passed without treatment. After hours of consults and meetings, they'd decided to work with a surgeon, who opened her legs painlessly, gingerly exposing scar tissue and mangled sinews, while the Vash worked from the inside, painstakingly piecing together fiber and tissue, reconnecting the tiniest vessels and veins.

Within a day, she was on her feet. In a week, she was jogging on a streamlined moving track. Within a month, the pain was but a ghost of what it had been.

The Vash were so honored that she'd sacrificed everything to seek them out, that they worked for free. The Valoran surgeon frowned, grumbled and also dropped his fees. He was grim but good-hearted.

Verda lay on her bed in the healing center, one leg extended in the air above her. She flexed her ankle, grinning when she felt the pain of a normal, healthy stretch.

"Today's deliveries."

Brock filled the door, a smile on his face and a huge pile of flowers in his arms. They'd become celebrities among the Vash . . . and other Coalition species as well. The slave girl and the gladiator—the story of their escape from the arena

231

and the journey up the mountain had leaked, probably from a survivor. Brock suspected Peri Stroop. Her miraculous recovery was being detailed in news publications and broadcast on entertainment networks. Storefronts featured limited edition images of the two, as well as old data books from Brock's fighting days.

Amazingly enough, local laws enforced subject royalties, so Brock and Verda were earning a substantial profit. Still, she was impatient to move on, back to anonymity.

"Crazy news coming in from Attigua." Brock placed the bundles of flowers on a dresser and then sat next to her on the bed. "The king was located, and when investigations revealed that he'd knowingly covered up the effect of the White Star on the planet, he was tried before a citizen committee. As it turns out, the effects of the solar waves could have been mitigated. Those scientists you knew provided data indicating the star's flare cycle will soon end. Jamis was sentenced to death."

Verda let out a long breath. "Who pronounced the sentence?"

"His daughter Janine." Brock took her hand. Verda felt dizzy. "She wept. And then she oversaw his execution."

She sat very still, staring down at her legs. The scars were all but invisible. The pain was a phantom of what it had been. Her uncle had ordered those injuries.

"I can't imagine the cover-up being worthy of a death sentence. Perhaps exile, or imprisonment."

Brock bit his lip. "He wasn't executed for the cover-up. There was another charge."

She looked at him in question.

"Regicide. Fratricide. He was convicted of killing the king and queen. Your parents." She said nothing, so he continued. "Witnesses came forward on your behalf, recounting his mistreatment of you, and the maiming of your legs."

"This case was argued before his daughter?"

Brock nodded.

Her heart was beating so hard that Verda felt like she was panting. "Do you—you knew her in a different way than I did. Do you think this is a power play on her part? To claim the throne?" Yet who would want to reign over a broken planet?

Brock shook his head. "She sent an offer to you. A fiscal settlement and the throne. She says she'll accept exile, if necessary."

Janine. Janine was offering Verda the throne. Riches. She shook her head, as though to clear it. "Message her. Say the proper thing, Brock, but I don't want the throne. The money belongs to the people of Attigua. It should be used for the recovery." She nibbled her lip. "I believe my cousin might be exactly the right ruler for the planet now. She's obviously got a conscience. And she's tougher than I'd be. I may not like her, but I have to admire what she's doing."

Brock reached for her hand and squeezed it. "Now that all that is out of the way, I'm told that you're being discharged."

"When?" She sat up, excitement warring with the pain and grief. "Where will we go?"

"Are you ready to go home?"

Verda looked at Brock, marveling over how happiness had changed him. His step was light, he no longer looked surly or suspicious. Or lonely.

"I think we should go on a honeymoon. Your family couldn't begrudge us that."

"One has to be married—" He blinked. "Are you finally saying yes?"

"It's what people do when they love one another." She squeezed his hand. "I just want you to tell me one thing. Why did you leave home all those years ago?" Verda stroked his cheek. His color was good. This planet was light and clean, and they both spent time out in the sun. Brock grew restless when she napped, so he'd resumed training, though not for fighting. He was practicing the forms she'd taught him to keep him alive in the ring. Her parents' arts wouldn't die with Verda. She and Brock would teach his nieces and nephews, and anyone else who wished to learn.

Maybe someday their own children.

Brock looked up, out the large window of her room, out to the copious garden that filled their patio. "I left looking for adventure. I thought I could make money fighting, then leave when I chose." He smiled at his own foolishness. "I never wanted to be famous. I just wanted to see the universe. To chase stars and see amazing sights."

"Then let's go see the universe. Let's go find adventure. Your family will understand, and your home will still be there."

Brock clasped her hand and kissed her knuckles, and then her lips. He rested a hand over her heart. "Verda, my love, my home is right here."

About Belinda McBride

Belinda is an award-winning, top selling author of erotic romance, speculative fiction and LGBTQ romance. She lives in far Northern California with her family and a pack of Siberian Huskies.

A graduate of CSU Chico, she managed to attend the notorious party school without once getting drunk, arrested or appearing in a "Girls Gone Wild" video. Her main focus of study was classical and archival history, cultural anthropology and theatre arts.

After several years in the workforce. Belinda purchased a laptop computer and from there, knew that her childhood dream of being an author would come to life.

Xanadu
By
Astrid Cooper

XANADU

"Is the bitch coming to the party?"

"By that, do you mean Doctor Duran?"

Suleah gasped and swivelled around in her chair to confront the speaker. She grimaced. Someone had left the audiocom switched on. As she reached out to disconnect, another voice joined the others.

"Even the ice-maiden has to celebrate Empire Day!"

"I'd rather not with us."

As Tracey laughed at Mik's retort, Suleah snapped the connection closed. For a moment her eyes flooded with uncharacteristic tears. She *was* a bitch. A cold-hearted bitch. She had worked long and hard to earn the distinction. A slave to her profession, ice-water flowed in her veins—these taunts, and more, she had heard from colleagues on every assignment she had taken.

But today it hurt. *Today* . . .

She pushed away from her console and strode to the wall. At the wave of her hand, part of the wall grew transparent. She gazed upon a vista from hell. Red sky, red soil, it was difficult to tell where heaven ended, and earth began. Overhead the single red sun shone feebly. A dead world with a dying star—nothing to interest Imperial Exploration, except for the disappearances.

A thousand beings in the last ten years had vanished within the star system, one scientist from the planet's surface. Not a great number in comparison to the millions who traversed the space-lanes, but an anomaly to interest some

237

bureaucrat, perhaps prodded by the relatives or friends of the missing.

Missing—how she hated the word! Suleah bit down the regret, the recriminations, her attention diverted. Outside, thirty feet beyond the base perimeter, she saw the twisting rainbow. On this world, the light played strange tricks on the Earth-born. They saw coruscating lights that did not register on any sensor, and rainbows shimmering over land where rain had not fallen for millennia. These miniature light-tornadoes were the only remarkable thing on the planet, that had, so far, defied explanation. She squinted at the apparition until her eyes stung.

Ah, Suleah . . . Sweet Suleah!

She gasped at the words echoing in her mind. *His* words from a time long ago.

Turning away, she saw the bottle of *Moet* on the table. Vintage champagne; nineteen-ninety-nine. Bottled two-hundred and forty years before he had died.

He'd given her the *Moet*. His, an old family, wealthy beyond imagining, thought nothing of such gifts, such indulgences. Yet, he had not evaded his duty to the Empire, though his family connections could have seen him take a safe posting. No, he loved the danger, the adventure. A commander of a fighter squadron, he'd flown that extra mission, standing in for a friend, just hours before the truce. He had died for nothing, as others before him . . .

War never decided who was right, only who was left—a Terran saying, centuries old, but still apt. She'd used it often to challenge Gilland's commitment to the war, the futility of blasting and being blasted out of existence. And for what? Possession of a disputed piece of space, when there was, surely, enough space for everyone? Gil had said she didn't understand. He was born into politics—she was not.

Suleah walked to the table, voice activating the 3-d memory disc. The hologram hovered before her.

She saw his face, the lop-sided smile, his dark hair tied elegantly back with the black and gold Imperial Ribbon. The black, high-necked uniform hugging his tall, lean torso. She closed her eyes to remember the feel and smell of him. Now, so difficult.

Oh, God. Panic clawed at her. Her memories were fading! She'd clung onto those images, with the hope that one day he would be found alive, as others before him were found alive, having been presumed lost in the far-flung battles for independence.

Four years she had waited. Four long, lonely years. She had studied and finished her planetology and terraforming degree, her distinctions allowing her to choose whichever lucrative post she wanted. To forget, she took the distant and the difficult. But she could not outrun the pain.

On every anniversary of Empire Day, the day the old Earth confederacy had gained its independence from the Jalak oppressors, the memories returned, biting deep. Haunting.

Just this once she had thought to share the celebration, to break open the *Moet* and drink to life with her outpost colleagues. To call a truce to her own private demons.

Is the bitch coming to the party?

I'd rather not with us.

Suleah grasped the bottle and ripped off the foil wrapper, wincing as her third finger caught on its jagged edge. She ignored the cut, eased off the cork and poured the bubbling liquid into the glass. Delicate gold-edged crystal, it was an anachronism amid the plastic and metal of her quarters. The goblet's mate she had broken the day the space-gram arrived . . . *Commander Gilland D'Ambrose missing in action.*

Missing implied a possible return. Offering hope.

It had taken her months of persistence to discover the details. Years to understand that 'missing' meant lost forever.

Gilland was gone, but she remained with one glass and an

ancient bottle of champagne—his last gift to her, delivered with his last kiss.

Suleah drank the first glass without thinking. The second glass she savoured, as Gilland had taught her. He'd taught her a lot. His aristocratic ways, his tastes. How to love.

The third glass of champagne caressed her mouth and throat, warming her emptiness, its sweetness replacing the bitterness.

Sully . . .

The hairs on the nape of her neck lifted. Only Gil called her that. She glanced over her shoulder, half expecting to see him leaning against the wall, arms folded, that smile of his, which turned her inside out . . .

"Suleah! Doctor Duran, are you there?"

She drew in a breath. Not his voice, but Connor's, the CEO of outpost twenty-three, Rigel sector, coming from her wristlet hailer.

"Yes, I'm here. What do you want?"

"Sorry to worry you. I need someone to check out station six. It's not registering. Can you?"

Was this a clever ploy to get rid of the bitch, so they could party on without her? Suleah forced a bitter smile. "Sure."

"When you get back, join us in the lounge. We always celebrate Empire Day."

I don't, she wanted to scream.

"You will come, yes?"

"I'll try."

Connor's eyes had been warm, frankly admiring, the last time they had spoken. He'd continued with his pursuit, even in the face of her frostiest responses. The man must be space-happy, or desperate. Probably both.

Suleah downed the last of the champagne, ignoring the giddiness. She hadn't been drunk in . . . *stars!* Four years. Hadn't been laid either in four years. That thought she quashed. Ice-water ran through her veins.

The small reconnaissance ship flew over the flat terrain. Occasionally the vehicle bucked, caught in a crosswind. The movement made Suleah queasy. Too much champagne on an empty stomach.

She halted the rover, and it settled with a hiss against the sand. She checked her enviro-suit one last time and dragged on the helmet.

The door slid open, and she stepped outside. The dust, like fine powder, floated up, swirling around her. It stuck to everything, that red dust. Invaded, permeated. Long after she left the planet, she knew she would remember its gritty, bitter taste. Even with the pressure locks, the sand managed to infiltrate every building of the outpost, glitching equipment and giving everyone a rash.

Suleah strode to the monitor, sending up puffballs of dust in her wake. "Stars curse it!" She saw the equipment casing had broken free and a dozen fibre wires dangled from the mainframe, the wind, and the dust acting in concert— planetary saboteurs against the alien intruders.

"Suleah!"

His voice, again. The wind whipped around her, whispering, dragging at her body like fingers. She shook her head.

"Suleah, remember! Remember!"

"Go to hell!" she yelled at the tormenting wind. The champagne made her think and feel things better left unthought, unfelt.

"Suuulllllyyyyy!"

She turned. In the distance, maybe twenty feet away, she saw it—a twisting cyclone-rainbow of red, gold and blue. The phenomenon was rarely seen so close.

Suleah fumbled with the recorder at her belt and aimed the sensor. Nothing registered; it never did. The light edged closer, retreated, moved closer, before vanishing abruptly.

She returned the recorder to her belt sheath.

Suleah laser-joined the wires and snapped the housing closed, soldering it for good measure. The wind stepped up its moaning and its speed. *Time to get back to base.*

She climbed into the rover and tore off her helmet as the hatch sealed behind her. Outside the wind whipped up the dust so that it scraped against the sides of the rover like a million scratching nails. The noise always set her teeth on edge.

She switched on the engine. Nothing. *Stars!* She tried again. *Deader than . . .* Suleah bit back the thought. The rotors wheezed and slowly kicked into life. She punched in the autopilot and co-ordinates.

The rover shuddered amid the squeal of protesting grav-rockets. The thing would have to be serviced and soon! Like everything on the outpost, it was falling apart because of the dust. The ship finally reached altitude, fifteen hundred feet, just above the seething cloud.

She settled back and closed her eyes. An hour to base. Time enough to get rid of the lethargy from too much champagne. And then what? Return to her quarters or join the party. So not spoiled for choice.

The rover lurched, startling her awake. Another jolt sent the vehicle dipping sideways, flinging her from the seat. She had forgotten the basic safety precautions of the harness and paid the price as she collided against the instrument panel at her left.

Suleah dragged herself, hand over hand, to the control panel and flung herself into the chair, snapping on the harness.

The rover coughed and bucked. For a moment it halted, before slowly rotating nose first towards the planet's surface. The cyclonic wind lifted the vehicle, flipping it end over end.

Suleah desperately fought the controls, trying to re-start

the engine, while the computer screamed *Danger. Proximity.* The rover fell metres, then heaved upward in a cyclone stream. Up and down.

She punched out a distress call . . .

Suleah awoke to the distant sound of running water. A fragrant coolness soothed her skin. Familiar, that scent. Through the fuzziness, she struggled to remember. Honan, the rarest of spices. Six-months pay just for a drop. On leave, before his last mission, Gilland had massaged a full bottle of it into her body, lavishing her with his hands and his kisses.

She snapped her eyelids open to find herself lying in a rose-covered arbour, naked save for the sheet of white silk draped over her. Beneath her were cushions of velvet and satin. *What the* . . . She pushed herself upright.

"Awake at last. You've slept the day away, darling."

Suleah gasped and turned. Smiling, Gilland strode to her, dressed in a long flowing robe of azure silk. His grey eyes were alight to her.

"Gilland?"

"Who else?"

He laughed, and the sound of it was like . . . It had been so long since she had heard his laugh! So long. She struggled to remember — something important. But what . . .

Her, but not her, crashing some stars-forsaken machine in a hell-hole. She shook her head. No, it was only a dream. Gilland was not dead. He was here with her in their garden.

He squatted before her, stroking her feet. His smile was teasing, light. His hands touched, while his eyes promised. Ah, what they promised!

Gilland leaned forward, straddling her, his mouth over hers. For a moment she melted into his embrace. His strong arms about her provided a gentle sheltering. She breathed in his spice-scent as she kissed him. A soft, intense kiss . . .

But not Gilland. Not as she remembered . . . Something, a subtle change. She tore her mouth from his. "Who are you?"

He laughed. "How can you forget me, the man who worships you with his body? Ah . . . Sully, now I understand. You are disoriented. I gave you too much honan."

She glanced down. Her skin shone with oil, and she smelled the unmistakable honey-musk. Silence stretched between them, and the only sound, her heart thudding in her ears.

Suleah swallowed against the panic in her throat. The panic of her dream. "I was asleep?"

He grinned. "You needed to rest, after my demands of last night . . ."

Her blush heated her skin from her head to her heels. Their appetites for one another had always been voracious. How she wanted him inside her, now, filling her with that distinctive, intense possession of his. Her body ached . . .

She drew a hand over her face. No! Gilland was dead, four years dead. She knew it for a certainty. *But how? How?*

"I'm dreaming because Gil is dead."

Smiling, he sat back on his haunches, his eyes darkly intense. He held out his hands, flexing his fingers. "I am alive. Touch me, feel me. In fact, I insist you touch me, just to make certain."

"I—"

His gaze traced over her and she snatched up the sheet to hide her breasts.

"Sully."

"You know my name?"

"Of course I do, as I know you in all ways."

"You aren't Gilland."

"Then who am I?" he demanded, irritation crisping his voice.

"I don't know. I remember an accident. I was in the rover

on . . ." A hand flew to her mouth. "I must be dead. Or delusional."

Gilland frowned. "Neither. You are being difficult. Too much honan, too much champagne, too much sex. I shall have to ration you."

Suleah gasped. These words of Gilland's had been spoken so long ago in the heat of their first quarrel. Their acrimony had dissolved as they had both laughed. Who would be the rationer and the rationee? They could not make a decision, so had retired to bed for an intimate debate.

Tears stung her eyes as she stroked Gilland's hand. "*Cheri*," she whispered.

A disc-servitor hovered nearby, chiming.

"It is dinner time." Gil stood in a quick, fluid movement that rustled his robe like dry autumn leaves. He raised her to her feet and held out a cream silk gown. "Do you intend to walk to the house naked, or wrapped in a sheet?" The deep timbre of his voice rippled with laughter.

Suleah turned and thrust her hands into the sleeves, shrugging the robe over her body. His fingers lingered on her shoulders, searing her skin. She leaned into his body, to savour him. Intoxicating, this man, an addiction, like some heady drug.

He gently pushed her forward. "If we stand here any longer, Sully, we will be late for dinner. To distract me, tell me what you were dreaming. You looked at me as if I was a ghost."

"I thought you were." She turned and pressed into him, her body inch for inch against his length. No ghost, this man. Warm, lean, hard. All man, her Gilland.

Laughing, he lifted her away from him. "You want me again, so soon?"

Suleah frowned. Gil had never said that before. Always voracious for each other, neither had ever said no to the other's demands. Maybe he was tiring of her? His friends had said he would — sooner or later.

His family and friends hoped sooner . . . Some of her friends, too, wanted the *mesalliance* to end. Their betrayals had hurt the most.

Above her the protective transparent dome rippled, sending shadows like birds of prey swooping across the grass. She glanced up. The screens had turned opaque.

"What's happening?" she asked Gilland. She'd never trusted those screens. Gilland had built a transparent dome around their asteroid to appease her — she couldn't imagine the construction cost.

"Just a . . . an energy fluctuation. Nothing to worry about, sweetheart."

The artificial asteroids circling Polarium were home to the super-rich and powerful. Gilland owned two asteroids, their house built on the largest, and most distant, so they could watch the swirling oceans of light tearing across Polarium's crystalline surface. Sometimes chunks of crystal were flung into space to form rings around the giant purple star. Gravity eventually brought the crystals back to Polarium, but until then, the sun refracted the rings, illuminating the night sky like hundreds of fairy lights.

Unique, Polarium — no wonder so many travelled the galaxy to watch the formation and destruction of the rings.

Our own special theatre, Gilland had said, insisting that the screens and the dome would never fail, their home forever safe.

Suleah relaxed as the vista returned to normal. The giant star and its swarm of asteroids with homes and spires built impossibly high, and gardens under screens that protected them from the vacuum of space. If a screen should ever fail — Gilland had always laughed at her fear of dying —

Dying . . . dead planet. Rigel Alpha 23 . . .

Suleah gasped as pain lanced her side. Gilland turned to

her.

"What is it, Sully?"

"Nothing." She shook her head. *Nothing. Just a bad dream.* She took Gil's hand, again. "I love you."

His smile was the caress of summer. "*Mon amour.*"

Gil always had the touch of the theatrical. *Mon amour,* 'my love' in his ancestral tongue.

Ahead of her, the three-storied chateau glittered in the afternoon sun. She always loved this home, their retreat. Built from fire-crystal, the walls shimmered with the colours of the Polarium spectrum that in addition to the Terran rainbow comprised of gold and silver. Above the main building, with its four copper turrets, the bronze dome, resembling an ancient cathedral dominated the skyline. Xanadu. They named their home after the old Terran poem — Xanadu with its stately pleasure dome . . .

The crystal-embossed doors slid open with a sigh, and immediately they were besieged with servitors. No humans lived in their retreat. She and Gilland favoured privacy. They rarely invited friends to their home; rarer still were the visits of the few family members who maintained contact with Gilland. He, the errant son, who chose his woman and his life, and be damned to family expectations.

Suleah followed her servitors to her own apartments, while Gilland strode down the opposite passageway. They kept their own apartments, to pursue their own work, and hobbies, coming together at night.

Once inside her room, she slipped the robe from her body and stepped into the cleansing cubicle. She chose water instead of laser beams. Warm, fragrant liquid swirled around her, over her, cleansing, soothing, reminding her of Gil's touch. Gil's touch . . . her body pulsed with wanting him. Again. After dinner, she would have him. She'd bed him in a new way, tease him. Gil enjoyed her inventiveness. She'd read *Kama Sutra* so often to keep Gilland amused.

The cleanser fanned her with warm air, drying her. Returning to her bedroom, she smiled to see the fabric arranged on the four-poster bed. Copper chiffon, decorated with crystal seed pearls, another gift from Gil.

She stepped into the gown and servitors flew around, lifting the diaphanous garment, fastening it about her body. She raised one foot and then the other for the machines to place sandals on her feet.

Suleah sank down onto the chair while the servitors hovered, like fireflies, brushing and styling her hair.

"No," she said, frowning at the reflector. "Leave it loose." She waved away the jewellery proffered by another machine. Suleah leaned forward, studying her reflection. The copper gown matched her hair. In stark contrast, her eyes were dark, her skin cinnamon. She programmed the servitor to replenish her makeup. Her eyelids were metallic green, her black lashes long and thick. Her lips shimmered an opalescent pink, and her cheeks a faint rose.

The servitor offered her a range of perfumes. She chose 'Egyptia,' her favourite. It reminded her of the times she spent in her mother's house in Old Cairo.

The doorbell chimed.

"Come," she said, turning.

Gilland strode into the room and halted. His grey eyes widened, as he gazed upon her. She tossed her head.

"You stare at me so, sir."

He paused as if struggling to find the correct response. Gil was never at a loss for words. "I admire loveliness, Suleah. *Stars!* You are beautiful!"

She admired him, too, the deep crimson of his tabard, hugging the width of his shoulders, the black 'tards highlighting his long, muscular legs and the soft, jewelled slippers that on another man might be considered effeminate.

But not Gilland. He wore his hair loose about his collar. She much preferred it that way to the austere tail required by Imperial Star Service regulations.

"I have something for you," he said, holding out a long black velvet box.

She rose to her feet and accepted it. Opening the container, she gasped in shock. Exquisite and so rare, the strand of pearls, since no one killed oysters, the shells died of natural causes, their jewels collected over many years.

"Gil, you shouldn't have."

Again, that perplexed frown at her outburst. "I thought it would please you. If you prefer, I will gift you something else?"

She shook her head. "The pearls are perfect. It's just you spoil me. Too many gifts." She felt the imbalance—his gifts, her acceptance of them. Rarely could she reciprocate. What did you give a man who could buy the star system of Polarium?

"Ah." He smiled. "It gives me such pleasure to . . . spoil you."

"Will you fasten them for me?" She turned around.

After a brief hesitation, she felt him lift the hair from her nape. She shivered as he leaned into her, a deliberate movement to contact her body. He fastened the catch and drew her back against him. They regarded one another in the mirror. She moved in his arms and raised her face for his kiss.

His lips touched hers, a tentative exploration, deepening suddenly, tongues questing, bodies entwining. The thick velvet of his hair slipped between her fingers as she cupped his neck, holding him still for her kiss. She raised her leg and his thigh settled between hers.

He broke away from her and held her out at arms' length. "Kiss me like that, again and . . ."

"And?" She arched a brow.

"Our dinner will spoil."

"Perhaps I should eat you instead."

She laughed at his stunned look. Despite his experience with women, Gil was often shocked — when she set her mind to teasing.

He offered her his arm, and they walked down the passageway, to the great dome. Their stately pleasure dome.

Inside, the room was hung with filigree brass lanterns. In the centre of the floor, a round carpet of mottled green and blue and red was encircled by many large cushions. An ornate copper brazier, burning sandalwood, cast a red glowing shadow over the opalescent walls.

They sat opposite one another on cushions, while servitors floated before them, offering food and drink. All her favourites were displayed on the platters.

Suleah bit into the sliver of carris root. "Ugh! There's something wrong with the dispenser, Gil. This doesn't have any taste. Well, that's not true. It tastes like . . . dust." Dust — something she should remember. Red dust . . . clinging to everything . . . Her temples pulsed as she tried to recall —

"Come here, Sully."

"Patience, Gil."

He laughed and joined her side. Taking her into his arms, he kissed her deeply, thoroughly. His mouth slipped to her cheek, to her neck, to the hollow at the base of her throat. Now, this was more like Gil, taking the initiative, slow, thorough. She arched back to accommodate his questing.

Gilland pulled away, and Suleah regarded him, puzzled.

What was he up to, playing the reticent, inexperienced lover?

"I prefer to sample you in small doses, for now. But later . . ."

His smile and his eyes made promises that made her writhe from inside to out.

A servitor, carrying a bottle of champagne, hovered at Gilland's elbow. *Moet.* Their favourite.

"Allow me," Sully said. Gilland waved the servitor to her, and she carefully took the bottle from its mechanical claw. She sat cross-legged, the bottle between her knees.

"I envy that bottle," Gilland said, reclining against the cushions, his dark gaze sultry. He'd said that a long time ago, their first night together in Xanadu.

Suleah smiled to remember. and lifted the foil with her fingernail. "Ouch!" She drew back her hand as the metal wrap sliced through the skin of her second finger. "I . . . Oh, no!"

The world, her mind, turned inside out with the memory. Dread seeped through her veins.

"What's wrong?" Gilland asked, sitting up, no longer smiling.

Suleah studied her hand, the wound on her second finger. The older wound on her third finger. Both from a *Moet* wrapper. Now and . . . *stars!* Before. *Before!* Red dust clinging—now she remembered. The pain, the fear as she fought to regain control of her flyer. Her side ached, her temples throbbed from injuries inflicted but somehow healed. Or, was it all a dream?

Flinging the bottle away, she jumped to her feet, staring at him. His troubled gaze met hers. For a moment his grey eyes were lit by rainbows.

"Who are you?" she demanded.

He frowned. "This grows tiresome, Sully. If you are in the mood for a game, I know something more entertaining than this feigned loss of memory."

She stared at him. A typical Gilland response. How she wished he was her Gil. But his kiss, his touch was different, subtly different. She had wanted to believe.

"I cut my finger," she said. "Just now. Just like before on

the Rigel outpost."

"Your dream!" A hint of ice had infiltrated his voice, so, too, his eyes.

"No! A dream doesn't do this!" She held out her hand, indicating her finger. The one bloodied, the other with a faint seam of an old scar.

Her gaze met his. His eyes swirled with rainbows, red dominant. Oh, stars!

"What are you?" she whispered.

Gilland flung himself to his feet and spread his hands.

"Don't come near me!" Suleah bent down and lifted the *Moet* bottle, brandishing it.

"It will be the first time anyone has used champagne as a defensive weapon against me."

How much like Gil, that last remark. She swallowed down hard. This was not *her* Gil — *must remember that*!

"I know you aren't Gilland D'Ambrose. Who are you? What are you? I want explanations, not lies."

He sighed. "Will you sit down?"

"No." She glanced around. "This place isn't real. Is it a hologram?"

"What is reality, Suleah? By your definition, this place cannot exist. Yet it does. It is real."

There was a shifting of substance around her and where moments before she stood in the chateau, now she found herself in the leafy courtyard garden of her family home and in the distance the hazy outline of the great pyramid. Her mother squatted down before one of the garden beds, weeding it meticulously. Her mother, young and beautiful. Her pet kitten, Khan, wound around her mother's hands as she worked. Khan was now eighteen years old. These were her childhood memories, dredged up by whom? By *what*?

Suleah forced her gaze to Gilland. "No lies. Who are you?" The silence lengthened between them.

"I am Gilland. As much as I can be."

Another blurring and the next reality found them both in Suleah's stark outpost apartment. Yet she knew it for the illusion it was. Gilland stalked around its confines.

"To live in such a place, no wonder your species is so unhappy. There is neither beauty nor grace. I much prefer the other."

Suleah blinked and found herself, once more, in Xanadu. From somewhere she heard music. Gentle, low. *Parsifal* — her favourite opera.

"This is all done for you, Suleah, for your comfort."

"I was killed in the crash. That's it, isn't it?"

He took a step towards her. "In a manner of speaking."

She again brandished the bottle of *Moet*. "Stay back!"

"I mean you no harm, Suleah. Least of all you."

"Is this heaven, Gil? We're both ghosts. You can tell me the truth. I've never feared my death." *There are worse things in life than death. And if you are with me . . .*

"There are worse things in life than death," he said, frowning. "What has happened to make you believe this?"

"So we're ghosts, and you can read my thoughts?"

Gil cocked his head to one side as if listening to something — maybe someone? Cold tracked up Suleah's spine. "It is true; we are ghosts of our former selves. But so much more in this reality. In time, we will be able to communicate mind to mind, although I do enjoy the sensation of speech. The resonance of the mind has its beauty, but so too, the spoken word." He paused. "You were brought here, Suleah. Oh, how can I explain all that I must? Live here with me. We can make it heaven if you wish."

"Where is *here*?"

Again, he cocked his head to one side, his eyes turning glassy. She caught another's thought, a sensation of surprise. "They said you would be difficult. Your transition was — "

"My what?"

"Transition." He spread his hands. "You are on the planet you have unimaginatively named outpost twenty-three, Rigel sector."

"That's not possible. Only the survey team lives there."

"True, in the reality you know, but we both exist in another reality. This place we now inhabit was untouched by destruction." He paused. "I will not hurt you, Suleah. Can we at least sit and talk over the champagne? It is a shame that it goes to waste."

"I'm not sitting and talking to you. And you can have your damn champagne all to yourself. I want out of here. Now. I want to return—"

"That is impossible."

Suleah swallowed the panic and the fear. This person, no, this creature, had lied to her before, why not now?

"I am not lying. I cannot do so to you, or any other."

"All humans lie."

"But I am not hu ... Ah! *Touché!*" He smiled bitterly, admiration in his eyes. "Clever of you, Sully, to entrap me thus. I am not human, but I can be so many things to you."

"Then what are you?"

"I am a who, not a what. I am as real to you as you ..."

"You aren't Gilland."

"I am more than Gilland. Or so I could be to you if you would allow it. Allow me, please."

Suleah studied him, trying to remain detached. Stifling her fear, her anger, her outrage. Become the scientist, Sully. Become the cold-hearted bitch, the ice-maiden—analytical, unemotional. So hard to do, because this creature looked like her Gil in every detail. She wanted him to be real. Perhaps ... she shook her head. No, it was a nightmare, not a dream!

"We always dared to dream, you and I, Sully. Why do you resist this? It is your desire."

"Damn it all; it's not my desire. And I no longer dream. Dreams are lies." She blinked against the sting of tears.

"Words and dreams are only lies if you make them so."

"Then what is this about us, if not a lie?"

"A different perception of reality."

She laughed without humour. "A fancy way to say a lie."

"I exist, as you, in this dimension. It is our Retreat."

Retreat from what? Who? She was scared again.

Gil shook his head. "Have no fear here, Suleah. Outside this Retreat fear and pain exists. Here, there are only ... dreams. Dreams that can be real. My species was once like you, flesh and blood creatures with ambitions and passions and a tendency for self-destruction. Your kind managed to evade the desolation we inflicted upon ourselves, our world. A few sensed the oncoming catastrophe and escaped."

"To space?"

"No. We long ago ceased to travel the cosmos. We had more than one universe as our playground."

"So you were able to move between the layers of existence?"

His eyes glowed, his look one of pride as he studied her. "Few who come here understand this so quickly. You are special, Suleah." He smiled at her derisive snort. "In our folly we shaped dimensions. We forged a Retreat by the very same process that made a wasteland of our planet. Now, we exist on our world, but in a different dimension. In time, we learned to harness other powers to shape-change our Retreat, so that it could be anything we desired."

"How long have you been here?"

"I? Three thousand years."

"Then you're immortal?"

"No. In my other form, I could exist for four millennia, but I do not wish for longevity. To live forever alone is the worst existence. You know that, as I." Sorrow shadowed his face.

"You know a lot about me," she challenged.

"I watched you from the first day you arrived."

"You *watched* me?" Hair prickled on her nape.

"From the window. You saw me as a pattern of light, a rainbow you called it. That is my reality before I undertook the Change."

"I don't understand."

"Of course not. So much to explain. I would have come to you in dreams, prepared you, to avert the horror you feel now." He spread his hands. "Your accident meant there was no time for the usual initiation. We choose our companions with care. Those who are alone, sad, sometimes dying. We restore them, give them life and hope. And love." He smiled. "While you slept I intercepted your memories, of your lover, of your Xanadu, so that you would awaken in familiar surroundings. There is so much I do not understand, so much I wish to learn."

Suleah stepped back from him. "You crawled around my mind without permission, extracting memories, feeding your illusions to seduce me. It's disgusting!"

"No."

"Yes, I say."

"I meant no harm, Sully."

"Don't call me that. Only Gil was allowed, and he's dead." Hope flared within her. "You said you can restore . . ."

"We can only retrieve those who are within our star system. Your Gilland died a thousand light years from here."

"But you said you can traverse the dimensions . . ."

"Once, we could. The ability is now lost to us. We expend all our energy to maintain our Retreat."

"And to kidnap people here." Her accusation made him blanch. His eyes sparked red before returning to Gilland-grey.

"There is always choice, not force. All come willingly. There are many existing here. Your kind and mine. Other species, as infinitely diverse as the cosmos. We live here in peace" He waved his hand. "But beyond this Retreat, there is much discourse."

Suleah frowned, intrigued despite herself. Many alien encounters ended badly for humans—the Jalak war was one such tragedy. Now, aliens gave humans wide berth. The Jalaks called humans a scourge on the galaxy, not without some justification. Star systems had been devastated by the war, dying suns testament to the depths some humans descended to gain victory over their oppressors. The Empire was trying to right the wrongs, but the Jalak Federation and their allies were unforgiving.

"Was the accident so bad that I would have died?" she asked.

"Yes. To save you, I brought you here, before you were prepared. Before I asked your permission. I would have explained, but there was no time." He paused. "You discovered the deception with the wound on your finger. The transference heals all injuries. The small cut was overlooked."

Suleah folded her arms. "I want to go back."

"Impossible."

"You said you can enter the world, my reality, then why can't I?"

"I can no longer traverse the dimension since I have taken this form, this substance. I am human."

"Hardly human," she said.

Rainbows flared in his eyes, the red sparks she now knew were anger. What did he have to be angry about?

Because, Suleah, you and I are matched.

Matched. Another word for mated. The idea was horrifying.

"I don't want to be here, with you, or anyone else. I have my own life, my own work."

"You can have both here, Suleah. More life than even you can imagine." He held up his hands, examining them. "This frail casing you call the body contains a universe of experiences and emotions. Nothing in my former existence compares to this."

"You had no substance?"

"We were once flesh creatures, but the destruction altered us. We lost the corporeal form. We lost many things. But by becoming human, I have gained so much. The ability to touch you, to smile and laugh." He paused, his eyes muted rainbows. "To love you."

"You don't know the meaning of the word, to do what you've done to me." She swallowed more recriminations. His bewilderment showed her the creature had no understanding of what it meant to be human. "What am I supposed to do here in this reality of yours?"

"Our reality, Suleah. This is for you. I am for you. We are together."

She backed up. "I don't want you."

He frowned. "I am your Gilland. More than Gilland. I can be—"

"You aren't Gil. You can never be him. Never! I want to get out of this horror."

"Even if it were possible to leave, why would you prefer to return to those of your kind who scorn you? To a world that has nothing to give you, when I can offer life and love?"

"You can't offer me love."

"You are wrong." He took a step towards her.

"Stay away from me. Just stay away."

He retreated. "If that is your wish, then I will stay away for as long as you want. But realise this. You cannot leave the Retreat, Suleah. To bring you through the dimension, the transference altered your physical composition. You would die if you tried to return."

"Then I'm your prisoner?"

"No, Suleah. Never that." His look was pure horror, his voice hoarse. "You are free to go where you wish. Except return to your own world. Here, all that you desire can be yours. Just allow me—"

"Go to hell!" She flung the *Moet* down on the cushions and stalked from the room. Once free of the dome, she hitched up her robe and ran down the passageway through the chateau entrance and out across the lawn.

She turned to look up at Xanadu and was it her imagination, but at the top window, she saw the silhouette of a man . . . No, not man, an alien who had brought her to this place for his—its—own antidote for loneliness. The utter bastard.

She turned away and walked . . . and walked. Sometimes, she ran—away from him . . . it—and her own horror. She had always hated to be controlled, confined, Gil understood that and gave her as much space as she needed—when it suited him, she reminded herself.

But the creature in the chateau, when would it invade her privacy, her thoughts, impose itself on her?

She ran until her heart and lungs burned with fire. When she recovered her senses, she found herself on blue sand, grit chafing her sandaled feet. In the sky a large ringed planet circled by ten silver moons—Daedalus—she recognised it from the last holiday she had with Gil.

"Get out of my mind, you monster!" Even now the alien was probing her mind for memories in order to seduce and subdue.

The dazzling azure beach she had once walked with Gil stretched as far as the eye could see. In the distance, she saw a silver obelisk, and in its shadow, figures moved.

People!

She raced towards them, but no matter how long she ran and then walked when she could run no more, the people remained distant.

Suleah turned away. Was this another Retreat for another prisoner and their alien keeper?

No, Suleah. His mind touched hers.

"Go to hell." She turned away and stalked across the beach, halting before a gently rolling sea. Creatures frolicked in the golden water. She could go no further that way.

Suleah walked for hours, crossing more territory, some of it almost like home. One vista she saw was Terran-inspired because of the replica of the ancient palace. Taj Mahal, they had called it. Built for love, so the legend said.

No matter how beautiful, no matter how exotic, there was no escape from this horror-reality. Her intellect accepted it, but her heart rejected the prison.

She returned, exhausted, to her own Retreat, and sank down beside the stream cutting through the fragrant grass and cooled her feet in the clear water. She hugged her knees to her chest and rested her face on her knees and wept.

"Suleah." His hand on her shoulder made her flinch. "Please do not do this."

She shrugged off his touch, her skin crawling. "I saw others here."

"Yes. There are many."

"The missing persons from this sector and from the planet, they're all here?"

"And from other places."

"Then why can't I meet them?"

"In time you can." He sat down beside her. For a moment his gaze rested on her feet and ankles. "You came here without knowing, without understanding or accepting. Your anger would disrupt the others."

"So I'm a caged pet until I accept the rules and behave?"

He frowned. "It is not like that."

"Then how is it?" She jumped to her feet. "I don't belong here. I don't want you. Do you understand? I hate you for what you did."

"Would you have preferred I let you die?" His gaze searched hers. "Then I am sorry."

"Isn't it too late to say sorry?" She turned on her heel and walked away. She would never see him again, have nothing to do with him. He might be her keeper, but she would not be tamed. He would regret the day he had brought her to this place.

Yet, in bringing her to the Retreat, he had saved her life. So he said. Perhaps another lie?

Death was preferable than this existence.

If you truly wish for death before your time, there are ways, Suleah, he told her. *Ways we take when the loneliness is too much to bear.*

"Stay out of my mind!" Reaching Xanadu, she ran down the corridors until she reached her apartment. She flung herself inside, the door sealing behind her. She activated the lock and leaned against the lintel, struggling for breath.

The next morning, on the dispenser tray, Suleah found a red rose. As she stared at it, it fell apart like confetti.

Next day, he sent her another rose, the petals misshapen. Subsequent roses were better crafted. One even had a faint rose scent. She spurned each one.

The next rose, she could only call it that by its shape, was made from pink crystal, its transparent stem filled with sand that swept up and down the stem in a never-ending circuit. Its scent reminded her of red dust. So utterly alien.

She kept this and every rose thereafter, enjoying the beauty of the flower for its own sake, however bizarre, but not acknowledging its creator.

How many days, how many weeks? Suleah lost track of time. She established her routine, the opposite to his. From her window, she had seen that he walked in the garden during the morning, so she made it her domain in the afternoon. It appeared he respected the arrangement, because she never encountered him outside, or in the chateau.

Where he ate — *if* he ate — she cared not. She ate her meals in her room, the tasteless food dispensed through the computer console. How could she ask for real food without interacting with *him*?

The console gave her everything she asked. Clothes. Discbooks. She read, she studied, she slept, the pattern of her life comforting in its monotony. She saw no one, just him in the garden at a distance, tending one of the flowerbeds, trimming a rose bush, with a servitor hovering nearby, offering tools and refreshments.

She dreamed at night. Of Gilland. Not the alien-Gilland, *her* Gil. She awoke sometimes crying for him, wanting him. Dying for him. And on those mornings other gifts would be awaiting her at the dispenser.

Once, a book of poetry — a real book made from paper with hand-written verses from an alien poet whose name she did not know.

Other gifts were dispensed, always exotic. Perfume, or a statue, or a hologram picture of an alien landscape, she collected them all, curiosity overcoming abhorrence.

The line of gifts extended along the shelf built into one wall. Fifty gifts. Fifty days. Fifty days or fifty years? What did it matter, the passage of her imprisonment?

But one day, she decided, it did matter. This half-life was unendurable.

Because she had not spoken to another for so long, she found herself talking to the walls, singing the songs she wrote each day, playing the music she composed on the dulcimer.

The first instrument had arrived in the dispenser, mis-shapen and stringless. Each time she mentally pictured the dulcimer, a new version would arrive, better-formed than its predecessor. Many days later, having learned how to project clearly, the dispenser had produced a beautiful dulcimer, perfect in every detail. Its satin-smooth wood inlaid with red roses.

Stroking the strings, Suleah had cried for its perfect reso-nance. She had not had the time for music before. But it had been her love for as long as she could remember. Had she not become a planetologist she might have studied music at the Academy.

No! That was a lie. Her music had been forbidden, her fa-ther insisting that she follow in his footsteps. Her father was not a man to deny. Her mother had learned that early. Suleah had rebelled, but in the end, she had acquiesced. As her mother before her. She had hated her father for his tyr-anny for so many years, had not spoken to him, or seen him in . . . how long? She had lost track of time.

She had been off-world when he had died. The funeral was long over before she came back home to make her peace with the man whose remains had been enshrined in the Star Service Academy garden. A great man, her father. Com-mander Devereux — well loved by his peers, but a bastard.

It had been Gilland who had healed her of her hatred, turning her anger to understanding and then to respect. But love? Never that. Even Gilland could not coerce her to love her father.

Gilland — who fought his own demons and understood the hurt carried by others . . .

At his memory, tears came to her eyes.

She snatched up her dulcimer and her papers and fled to the garden. It was afternoon. Her time. She would be safe from him.

She rounded the corner and halted. Alien-Gilland turned to her.

"You—" The words froze on her lips as she saw him. He was paler and thinner than she remembered. Something of the sparkle had gone from his being. Or, perhaps it had never been there? She was seeing him in his true form. Weeks of isolation had hardened her, quashed the romantic memories. She had refused to allow him to access her mind, so he had nothing to feed off. Without the memories, he faded. His species was vampiric in nature. A simple explanation. Logical. Somehow unconvincing.

"I am sorry,' he said. "It is later than I thought. The garden is yours." He turned away, striding across the lawn, his blue robe flapping around him in his haste to depart. He couldn't wait to get away from her, as much as she wanted him gone from her, it seemed.

Suleah took her customary place in the white rose arbour and strummed her dulcimer. Today, the music brought little comfort. She set aside the instrument. On the ground, she saw a sheet of paper, fluttering, the breeze trapping it against the trellis.

She captured it and saw the lines of a poem, written in a bold hand. Lines crossed out, new words substituted. Some of the words were Terran-standard, French, others alien, a swirl of colour. His language, she presumed.

She knew enough of Gillan's native tongue to read the scrawled French, and like a Frenchman, the words were about love, loss, and sorrow. But what did the swirls of colour mean?

Her gaze, of its own accord, returned to the house. Was the alien writing poetry? The book of poetry with its unknown poet, was alien-Gilland its author? She shook her head. The real Gilland enjoyed poetry but never wrote it. His

eloquence was not derived from the written word. His loving and his smile were poetry enough for her.

Suleah dressed slowly that evening. She and Gil had always dressed formally for dinner. It made the undressing
that much more tantalizing. She laughed. Even alone, in captivity, she kept to the custom they had established so long
ago, dressing for dinner, sitting at a formal setting of fine
white china, silverware and crystal glasses. Light from can-
dles burning from silver candelabrum. The dispenser had
managed to produce all this after many bungled attempts.

Before she changed her mind, she left her room and traversed the passageway, the servitor escorting her, illuminating her way.

The curtains parted as she stepped into the dome. She
saw him reclining on the cushions. Strange that he should
keep to the decor of their first night together. Perhaps he enjoyed Xanadu for its own sake?

His servitor chimed a greeting and Gilland stood slowly.

"Am I disturbing you?" she asked.

"No." His gaze was dark, impenetrable.

"I found this in the garden. It is yours?" She stepped forward, holding out the paper.

He took it carefully from her, not wanting to touch or to
be touched, it seemed.

"Thank you," he said.

"You're a poet?"

"Do you think poetry is confined to your species?" A
touch of reprimand in that tone. Yes, she deserved it, she
acknowledged. Typical human arrogance to think that poetry was confined to one species.

"It's just that Gil never wrote poetry."

"I am a hybrid creature, Gilland, and the original alien. I
am finding my own self within this new life." He studied her

deeply. "Will you join me? I am tired of dining alone. Would you like *Moet* to drink?"

"I'll stay for a while, but nothing to drink. Champagne is for celebrations."

"Is it?" He went to add something but instead turned away.

She settled on the cushions facing him. A servitor hovered before her offering her platters of food. She sampled the cuisine and wrinkled her nose.

"Like last time, it doesn't have a taste," she said.

"What is taste?"

"It's . . . when you eat something, your mouth . . . Stars! You've never *tasted* anything?"

"The word has no meaning for me. Will you explain taste?"

She thought slowly, discarding various explanations. How to explain a human sense to an alien? "Everything has a particular flavour. It's like smell."

Gilland frowned. "Ah, I think I understand. The roses in the garden have a pleasing smell."

"Food also, and you can sense it with your mouth when you eat. That is taste."

He stabbed the food on his plate with a silver fork. "It has no smell, no taste. How can I give it these sensations?"

How indeed, Suleah wondered. "Maybe growing spices might help."

"Spices?"

"Plants grown for their smell and taste. You can eat rose petals."

That astonished Gilland, by the sudden rainbow flare in his eyes. She was learning to read his emotions that way. "Not only beautiful to look at, but . . . culinary?"

Suleah nodded. "If you know how to present them, yes."

"And can you present them so?"

She shook her head. Those special meals had been constructed by Gil's human chef.

"Gil kept a human chef because he refused to let a machine cook for him. He was probably right in that if your dispenser is anything to go by." But maybe she could experiment? Nothing could taste as bad as the food he offered, the look of it was enough to turn her stomach. "What is this stuff?" She waved her hand at the plates of food.

"Organic compounds, transmuted. It contains all the necessary nutritional requirements."

"Maybe, but it tastes awful."

"Then perhaps you can re-program the main computers to include taste. The food you take in your room has taste?"

She nodded and stood up. "Wait here." Suleah went to the main console and activated the computer. The first dish to arrive from the dispenser shelf was disgusting. Gilland laughed at the face she made when she tested it. The last experiment, number eight, was successful. She placed it before him

"Now try this."

"What am I eating?"

"Poison," she said. "It'll turn your blood to water."

He looked at her in alarm. Alien-Gilland was childishly gullible. So, he still wasn't reading her mind. He'd kept another promise to her.

"It's lasagne, a simple dish. When I get that computer sorted out, I can program more ..." That implied her acceptance of her captivity, a role reversal—the kept feeding the keeper. She was a long way from accepting anything.

She watched him raise the fork to his mouth. He tasted the pasta tentatively. His face brightened.

"It's very good."

"It's passable."

Gilland ate the meal, quickly, neatly.

She studied him as he ate. "Have you always been a poet? I could call you Gilland, but that isn't your name, is it?"

He lifted his gaze to her. "My name is felt in your mind, rather than heard. One day I could show you my name. But I *am* Gilland, Suleah. I am he, as much as I can be. Does it concern you that I am Gilland, in form but not in reality?"

She shrugged.

"Then call me what you wish, if using Gilland displeases you. And I have always been a poet. It is a revered profession among my people, as is music. I did not know you were a musician."

"I'm not. I'm a planetologist."

"But music is your passion."

"A hobby."

"No, your love runs too deeply for a mere pastime. Why did you not choose it as your career?"

"Why, indeed." She heard the bitterness in her words. She explained to him about her father. About a lot of things, before she realized she had told him more of her life story than any man alive, the real Gilland included. Perhaps it was easier to tell an alien her deepest secrets because an alien didn't count for much . . . She winced at her own brutality.

Suleah ran a hand through her hair, conscious that his gaze followed her every move. She set her hands in her lap. "Tell me about your poetry. What did you write on the page?"

He glanced down at the paper beside him. "It is not completed. It is not as I wish. I tried to convey my feelings in your language and in mine. What I am feeling . . . in my former language, there are no corresponding words, and I am still not comfortable with this new identity." He smiled quickly. "Will you sing for me? One of the songs you wrote?"

"If you'll read me one of your poems."

"If you wish." He turned to the servitor. "Bring the dulcimer. Please. I should say please, should I not? It is polite to do so?"

"Good manners never hurt anyone or anything," she said, trying not to laugh.

The machine streaked from the room. Minutes later, it delivered the instrument to Suleah.

"Thank you," she said accepting the instrument from the servitor's claw. She was suddenly nervous, a little flustered. "I've never sung to anyone before."

"I am an alien, and of no account."

She felt the flush extend to her toes. "You heard that, Gil . . . I didn't mean it, how it sounded."

"So sometimes what a human says or thinks, is not what they truly intend?" He frowned. "A paradox, your species."

"Humans have been called a lot of things, but paradoxical . . ." She laughed.

"Then, will you sing for me, or play the music?"

She strummed the dulcimer, the notes of her latest composition echoing in the silence of the dome. When she had finished, she glanced at him, intercepting his gaze, the intense shifting of colours across his eyes. Strange how that rainbow had once frightened her, but now she found it . . . What did she see in the depths of his eyes? Understanding? Love?

You fool, Suleah! This sweet seduction was his game. To win her over, to make her . . . accept the unthinkable. She came to her feet, startling him.

"You are leaving me?" he asked, bewilderment creasing his brow.

"Did you think I would stay, that I was charmed by the talk of music and poetry? That's what you thought, wasn't it?"

"No, Suleah."

"I think, yes. Good night."

She stalked from the room.

"You do not wish to hear my poetry?" he called after her.

She pretended not to hear.

Suleah glanced at the roses on the shelf. They had been there for weeks, remaining as fresh as the first day they had been plucked and dispensed to her through the chute. Now, they were wilting, the crystal shattering. All life came to an end, she realized, even alien roses had to die sometime.

Her life had ended the day the rover had crashed. She paused in her pacing. No, that was unfair. She had been rescued from certain death by an alien who had wanted her for his . . . *its* own, and to that end had transformed itself into the semblance of the man she had loved. For her. For her happiness. She could only begin to imagine what he had sacrificed to become Gilland.

She hadn't seen alien-Gilland again. They kept to their separate garden visitations. In her cache of gifts, she found the book of poetry — his poetry — and re-read the verses. Lyrical. Sad. Evocative. The complexities of the syntax, equalling the complexity of the man.

No! Not man. Alien. Gilland was an alien, a rainbow with a façade of skin. Nothing more than a parasite who had stolen her memories to transform itself into the semblance of her real-life lover. She had to remember what he was. What he had done. But when faced with the beauty of his poetry . . . how could she maintain her hatred? A creature who could write such was not to be despised or feared. But loved? That was too big a step for her.

Suleah glanced at herself in the mirror. The grey work overalls fitted perfectly, but the dispenser had a mind of its own, and where she specified simplicity, the machine produced overalls that were embroidered at hem and sleeve with seed pearls and silver thread. Her work boots were also silver, but mercifully unadorned. She'd have to speak to Gilland about the dispenser, or maybe it was his sense of humour to add ornamentation to her clothing? Did the alien have a sense of humour?

She picked up the steel trowel with the carved gilt handle embedded with diamonds — for the star's sake — and her gloves and strode across the room, through silent corridors to outside.

Overhead the domed sky was muted to resemble early morning. Gone was the starscape of Polarium and its asteroids. The sky was red, the sun crimson. The Retreat was Xanadu in name only.

The garden was a mix of alien and human plants. Gilland, she knew, tended to each one with the aid of servitors. New crystalline plants grew under the shelter of green ferns and purple-leaved trees. The air was heavy with exotic scents and in the distance, she heard water trickling and was that a bird singing in a nearby tree? Gilland's attention to detail was remarkable. Transmuting reality from random matter was nothing short of magic.

A tray of crystal-stemmed seedlings, with orange and black leaves, rested on the ornate metal table. Next to the tray was a simple metal trowel — Gilland's she presumed.

A section of soil had been prepared, ready for the seedlings. She carried the tray to the garden bed and kneeling down, carefully extracted one seedling. She used her diamond-studded trowel to dig a hole, smiling at the incongruity of gardening with such an implement. After she had planted the first seedling, she removed her gloves. She always preferred to work without gloves; it had been Gilland who insisted on her wearing gloves. She smiled at the memory, then frowned as she remembered their argument over such a simple thing as wearing gloves—or not. How telling that she had instinctively ordered gloves. She threw them down on the soil, disgusted by herself, her acceptance of another's will, even after four years.

She sensed the alien nearby and turned to see him standing in the shadows. How long had he been watching? He walked towards her, his gait so unlike Gilland's confident panther-like stride—there were some things a replicated alien could not imitate.

"You enjoy gardening?" he asked.

She sat back on her heels. "You didn't see that when you were crawling around in my mind?"

He knelt opposite her and pressed a seedling into the ground. "I wanted to discover you for myself. Does that offend you?"

"No."

She planted the last seedling while he removed a dead fern leaf. For once the silence between them was less charged, more relaxed.

She wiped her hands on her overalls and smiled. "The dispenser will have a fit when it sees how dirty its creation is. You know that machine insists on making even a simple pair of overalls ornate."

He glanced at her. "You prefer simple to ornate?"

"For some things, yes."

"Then you must explain your preferences to your machines."

"I think the dispenser has a mind of its own. I did explain. I even drew diagrams."

Gilland laughed. It almost sounded human. "My dispenser, too, can be contrary. It insists it knows best. I have learned this is a human trait. I must have transferred it to my machine."

"Maybe we should threaten to pull their plugs?"

He looked at her horrified. "I could not do that, to kill a machine, it . . . has feelings."

She stared at him. "It does?"

"Yes." He paused. "It is attuned to our needs. Living in close proximity to life, it replicates itself . . ."

"As you did?"

He nodded.

Suleah ran her hand over the soil, smoothing it. "Gil always made me wear gloves. To protect my delicate skin." The dirt under her manicured nails, the tiny scratches—he would have had a fit to see them. "Gil disapproved of my gardening. He insisted the servitors maintain the grounds and the computer ran Xanadu smoothly. We argued once, because I worked in the garden with the servitors, pruning the roses. I cut my fingers on some thorns."

"He did not want to see you hurt."

She snorted. "No, we were going out that night to a ball . . ." Gilland had been furious that her hands were marred by unsightly scratches. She'd worn the long gossamer gloves he'd given her. "He refused to allow me access to the garden thereafter unless I was chaperoned. The servitor was his creature and was programmed to alert Gil if I tried to work in the garden." She paused. "He was used to having his own way . . ." They had argued, but eventually, she acquiesced. It just didn't seem to matter then, but now . . . she remembered the incident with rancour.

"He stopped you from doing something you enjoyed?"

"It's complicated. Was . . ." She spread her hands. "Relationships are complex. To work, they require a lot of give and take."

"I have read this. One gives, the other takes."

"Not always." She shrugged, sighing. "Well, yes, I guess that can be so."

The alien's eyes burned with rainbows as he studied her.

"Will you garden here tomorrow?"

"I'd like to. I might even prune the roses."

"Without gloves."

Was that a statement or a question? Had the alien under-stood her resentment? Funny how that resentment burned now, years after the incident.

She pushed herself to her feet and wiped dirt from her overalls.

"Suleah, shall I see you tomorrow in the garden?"

"I thought you'd rather have the garden to yourself."

"No. Yes, if you don't mind sharing it with me."

"I don't mind."

She stalked away. Once inside her own apartment, she stripped off her clothes and headed for the shower. The lav-ender-scented water sluiced over her.

After Gil had died, she had returned to her studies, finish-ing her terraforming-horticultural PhD in record time. Had it been a protest against Gil's control to do so? He would never have approved that she had become a gardener . . . Such menial tasks were for servitors, not his life-partner. Even though gardens were her passion.

She sighed. Realisation was bitter. She had allowed Gil to win too many times. When — why — had she become so com-placent, to happily live in his shadow?

To be loved by a man who gave her everything, not the luxury or the wealth, her own family had been old rich. Gil had been exciting, taking risks, defying convention. Oh God, was she just another way to thumb his nose at his family? No, Gil loved her. He gave her everything she needed . . . except the freedom to garden, to get her hands dirty.

I am so angry with you Gil. I'm angry with myself.

The anger bubbled through the layers of control she had built around herself. Not just the garden, but Gil insisting on flying that last mission. They'd known the truce was hours away. Every pilot was finding mechanical faults with their ships; every soldier dodging calls out. Every star captain ensured the men and women under his command were out of harms' way . . . Any death at such a time was futile. Gil had volunteered to fly reconnaissance.

No one knew what happened, but his ship disintegrated. Beeped on screen, then gone the next. Had he jettisoned? His family spent years and enormous sums of money to pay for the searches. Even the Emperor had added his call for an answer. It came — Missing in action.

Missing in action . . .

Missing implied a possibility to be found. *A lie.*

She slammed her fist against the wall. So many lies. His, hers. To herself. To stop the pain. To live in a shadow of life . . . The past years — what a waste.

And now she was trapped in the Retreat with an alien and no chance of ever living a normal life . . .

She slammed her fist against the wall again and again, until her knuckles bled, and the water ran red with blood.

The servitor beeped in alarm when she emerged from the bathroom. It flitted around her, trilling, like a demented wasp. A thin wire extruded from underneath its saucer, and after a few more beeps, it fell silent.

Her torn skin warmed, then burned as the servitor circled her, and to her amazement, the abrasions on her knuckles healed before her eyes.

The doorbell chimed, and the servitor flew to answer it before she could stop it. The door slid open. Gilland stood there, indecisive.

"It said you were injured."

"The servitor is your spy?" That was the bloody last straw.

"No, it is your creature. It informed my servitor you are unwell. I was concerned. I do not mean to intrude."

"But you bloody well are. All this . . ." She flung her arms wide. "All this is an intrusion on my life and liberty."

Gilland stepped forward, hand outstretched to her.

"I didn't say you could enter."

Immediately, her servitor blocked his path, amid much trilling, and the lights at its saucer base flashed an ominous red. So, the servitor truly was loyal to her, turning on Gilland. How far would it go to protect her?

"It could inflict upon me a great deal of pain before my own servitor rendered it inoperative," he said.

"So much for our equality, you admit you are dominant here. I'm just your pet."

"I have explained our relationship." He sighed. "You are being unreasonable."

She laughed. Unreasonable? "Is it any wonder?"

"Today, in the garden . . . you were different. What has occurred to make you angry?"

"I woke up. I realise how much of a fool I had been. Now I'm here, and it's all too late." She turned away, then confronted him again. He was still standing there, his eyes swirling rainbows, confused. Not understanding—never would he, because she hardly understood herself. "Do whatever you do in this prison of yours but leave me alone. Do not intrude, do not spy. And do not send me gifts via the dispenser." Gil used to send her gifts, expensive, carefully chosen to placate her. The bottle of *Moet* had been one such—sent to her that last day . . .

"I do not understand," Gilland said.

"It's simple, really. I hate it here. I'm a prisoner. The cage might be gilded—"

"But you have everything you need."

"Except freedom."

"You can come and go as you please. Do what you wish, whenever you wish. How is this a prison?"

"Your kind created it, to save yourselves. You retreat

from the world, humans confront it, full on, face first. We might blunder about and cause problems, but at least we are living a life, not existing within an illusion."

"The fabric of Xanadu is changing. It is becoming real." He spread his hands. "In time you can leave this Retreat, meet the others."

"Provided I submit to the rules?"

"For your own good."

"Get out!" She waved at her servitor. "Secure the door. No one gets in or out unless I approve it, Understood?" The servitor flew to obey, beeping rapidly, lights flashing. The door sealed against the alien's bewildered expression.

She barely noticed the passing of time. By the clock's reckoning, she endured her self-imposed exile for six weeks. In that time, she read, slept, cried an ocean of tears, writing in her journal every thought, every conclusion.

No relationship was perfect, however much she had thought Gil was perfect. Like so many women before her, she had surrendered a little of herself, to keep the peace. She had woven a fantasy around a memory, fuelled by grief and loneliness — made Gilland more than he had been, forgetting the reality.

The loneliness was unbearable.

Come to the garden. The hand-written note emerged from the dispenser that day. A coincidence? Or had he been spying?

She found him in the garden, sitting under the rose arbour. He looked paler, thinner than she remembered, much like her own reflection — thin and wan.

She sank onto a wide cushion on the grass opposite him.

"You are well?" he asked finally.

"Yes."

They chatted about inconsequential things — the garden,

their servitors, their days.

"I can still change this Retreat to whatever you wish," Gilland said. "If Xanadu now displeases you?"

She glanced up as the sky swirled, became the azure blue of home, with fluffy white clouds. In the distance, she saw the pyramid, the silhouette of Old Cairo beneath the glass skyscrapers of New Cairo.

"I prefer Xanadu."

"Why?"

"Because it reminds me that nothing endures."

He sighed. "You are torturing yourself."

"Not so much, because I have you to do that for me."

"I have never laid violence upon you." He looked truly shocked, and she had to smile.

"You don't have to. You are the façade of someone I loved, but who I need to forget."

"But love endures. All your literature says so."

"Depends on what you read, Gil," she said.

He smiled then. "You called me Gil."

"What else am I to call you?"

"I could teach you my name."

"Maybe." In the future. She could only take one day at a time. "I want to show you something." She waved her hand, and her servitor, hovering in the shadows flew forward, a wooden box clasped in is claws. The machine deposited it onto the table. Suleah unpacked the box and set the carved pieces on the board. "Come and take a seat, Gil, at the table. I'm going to teach you how to play chess."

"Ah, a game? I have read about them. These are for pleasure, a hobby?"

"Yes. It's also an ancient game of skill and strategy." She explained the various moves. "The aim is to capture the king to checkmate your opponent."

"What is opponent?"

"Er, who you're aiming to defeat."

"Defeat, as in how?"

"By out-thinking, by strategy. You beat them."

"No," Gilland said.

"No, what?"

"I do not beat any, cause harm to any."

"It's only a game."

"Perhaps, but the rationale behind it, is to harm, to beat, to win at all costs? I find that offensive."

She stared at him. "But didn't you tell me long ago, that your kind had a propensity for self-destruction? You must have had winners and losers."

"Long ago. Now, we support each other to exist."

Suleah sighed. So much for chess. She thought through other games. Poker — he lacked the subtlety, and she could read him most of the time, she realised with a shock. Gilland, unlike his namesake, was naive in many things. A creature of his own world. He lived in a Retreat — in more ways than one.

"I guess we could try cards."

"I sent you cards."

"These are different. Wait here."

Suleah returned to her apartment and keyed in the dispenser. Since her arrival, she found that she had honed her mental skills. It took little concentration to get the dispenser to produce what she imaged, though sometimes she suspected it teased her, delivering quirky goods, like the pearl-studded work overalls.

Retrieving the two decks of cards, she re-joined Gilland in the garden. When she sat down, she noticed that Gilland had ordered green tea.

"This is a card game called 'snap.' No challenge, no strategy, unlike chess, just eye and hand co-ordination." She explained the rules and the first few games were tediously slow, until Gilland understood. He was a fast learner. When he won his first game, he looked suitably pleased with himself. His laugh was so human . . .

"Suleah, there are other card games and board games?"

"Lots."

"Will you show me more?"

And for the days following, each afternoon, she introduced him to a new game. He would never be good at poker, but he enjoyed the complexity of backgammon. His favourite was snakes and ladders. Scrabble was another challenge. He learned Terran-standard words, and she learned words translated from his language into Terran-standard. The scrabble board was a mix of human and alien, challenging them both.

"You aren't happy, here," Gilland said as she packed up the Monopoly board. These places remind you of home?" He touched Mayfair on the board.

"Gil and I went there, to Mayfair. An old hotel. His family owned it."

"Ah. I could replicate it for you?"

"No. Some things are best forgotten."

"It holds unhappy memories for you?"

She shrugged.

"I do not understand this place. Go to jail."

"That's where criminals go. As punishment."

It took her a long time to explain these two concepts. He looked at her askance. "A person is a criminal if he, or she, breaks a rule? How do you know these rules?"

"You learn them as you grow up, get taught by your parents, or at school. Or laws made by legislature. You have laws here you must obey."

"Of course. Order must overcome chaos." He studied her, head askew. "You have laws, but yet you still have criminals on your world."

"Yes, because some people are evil."

"Define evil."

Crives. "I guess it's a matter of perspective. We called the Jalan Empire evil when we fought them in the war, and they called us monsters for what we did to them. Both of us evil, from a different perspective. Truth always lies somewhere in the middle."

He smiled. "Did you always think so?"

She paused, chewing her lip. No, she'd been like everyone else, not questioning, but here she had time to analyse every moment of her life, her beliefs and in some cases, she had found herself wanting. She slammed the box shut. "You'd make a good psychiatrist, Gil. You know that?"

He lifted a dark brow over rainbow eyes.

"You get inside someone's head and do stuff, make them think too much." She paused. "I can never be the person you need. One day I will find a way to escape this prison. Don't you ever want to leave here?"

"Why would I want to?"

"Because a prison is a prison, no matter how comfortable. Freedom is everything."

"I don't understand."

"And that is the difference between us, Gilland. You accept your prison. I do not."

"A prison can be of one's own making. Or it can have bars. Only a thought can set you free."

She stared at him, then turned on her heel and stalked away.

That night she left the Retreat, having locked up her servitor in her wardrobe. The machine, like a faithful dog, had beeped alarm as she flung essentials into a bag. "You can't come with me, Igor," she told the machine. The name had come to her, after reading a Victorian Penny Dreadful, dredged up from her library computer—a library that contained every known Terran and alien work. A thousand life-times of reading and she had chosen *Blood Murder on the Moors*—a shockingly bad novel of murder, myth and may-hem and a vampire who loved a mortal woman . . .

Igor whined and beeped as she strode through the large doors and into the garden.

No matter how long she walked, the shimmering walls of the Retreat remained in the distance. Around her, the land-scape changed, transforming to more lush gardens, blue skies, or a sky lit with unknown constellations. Something or someone was feeding from her mind, transforming images to reality. As she walked for days, she learned to keep her thoughts to herself, and slowly the red sky and the red sand stretched in every direction.

Come back to me, Suleah . . .

She blocked his mind-call time and again, and then all was silent. Ominous.

This creature is unsuitable.

She was chosen.

It was a mistake.

"Who the hell is speaking?" she demanded of the red sky.

We who exist here. In harmony. Your thoughts and actions are acrimony.

"Then let me leave."

You would die. You have been changed, so your form can exist here. This was explained to you.

"You found a way to make this Retreat, find a way to unmake it, so I can leave."

Their horror rolled over her.

To do as you wish would destroy the life within. Your life, and that of your chosen. Is death the price of your freedom?

She pondered that question over more miles of walking. By now the nutri supplements in her bag were gone, and the Retreat voices were silent.

Suleah dreamed of him again, that night. They danced the intricate court dances he had learned as a boy and which he taught her for their own private balls. She had never been to court, of course, but he had, and often. An Imperial son from old aristocracy, with blood ties to the Emperor, the palace had been his second home.

Gilland had met her at a science lecture in the Academy. To escape the rain outside, he had chosen the first building to offer shelter, so he had said. She was there to participate in the presentation. At the cocktail bar, Gilland had cornered her, asking her questions that left her in no doubt he had not understood one word of her lecture. His ignorance had been refreshing, intriguing . . . She had been with scientists so long, she had forgotten there was a world outside waiting for her to discover, and Gil was happy to act as guide. Their friendship had grown quickly into love. He defied his family and their rigid social expectations, to have her. He had the courage to defy, she had been the coward and acquiesced, done all that was expected of her and hating every moment of it. Until Gilland . . . had set her free. But in that freedom were his limitations. His and those he imposed upon her.

In the dream, he swept her around the room, her layered silver gown billowing about her. Closer and closer he held her, his hands fanning over the small of her back, pressing her to him. They laughed and kissed, ignoring polite, courtly convention. Escaping the palace, they had made love in an arbour of rainbow roses.

The dream-scape shifted. She found Gilland in the Xanadu arbour, alone and dying, not from an alien disrupter beam as her Gil, but dying from a broken heart. "You have a heart?" she asked, her palm against his chest.

His fingers rested against her hand, pressing her to his flesh. Beneath her fingers, she felt the slow, erratic beat of his heart. Cool, too cool, his skin. His smile was gentle, sad, as his rainbow eyes were full of regard for her. Only for her. As her Gil had once regarded her. His kiss was gentle, smouldering.

He retreated from her embrace; rainbow rose petals swirling around him as he fragmented into a thousand colours. She heard someone crying and struggled to find its source.

Oh, how it hurts, this emptiness, this sorrow, this chill, his words echoed about her, through her. The dark sky twisted in on itself, destroying the rainbows.

Suleah startled awake, to find her face wet with tears. The red-scape shuddered, and she found herself lying in her bedroom. On the shelf, the roses had turned brown. Near death, as he. She knew that. She mind-sensed him. No response.

She had walked for nearly four days, and in a moment, she was back where she had originated. The wardrobe door was broken, and on the floor, she saw Igor, shattered into a hundred pieces. She rose from the bed and lifted the machine into her hands. The servitor had destroyed itself to escape its prison—the one she had made for it.

"I will make you whole, Igor." She put the remains on the dispenser shelf and sent instructions for the servitor to be renewed. The dispenser whirled and clicked and scooped Igor into its maw with a tractor beam.

A prison, Gilland had once said, was made by one's thoughts, or actions. What was the nature of freedom? Freedom meant the ability to choose.

Alien-Gilland had chosen, so had she.

She searched the house and could not find him. Where could he be? As the shadows of late afternoon stretched across the lawn, she found him in the arbour. The white roses had shrivelled. Were they somehow linked to him? Did the roses reflect his life-force?

"Gilland?"

At her voice, he turned from where he reclined among the cushions. Beside him lay an empty sheet of paper and a discarded stylus. An anachronism: paper and a laser stylus to write his verses.

"I dreamed of you, Gilland." She frowned at him. His face was pale, gaunt, and his eyes were haunted. "I know you're dying. But why? How?"

He was silent for so long she thought he would not answer.

"It was wrong of me to bring you here. I thought . . . I was mistaken. And now you are here. Alone. As I."

"We learn to endure loneliness," she said.

"A living death, Suleah."

"Yes." She had prayed for death, but she had lived, while millions had fought for life and liberty, dying in the war. The universe's greatest irony. She had prayed she would die in the red dust. "Gilland, why are you dying?"

"It is the nature of my kind. Even after the transmutation from energy to flesh, we retain part of our former self. As your kind, we need more than nourishment to survive."

"You need love?"

"Yes."

"Gilland." She knelt at his side and touched his chest. He was cold. Fear constricted her throat. "Gilland! Live! Live!" She leaned over him, her lips a fraction from his. "Live, Gilland. I love you." She kissed him gently, fleetingly and then wrapped her arms around him, pressing her cheek to his chest. Against her ear, she heard the slow thrum of his heart.

I love you. She sent to him, mind to mind. For she knew she loved him, had loved him for so long. The real Gil gone forever, alien-Gilland, a mixture of her Gil and another who breathed new life into a man she could barely remember. She loved alien-Gilland. She loved his poetry, even if she could not understand it all, she loved his language, his smile, the play of rainbow-lights in his eyes. His frustrating manner when he played snap. His game of scrabble when he used alien words.

"Live, Gilland."

"I am so tired, so hollow," he whispered.

She sat back on her heels, her hands in his. "It's loneliness, Gilland. It's a living death. I've been more dead than alive these past four years, but in the last weeks, I've become alive again. Whole. Happy, sometimes. I have you to thank for that."

"I would not have you love me to spare my life. To deceive me. I will know. It will make no difference. Let me take the final sleep."

"No, Gilland." She leaned over him again. "I want you. Read my thoughts and know I speak the truth. Don't die. I couldn't bear it." She wept, her tears falling on his face, as she kissed him again. "The universe rarely gives a person a second chance at happiness. We both have this chance. Live for both our sakes!"

"But I have made a prison for you."

"A prison is just a matter of perception. I made a prison for myself outside this Retreat. I've made one here, denying myself, and you . . . I am so sorry."

With a sigh, he touched his mouth to hers and wrapped his arms around her. Turning on the cushions, he drew her to his side. He kissed her gently, then fiercely, dragging in life and love with every moment.

"Yes," she said. "Take from me what you need. I give it freely. I want you, Gilland. Now."

She felt the soft-as-down touch of his mind to hers. There was a moment of resistance as her mental barriers resisted his intrusion.

"Have no fear," Gilland said with his mind and his

mouth.

His thoughts swirled over her, through her. He probed, and she allowed him access. Areas she had not dared to read, to re-open, memories of childhood and later, the hurts and the pain and the desires, he learned them all. And in turn, she read his needs and wants and fears. She gasped mentally and physically.

Oh, how it hurts, this emptiness, this sorrow, this chill . . . Their thoughts merged. Both lonely, afraid, wanting love. Again, his mind touched hers. She finally understood.

Their kind could not survive *The Alone*. Before the bridge between dimensions and worlds had been established they had died, those survivors of the destruction, because they had been alone. A few star-farers returned with creatures willing to share their lives within their retreats. It was the beginning.

They sought the lonely, the afraid, finding them in the space-lanes, living their living deaths and the aliens visited them in dreams, offering them hope and life in a place where no pain would ever reach them. Thousands now lived within the Retreat, sharing life and love with the aliens who took on the form of those they saved.

Gilland, now human for his human Suleah.

She wept in his arms, and he stroked her body and her mind, to soothe. But the touch fanned dormant desires. She touched his body, to find his flesh hot and shivering.

Sully, I do not know this fever, this need. It hurts!

I do.

I am ignorant. You must teach me how to satisfy this craving . . . your craving and mine.

Yes.

She kissed him, her mouth and tongue blazing a trail over his virgin flesh. She laughed against his skin. Gil had not been a virgin. With all those court beauties vying for his title, he had been bedded at age twelve.

Suleah flung off her robe. His eyes widened.

"This is beauty!" he said. "The word had no meaning for me until this moment." He stroked her skin.

She pressed against him. "Harder, Gilland. You won't hurt me. I want you to touch me!"

"Like this?"

She moaned. He drew away, and she brought his hands back to her breasts.

"I hurt you," he said. "You cried out."

Suleah laughed. "Mind-touch me, Gilland. I've got a lot to teach you. Pleasure and pain is just a matter of degree."

"I do not understand."

"You will, I promise you." Suleah smiled.

His thoughts caressed her, an intimate touch that made her gasp and writhe. She drew off his robe and caressed his skin, the taut nipples. He gasped. Suddenly she felt the novice, unsure where to start her teaching of this man . . .

We must both begin anew. I will find what pleases you, and I will discover what pleases me. I did not understand the meaning of pleasure before.

This is only the beginning, Gil.

There is more?

Oh, yes.

You called me Gil, not Gilland. I am Gil for you?

Gil, yes, you are Gil. Never Gilland. You are my everything.

A rainbow of light, his spirit, swept into her body, warming, soothing, teasing. His spirit-loving drove her to the brink.

Their first flesh-joining was fast, furious. Their later couplings were taken at leisure, amid explorations and tentative forays into the pleasure of the other.

The warm breeze fanned Suleah's skin, and she startled awake. The scent of honan permeated her senses. With a cry she sat upright, cushions falling away. Igor, on the grass nearby, flew skyward with a beep of alarm.

"So you are awake at last, *mon amour*. You have slept the day away."

"Gil?" Had she dreamed it all? Doubt coursed through her.

I am here. He told her his name: a shifting of colours and sounds within her mind. So utterly alien, so terrifyingly beautiful.

At his mental caress, the tears of fear stinging her eyes became tears of joy.

Suleah touched his hand. "I was afraid it was a dream. You . . . a dream."

He smiled, his eyes and face alive. Beautiful again, whole again, her alien-Gilland.

"Dreams do come true. In the Retreat," he said.

"I understand that now."

He dropped to the cushions, sitting cross-legged. The folds of his robe parted, and Suleah gazed upon his flesh.

"I like your appetite for me." He smiled crookedly and reached for the bottle of *Moet*. "When I touched your body with my tongue and mouth, I understood, finally, what 'taste' means."

Suleah writhed beneath his smouldering look. What Gilland lacked in experience, he compensated with curiosity and inventiveness. He loved her fully, totally. More than Gil had ever done because while Gilland pleasured her body, his mind caressed. They shared sensations, and at the pinnacle of passion, back and forth, spirit to spirit, flesh to flesh, sharing, equals, taker and taken.

"We begin again, today, *mon amour*, with this liquid you hold in such high esteem. I saw you drink it that day, long ago. This time, and ever after, you will not drink alone."

Two glasses appeared at his side: two crystal flutes edged with gold. He poured the honey-coloured champagne into the glasses and handed her one.

"What did you drink to, that day I saw you?" he asked.

"To Empire Day. The day Gil died."

"But you said you only drink champagne to celebrate. Empire Day would not be a celebration for you."

"No. He left that bottle with me, to open on his return. He never did, of course. I think that day you watched me, I realized that memories were no longer enough for me. I had to live, to move on. It just took me a while to understand."

Gilland winced. "It was a difficult time for you."

"And for you, Gilland. I am sorry."

"Love means never having to say sorry."

"That's not true. When you love someone, you should never hurt them so that it's necessary to say sorry."

He smiled. "Then *sorry* is banned from our vocabulary. I promise I will not use it when we play scrabble."

"Even if it's a triple word?"

He inclined his head, laughing. "Even so." He studied her.

"There is something I need for you to consider, you and the others of your kind." She waved her hand skyward. "If they're listening?"

"Xanadu is now our private domain. I have forbidden them entrance."

She smiled. "That's probably just as well, given what we er . . . say and do. In and out of bed."

Gilland blushed. "And what is it you wish to tell them?"

"Polarium has the ability to heal. Our science has never been able to explain why. I suspect it's the crystals and the unique spectrum . . ." She shrugged. "If your kind could travel to Polarium maybe they can be healed without the need of the elaborate induction process?"

"I explained before, that because of what we did to our world, the destruction, and the Change, we are forever altered."

"Maybe our scientists could help? Perhaps if you could make contact with them?"

"Perhaps so. Humans are an ingenious, complex, infuriating species. That is why we favour them as our chosen above many others."

"Infuriating? Me?"

"Oh, yes." He smiled. "I will tell them about Polarium. But not today. Today . . . I understand it is customary we make a toast."

She touched her glass to his. "That day long ago I toasted to death. Today, we toast to life and love, to Gil's memory. To us. To a new beginning for both of us. No more memories, no more Empire Days. Let's toast to Xanadu, the palace of dreams."

ABOUT ASTRID COOPER

Combining the best of 2 fiction genres, Astrid has been writing science fiction romance since she could hold a pencil. Sometimes her romances are steamy, but always with a happy ever after ending.

Astrid's best-selling books regularly win awards. When not writing, she loves gardening, rescues cats, and restores her old home and antique furniture.